THE HAMTHOLOGY

HAM SANDWICH LITERATURE

Edited by David F. Shultz

The Hamthology: Ham Sandwich Literature
Edited by David F. Shultz

This is a work of fiction. The stories are products of the author's imagination and are not intended to be construed as real. Any resemblance to actual persons, living or dead, is entirely coincidental.

Published by tdotSpec Inc.
ISBN#978-1-9994039-5-9

Copyright Acknowledgements

ACKNOWLEDGEMENTS

This book would not have been possible without the volunteer efforts of a number of editors and readers. I would like to thank Adrienne, Calder, Marley, and The Itch, for serving as the front-line editorial/reading team. Thanks, team!

A special thanks is owed to The Itch, who runs the Toronto Horror Writers meetup, and in whose group the idea for *the Hamthology* was conceived. Thanks, Itch!

I would like to thank Justin Dill, our copy-editor, for giving the collection a professional polishing. Thanks, Justin!

Funding for the Hamthology came from a Kickstarter campaign. Our project backers made this anthology possible, providing funds for the authors. Thank you, project backers, for believing in and supporting this project!

Of course, this collection wouldn't be possible without the combined talent and efforts of its writers, poets, and artists. Thanks, contributors, for creating all the art that comprises *the Hamthology*!

And I would also like to thank you, the reader, for taking a chance on this unique anthology. Thanks, reader! I hope you enjoy this one-of-a-kind collection of ham sandwich literature!

-David

PROJECT BACKERS

Anand Mohan
autumnpsyche
Calder
Carolyn Rock
Crystal A Edwards
Dagmar Baumann
Dave Radford
Dr. Lisa M. Daly
Erich P. Alden
For My Hamo
Frances Boyle
Frank ham Soeren
Govneh
Graham Couch
Harris Bor
Jane A. Obenour
Jason Teal
Katie Sullivan
LARGELARRY
Lionel Ray Green
Marley Flowers
Matthew Frederickson
Melissa!
Michael Andersen
Mitchell Harris
Rob Schultz
Robert Perret
Robin Leigh
Sam Stockton
Shaun Hayworth
Sir Wilfred Neptuna
Suzie Olse

INTRODUCTION

The invention of the sandwich is sometimes attributed to John Montagu, the fourth Earl of Sandwich. However, the earliest historically documented sandwich is found in the first century BCE, crafted by the Jewish sage Hillel the Elder, who wrapped lamb meat and herbs in a soft matzah. Hillel is renowned as a sage and scholar within Judaism for his role in the development of the Mishnah and the Talmud, but his legacy in the culinary world is often overlooked.

The Wall Street Journal described the sandwich as Britain's "biggest contribution to gastronomy". It was in Britain that the sandwich evolved to its pinnacle form of the ham sandwich. By the mid-nineteenth century, seventy London street vendors offered ham sandwiches, one of the earliest forms of closed-face sandwich in the historical record. According to the British Sandwich Association, the ham sandwich is the most popular sandwich in the UK. And in France, ham sandwiches were found to comprise a stunning seventy percent of sandwiches, leading to the creation of a "*jambon-beurre*" economic index for the country. There is a certain irony in the evolution of the sandwich, from its first appearance in the hands of the

Jewish sage Hillel the Elder to its popular modern form in the ham sandwich, whose central ingredient is religiously proscribed by Judaism.

The sandwich is something of an enigma. Lawyers, legislators, and legal scholars have spilled much ink attempting to define the contours of this nebulous concept. In various states, contentious battles have erupted over whether tacos, hot dogs, and pita wraps are rightly considered sandwiches. The concept of "sandwich" remains legally indeterminate, shifting meaning across geographic boundaries. As for metaphysics, if there is a platonic form, the most likely candidate seems to be the ham sandwich.

Notwithstanding the legal attention it has garnered and its currency in the culinary world, the ham sandwich has attracted little in the way of literary attention. This books fills that critical lacuna. In "Art as Technique", the seminal work that became the basis for Russian Formalism, literary critic Viktor Shklovsky identified defamiliarization or "estrangement" as the essence of literature. Shklovsky gave the example of Tolstoy's story "Kholstomer", told from the point of view of a horse, which altered the reader's perception and allowed them to see the world anew. Shklovsky argued that deforming reader expectations and de-automatizing our perceptions is at the heart of literature. Throughout *The Hamthology*, ham sandwiches serve as a defamiliarizing device, acting as a prism through which to view our world and the human condition. *The Hamthology* is more than a collection of stories, poems, and art—it is an experimental feat in writing that operates at the very core of the literary enterprise.

The stories in this collection span a wide variety of genres, from fantasy and science fiction to mystery, horror, romance, and erotica. They cover such diverse topics as sexuality and gender expression, biological warfare, space colonization, religion, parenthood, crime and punishment, and mental health. Collectively, they comprise a broad look at various aspects of human life, and they explore a wide swath of philosophical terrain through diverse literary approaches, all united by the ham sandwich. Through these works, the ham sandwich comes to represent something greater than the sum of its edible parts, transforming into a transcendent symbol—of our hopes and dreams and fears, of who we are, from where we've come, and to where we might go. *The Hamthology* is, without a doubt, the greatest collection of ham sandwich literature ever produced in human history.

You should have a drink or two while reading the poems and stories—our editors certainly did! A ham sandwich pairs well with a white or rosé, but for *The Hamthology*, I recommend whisky, neat.

Thank you for reading, and *bon appétit*!

David

CONTENTS

Pig Collector

j. lewis

no need to look for pigs
they will find you
where you hide

at the bottom of the feed trough
buried in the muck of anonymity
lying still and quiet
beneath a forest oak
your truffle pheromones
an aphrodisiac

they will find you
consume you in retaliation
for endless ham sandwiches
for countless bacon mornings
press around you until
you finally confess
yes, yes, yes
i am, we are all,
just pigs

Beware Brown Bags

Karen Thrower

Dale drove down the winding, wooded road, his arm resting out the open window. Quail season started in the morning and he had to get the cabin ready for him and his friends. He reached for the radio knob when a buck jumped onto the road. Dale swerved left to miss the outstanding creature. Killing it with a truck was cheating, after all! The tires squealed on the worn road as the buck jumped off to the right, safe from Dale. POP! Dale looked in the rear-view mirror and saw he had run over a brown bag.

"Hope it's empty." He pulled to the side of the road and walked over to his unintended victim. The tires had left their tread on the bag and something white poked out. He grabbed a nearby stick and jabbed it. "Oh. Just a sandwich." Dale jumped back in his truck and headed for the hunting cabin.

•

Dale pulled into the yard and jumped out of his Ford F-150. POP! He flinched at the noise and looked at the ground. He seemed to have landed on a brown lunch bag. Weird, he thought and went to grab the guns out of the back of the truck. But as he opened the tailgate, he smelled something. "Is that... ham?" The smell got stronger as he pulled three gun bags towards the tailgate. Dale opened Randy's gun bag and jerked as over a dozen ham slices fell out of the overstuffed bag onto the ground. "The hell, Randy?" Dale grabbed all the slices he could find and threw them into the woods for the racoons. He knew he had to give Randy hell for that awful joke.

Dale opened Jon's bag, but when he reached in for the gun his fingers touched something slimy. "Ew!" He forced the opening wider and saw Jon's shotgun covered in tomato slices. His friends were avid hunters; there was no way they would treat their guns like this! Dale scoffed at how much their joke had backfired. "More quail for me then!" He pulled his gun bag close, but his fingers hovered over the zipper. "Come on, Dale," he said, psyching himself up, just in case. He unzipped the bag, and his eyes went wide as slices of bread and cheese burst from the opening. "Damn it!" He stomped his boot in frustration. POP! Dale jumped back and saw another brown bag on the ground. "That was not there before!" he yelled and ran for the cabin.

Dale slammed the door shut and rested his forehead against it. He couldn't believe such a thing had scared him. Sandwich fixings? When his heart finally settled, he turned.

POP! Dale jumped in the air and saw another brown bag on the floor. "Stop it!" he yelled to no one. "Damn food," he mumbled as he walked into the kitchen and leaned against the island. As he looked back to the bag by the door, it made him think about the one he'd run over earlier.

Dale laid his forehead on the cool marble, stretching the long drive out of his arms. Something cold slapped on the back of his hand. He jerked up to see a piece of ham on his skin. "Aah!" He scrambled back, throwing the ham against the front door. He wiped his hand on his cargo pants but stopped when he felt something in one of the leg pockets. Ripping the Velcro open, he reached in with shaking fingers. They wrapped around something slimy, and he pulled out four slices of tomato. Dale yelled and threw them on the ground. He stomped on the perfectly sliced fruit until his feet were covered in mush and the floor was slippery with seeds. "What the hell is going on!" He rifled through his coat and pulled cheese out of a breast pocket. He threw it on the ground then found bread stuffed in his back pockets. Next, he pulled lettuce from his shoes. Dozens of mayo and mustard packets had been shoved in other zippered pockets of his pants. It didn't take long before the sandwich ingredients covered the floor. He peeled the rest of his clothes off, yelling at the condiments.

"No, this can't be real!" Dale stood in the living room, wearing only tighty-whiteys. His eyes darted around the cabin in fear. The door to the bedroom slammed open. Dale jerked his head over to see a parade of bread, cheese, tomato, and ham rushing towards him. The cheese jumped on him and slapped his face. The bread careened into his legs, toppling him to the floor. Tomatoes slapped against his skin, covering him. He looked down his body and saw four ham slices slinking their way up his torso. They stopped on his chest and seemed to stare him down. "I'm sorry, okay! I didn't know you were in the bag!" The ham slices swayed left to right. He choked as they shoved their way into his mouth, dampening his yells. He struggled against the sandwich bits, but they seemed unending! His eyes bulged out of his head as his ham-flavored screams were silenced.

•

Around eight the next morning, Randy and Jon made it to the cabin. They opened the door, and both men screamed at what greeted them. A naked Dale, lying on his back in the middle of the living room. His open eyes staring at the ceiling. He was dead! Ham sandwiches covered the cabin, in varying states of decay. A line of sandwiches lay along his body, perfectly made but never eaten. The one on his forehead looked particularly delicious.

Ham Sandwich Recipe

C.H. Williams

Ingredients:

Bread

Butter

Ham

Method:

Tackle

baby into a vest and onesie. Do up all the poppers. Unpop the last three and adjust along the left leg until fastened correctly. Breathe a sigh of relief.

Undo

all of your hard work. Strip baby back down in order to change the nappy baby had waited so patiently to soil. Redress baby.

Put

baby in the direct centre of the bed and repeat the phrase "do not move," continuously while you attempt to dress yourself. Hop around in odd socks while staring at baby, still repeating the aforementioned mantra.

Find
comfy pants, failing that, find clean pants, failing that, grab the pants you wore yesterday. Continue staring at baby while you glare at your favourite pair of jeans that no longer fit.

Pull
on loose jogging bottoms that cover some, but not all, of your newly acquired stretch marks. Take your eyes off baby for a full five seconds while you pinch the excess skin on your belly where your bump used to be. Refocus on baby.

Continue
to wear the nursing bra you have been living and sleeping in for a week and a half, just change out the breast pads if you feel so inclined. Find an oversized t-shirt, if possible one without dribble, snot or poop on it, failing that, wear whatever top you can find. Praise baby for not moving.

Debate
whether you really need to pee or if you can hold on until after you've made your ham sandwich.

Carry
baby downstairs and pray you still have some control over your pelvic floor.

Balance
baby on your hip and jiggle up and down while grabbing the loaf of bread with your free hand. Switch baby to the other side when you find you are unable to release the tag left-handed. Hold bread bag from the top and marvel at the simplicity of it untwisting of its own accord. Place open bread bag on the side in the kitchen. Readjust baby.

Take
out precisely two slices of half-crumpled, starched white bread and plonk them down on the side. You can reseal the bread again later. Carefully venture over to the fridge and search for butter. Pause search in order to calm baby, who has now burst into tears at the sound of the fridge door opening.

Abandon
kitchen completely to change baby's nappy again. Ignore your tummy rumbling as you feed baby. Burp baby while fighting off yawns. Give up and yawn in baby's face. Show them how tired you are, but don't openly blame them for it.

Go
back to the fridge, and with a beaming smile, sing nursery rhymes to baby while you cautiously attempt the fridge door once more. Grab butter and gently close fridge.

Juggle
with baby, butter and a spoon, as you can't locate a clean knife. Avoid green, fuzzy patches on butter and apply messily onto the bread, ripping holes in the slices as the butter's too cold to spread. Swear internally as the bread mocks you with its lumps of cold butter between gaping holes.

Rock
baby and sing as you return to the fridge for a final time. Search high and low for ham. Swear loudly, with every expletive in your vocabulary, and slam the fridge door.

Difficulty level: Almost on par with childbirth
Cooking time: 3 hours minimum
Servings: Sod it all

The Ham Sandwich of Doom

Jan Karlsson

Cheddar-Ham Coast

E.E. King

Jean was an academic writer. She spent her days typing out text as arid as her imagination, as dry as the valley between her thighs. She viewed the world through horn-rimmed glasses, preferring the safety of code to the complexity of creation. She never took a vacation, or even a day off, favoring the sleek uncompromising lines of her laptop to the infinite variety of sand and shore surging only a block away from her Santa Monica office. She disdained even the thought of the bronzed bodies that frolicked in the surf as if there were nothing more important than play or laughter.

But when the sea wants you, it calls with a roar so powerful that even if you plug your ears with wax—even if you fasten yourself to figures—you are not secure.

When it was noted that Jean had five years of vacation due, she was given a mandatory two weeks off. Zipping her laptop into her sleek black bag, she left the office and wandered home. The sky was a clear endless blue; it tingled with the tang of salt. Sea breezes tugged at her linen suit and ruffled her bangs. Jean tightened her mouth and marched on.

Once home, she turned on her laptop and stared at the pulsing screen. She considered looking for some freelance writing, but the sites she found seemed too bright and full of promises to be genuine. Jean distrusted promise.

At lunchtime, she toasted two pieces of slightly stale white bread. After adding cheddar cheese and a slice of ham, thinner than a contract, between them, she cut them in half. Even though the cheese was barely warm, orange goo began to ooze out of the half sandwich on her plate.

As she watched, the toasted bread lengthened, each grain becoming visible, even though it was white bread. The slice of ham rose up, displaying an underbelly deep and blue as an endless summer. White foam fringed its top and little flecks of moisture, tasting of salt, sea, and toasted ham, wafted toward her.

As Jean gazed up, open-mouthed, grilled cheese dribbling from her lips like disbelief, she realized she had shrunk. Either that or the sandwich had grown, because she was now standing, neat black pumps buried in grains of what had once been bread but was now unmistakably sand.

She was alone on the beach—for beach it was—a blinding infinity of sand white as Wonder bread streaming in either direction. The indigo ham curled above her, drawing back the pebbles and flinging them at her shoes.

She looked around, trying to absorb the metamorphosis of her lunch.

Gliding toward her down the shore coasted a flying saucer. It was an unnatural bright green—but then, nothing about this day was natural.

As it approached, skimming the surface of the sand, she saw that it was being chased by a large, hairy yellowish creature—a golden retriever—tongue flapping in mindless delight. His paws punched softly into the sand, making tiny declivities, which shone in the sun before being damped by the rolling tide.

It was a Frisbee, Jean realized, just a Frisbee. She felt tremendous relief at this minor normality.

Behind the joyful dog, almost keeping pace with him, ran a man—strong honeyed limbs pumping, white teeth flashing, eyes as blue as dreams.

Cheesy ham drooled from Jean's mouth, heated by an internal fire. All the dry spaces inside her became moist. The dog leapt up, curving a perfect ellipse in space, as he grabbed the Frisbee and deposited it at Jean's feet.

The man arrived a minute later, breathless and laughing. Jean was breathless too. She had never seen anyone so alive.

"RIIIINNNNGGGG." A sound louder than the ocean's roar, more incongruous than the change of bread to beach, shattered the silence.

Jean blinked in the morning light. She was in bed, the alarm clock sounding like a judgment. Jean always set her alarm, although she had never needed it before.

It was just a dream, she thought, *but so real.*

She got up to brush her teeth, but as she looked in the mirror—for one brief instance—instead of her pale, tight face, a sun-bronzed goddess looked back. Shaking her head, the woman in the image vanished—the flashback of a dream so tangible, even now she could taste the piquant salt air and smell the rich, live, hammy sea.

Without letting herself think, she took off her cotton nightgown and, trying not to look at her clam-pale body, dug through her drawers like a manic puppy. Hidden beneath her underwear, she found it. A tiny bikini, striped like a candy cane. It had been a prize won at an office party where Jean had calculated the exact number of pinto beans in a jar. She had meant to throw the suit away, or give it to Good Will, but instead she had buried it beneath mounds of sensible cotton undergarments.

Squinting at herself in the mirror, she could almost see the tanned goddess. Before she could change her mind, she grabbed a towel, slipped on her thongs and ran the three blocks to the waiting beach.

She didn't even notice that surrounding the white plate on her table, tiny bits of sand glittered like promises in the morning light.

Famished Upheaval

Ethan Hedman

The King's own patch of golden wheat
Was discovered cut in ragged shreds
Not a grain remained for the kingdom's elites;
The peasants ground it for their bread

The Queen's prize boar had gotten loose
Escaping from its gleaming pram
It met its end and found new use;
The peasants smoked its legs for ham

The Prince and Princess gardened well
And sprouting veggies soon accrued
But their young anger would not quell;
The peasants absconded with their food

The castle's knights tore through the town
Fraught to locate the royals' things
In every home, the same was found:
A sandwich feast befitting a King

Dill's Song

Lionel Ray Green

I ordered the ham and cheese on wheat from Mill Street Deli.

The lady behind the counter—her nametag read Edie —piled the slices of Black Forest ham and Swiss cheese onto the bread.

Edie smiled, wrapped the sandwich, and placed it inside a brown paper bag with the Mill Street Deli logo. She rang up my order.

"That'll be fifteen dollars and seventy cents."

It was expensive but worth every penny for a taste of the tender gourmet ham infused with a hint of honey.

I paid, exited the deli, and stepped outside into snow flurries and winter wind. The tall downtown buildings did nothing to shield me from the arctic assault. They funneled the cold currents of air into bone-chilling bullets of icy numbness.

I only need to survive for five minutes until I reach my office, I thought.

Ahead, an elderly man, a young boy of perhaps ten or twelve years old, and a black-speckled gray mutt had set up camp on the sidewalk between a jewelry shop and a clothing boutique.

The man wore a faded camouflage coat and sported an unkempt gray beard. He had a cardboard sign on his chest that read: HOMELESS VET. WILL WORK FOR FOOD.

The boy was bundled in multiple flannel shirts and wore a tan cold-weather hat with ear flaps. He rubbed the dog's belly, and the mutt's back legs twitched involuntarily.

I'd avoided this motley trio for three weeks since I transferred to my new job downtown. When I saw them, I'd walk to the other side of the street until I could safely cross back to my side without the chance of an encounter.

Today was too cold to extend my walk an extra two minutes. Head down, I scurried by them.

What's wrong with me? I thought.

Three steps past their spot, I stopped and returned to stand in front of the elderly man. He was asleep.

"Need something, mister?" the boy asked.

"No, I was just going to give this man my ham sandwich."

Excited, the boy grabbed the old man by the arm and woke him.

"Dill," the boy said. "This guy wants to give you a ham sandwich."

Dill adjusted himself to sit up straighter, causing the HOMELESS VET sign to fall facedown on his lap.

"Much obliged, sir," said Dill, noticing the logo on the brown paper bag. "I've been craving some Mill Street Deli for a while now."

Dill pulled the ham sandwich from the bag, unwrapped it, and breathed in the aroma.

"No problem," I said. "I hope you enjoy it. Thank you for your service."

I walked away, feeling proud of myself for helping a homeless vet.

Until I looked back.

An irritating anger replaced my pride as I watched the old man Dill hand a slice of wheat bread to the boy, keeping the other piece of bread for himself.

Then, Dill tossed the ham and cheese to the mutt. The dog gulped it down in two bites.

Are you kidding me? I thought. *What a waste.*

I watched Dill and the boy as they ate their bread, savoring one bite at a time. They were smiling and talking.

The boy wrapped his arm around the mutt's neck, and the dog licked the boy right on the mouth. I heard the boy say "gross" and giggle at the mutt's drool-drenched affection. Dill laughed so hard that he slapped his knee a couple of times.

Witnessing the joy of the moment did nothing to quell my anger.

When I arrived at the office, the grumbling of my stomach reminded me of my wasted fifteen-dollar-and-seventy-cent ham sandwich. The image of the dog woofing it down needled my thoughts.

I avoided the homeless trio for the next couple of weeks. I'd see the old man Dill, the boy, and the dog camped at the same spot every day, but I'd skirt their perimeter by walking on the other side of the street.

One day, while heading to Mill Street Deli, I noticed they were gone. No old man, no boy, no dog. I paused at their spot on the sidewalk and looked around. Nothing.

Maybe the cold convinced them to go to a shelter, I thought.

Three days later, as I walked to Mill Street Deli to purchase my ham-and-cheese sandwich, I heard the familiar voice of the boy.

"Mister?"

I kept walking.

"Mister? Wait up. I just want to thank you."

I stopped and turned to face the boy. The black-speckled gray mutt was at his side with a short rope tied around its neck.

"Thank me? For what?" I asked.

"For that sandwich you gave us," the boy said. "That was nice. It really brightened ol' Dill's day."

"You're welcome," I said. "It was just a sandwich."

"Yeah, but it made ol' Dill happy," the boy said. "It was a good day."

"Where's Dill?"

The boy glanced at the dog before answering.

"He, uh, passed."

"Passed? Like died?" I was shocked.

"Yes sir. He passed quietly in his sleep, just like he wanted."

"I'm sorry to hear that."

"I was looking for you because the last thing he told me was to find you and tell you how much that meant to him," the boy said. "The day before he died, he told me, 'Don't never take no kindness for granted.' I think he knew the end was near."

"I'm so sorry."

I reached down and petted the dog.

"Is this Dill's dog?"

"Yes sir."

"What's his name?"

"Pickles," the boy said. "His name is Pickles."

"Of course," I said, grinning. "What's your name, son?"

"Sam."

"Would you and Pickles have lunch with me in honor of Dill?"

"Sure."

I ordered three ham-and-cheese sandwiches from Mill Street Deli.

We stood and ate them at the spot where I first met Dill and Sam.

Pickles gulped his sandwich down in two bites.
This time, I laughed.

Read My Crust: a Brief Linguistic Analysis of Talking Ham Sandwiches

Kelly Robinson

The ancestral roots of the ham sandwich have been well documented, from its breadless beginnings in Spain's Iberian Peninsula to its first appearance in its modern sandwiched form in Elizabeth Leslie's 1840 cookbook. By 1850, the ham sandwich was a favored offering of London street vendors, and today, it is the preferred sandwich of both Americans and the English. Despite this ubiquity, an in-depth linguistic analysis of ham sandwich speech has yet to be undertaken. While comprehensive research is still needed, we can make a brief study of the subject by looking at the semantics and sociolinguistic variables of talking ham sandwiches in film and on television.

The scarcity of written records of ham sandwich speech presents obvious limitations, but an advantage of filmed documentation is that we can observe not only semantics, but also vocal stylistics (dialect, emphasis, etc.). The sample size of talking ham sandwiches is small, but it is considerably larger than documented samples of other sandwich varieties. Though multiple examples exist of ham sandwiches in conversation with other kinds of food, we are missing documentation of two ham sandwiches conversing with each other. This presents difficulties in knowing if the ham sandwiches have altered their speech (or code-switched) in a pragmatic effort to better socialize with humans, celery, and leftover spaghetti.

One of the most consistent markers of ham sandwich speech is the use of paronomasia, or puns, which appears in nearly every single instance of recorded conversation by both fridge-dwelling and extro-fridge subjects. "Read my crust," says the ham sandwich who appears in a series of Florida Orange Juice commercials. A particularly intriguing example appears in the film short *Meltdown*, in which the ham sandwich pleads "Have a heart, celery!"—showing that punning is such an ingrained speech pattern that it shows up even under duress. A rare print example of ham sandwich speech supports the persistence of punning. It appears in *The Muppets Big Book of Crafts,* wherein a ham sandwich is captioned as saying, "Yeah, well you're full of baloney." Given the number of talking sandwiches of several varieties that appear in various Muppet enterprises, we can presume that the Henson Workshop is familiar with their speech and has provided an adequate transcription.

Ham sandwich speech typically makes use of consistent phrases for opening and closing conversations. To open conversations, the most frequent starter is "Hey!" Examples include:

1. "Hey, mopey!" (*Muppets From Space*)

2. "Hey, open up, open up!" (Florida Orange Juice commercial A)

3. "Hey, right up here, next to this poor neglected jug of orange juice." (Florida Orange Juice commercial B)

4. "Hey, ya cheap @#*!, bite me!" (comic strip *One Big Happy*)

5. "Hey, guys." (MTV's *The State*)

In *Meltdown,* the ham sandwich does not begin conversation with "Hey," but it should be noted that the orange, who speaks first, opens with "Hey, guys," and the ham sandwich is the first to respond. This may be a case where the ham sandwich has recognized the orange's choice of "Hey" as a social cue meant to gain *his* specific attention, despite the fact that the whole group was addressed. This form of language bonding is similar to a moment in a Florida Orange Juice commercial when a person tells the ham sandwich to "chill out." The sandwich responds favorably: "Chill out... refrigerator humor, I like that." He has bonded with a human over a shared language style, i.e. the use of puns.

Another ubiquitous language marker among ham sandwiches is the use of a closing retort, or "zinger." In fact, it's rare to observe a talking ham sandwich that doesn't use one as a signal that a conversation has ended. This can even be observed in cases where the existence of a talking ham sandwich is temporal. In an episode of *The Muppet Show,* guest star Linda Lavin asks Scooter to make her a sandwich. Scooter says, "Okay, you're a sandwich," at which point Ms. Lavin is transformed into a ham sandwich long enough to deliver a zinger: "Everybody's a comedian." We see similar behavior in *Muppets From Space,* in which a talking sandwich is inhabited by an alien. It's tricky to know how much of the sandwich's speech patterning is alien-derived and how much is part of the sandwich's natural syntax. A clue lies in the sandwich's closing zinger ("I'm just a sandwich. Some things you gotta figure out for yourself"), which not only follows typical ham sandwich conventions, but explicitly states the character's sense of self as being *sandwich.* In other words, the sandwich and not the alien possessor speaks this line.

Some ham sandwich outliers exhibit speech patterns that vary from the norm but offer insight into the ways the dialect has spread and changed. A ham sandwich appearing on the MTV sketch comedy show *The State* mimics the nasal whine of the humans who appear in the same sketch. The sandwich ("Frank") maintains a steady, deadpan tone of delivery at odds with the hot-cha comic delivery seen in most ham sandwich speech samples. As unusual as Frank's delivery is, he still exhibits some of the classic markers of traditional speech, opening with "Hey, guys." We also know that Frank makes jokes, though they are hard to recognize, which are deemed funny to his odd companions. "Waiter, do you have fried bumblebees today?" is followed by monotone laughter from the group. As the question is also Frank's closing line, that means he has followed ham sandwich convention by closing with a zinger, even if it lacks the typical zing.

Of particular interest are speech samples from ham sandwich components. Though their dialects sometimes differ greatly from that of their more-evolved compatriots, they offer some insight into the origins of ham sandwich speech. The use of puns by tomatoes (exemplified by the lyric heard on TV's *The Young Ones*, "I've just got to ketchup with my life") suggests the possibility of paronomasia being a trait that derives specifically from the inclusion of tomatoes on a ham sandwich, rather than an inherent fixture of the sandwich *in toto*. Further research is needed to determine if ham sandwiches with tomatoes are more inclined to punning than their non-dressed counterparts.

Segments of the television show *Pee-Wee's Playhouse* feature several varieties of talking food, including a whole ham. This ham is not only an ancestor to the ham sandwich, but it's also a special case in that it may be some sort of primordial ham. (Note that Pee Wee's home also houses a dinosaur family.) The frigid temperatures of the refrigerator and freezer may have led to a sort of Ice Age for some (though not all) of its denizens. Hams have notably long shelf lives, and this one seems to be a particularly primitive ancestor of the ham sandwich, not only lacking bread flaps with which to make speech (he has merely a strip of pimiento), but also lacking olives for eyes. When we first see the ham, he is visibly upset at the noise levels of The Crinkle Cuts, a french fry rock band performing in the freezer compartment. As the ham bangs on the top of his fridge compartment with a breadstick, he makes audible protests, but his sounds only barely resemble speech. His rudimentary moans and grunts represent a sort of ham sandwich ur-language. Further study is warranted.

While we now know some of the main components of the dialect, we still have no examples of ham sandwich-to-ham sandwich communication and very little insight into written speech. Further study should also be made into spokes-sandwiches, who do little more than parrot brand slogans ("That's not French's!"). Studies of sandwiches with fillings other than ham could provide insight into language development (see the nightmare meatball sub from *The Cosby Show* and the talking turkey sandwich in David Schwimmer's Skittles commercials, for example). And, as mentioned earlier, components that make up ham sandwiches have room for further exploration. What relationship does bread type play in syntax? Do sandwich spreads reduce or enhance the use of zingers? Do full-size sandwiches engage in code-switching when conversing with sliders? Ham sandwich speech is under-studied and under-recognized, and efforts should be made to fund further study. As the milk says of the ham sandwich in *Meltdown,* he is "the best of us combined."

The Zesty Garlic Pickles

Edward Palumbo

so much is stacked
upon

the zesty garlic
pickles

adorning the sliced
cheddar

within the ham
sandwich

Eating the Earl

Rachel Robins

For Lady Beatrice Wellington, *love* was the very last thing on her mind the evening her father's murderer was captured. She had unwillingly spent the last four nights wide-eyed and waiting, not for a paramour to join her, but for the faintest sounds of a trap well sprung. Once the stroke of midnight had long ago come and gone, and with it her delusions of rest, she cast aside her bedclothes. She'd given to pacing her chamber and fretting whether or not she had been most correct. Her, as well as her family's and her estate's, fate depended on whether her gamble paid off.

"Gamble, indeed." She rubbed her weary face. "I'm Papa's daughter, after all."

But then her straining ears caught a startled yell. A loud crash. The muted thud of something hard hitting soft flesh. The dragging scrape of shoes against cobblestones. Indelicate cursing.

Finally. Hope surged within her breast, propelling her to the bedchamber window. The sight below drove her heart to racing. Several dark figures in constable helmets flooded the alleyway. In the center of their confrontation, an old man, too distant and the light too dim to make out his features, struggled with a very familiar and comforting physique that handed the tramp to a pair of men.

The Lord Edward George Hamothy Montagu, the eighth Earl of Sandwich, stood sexily in the alley, somehow exuding confidence and complex masculinity. Towering at 6'4" by 5'5" wide, his rectangular shape was unmistakable, although the white of his bread was wrapped tightly in an overcoat to guard against the night's wet. He conferred with a constable for a moment before glancing up to meet her eyes through her bedroom window. The literal sandwich lordling gave her a barely perceptible nod before leading their prisoner to her doorway.

It had worked.

She scarcely had time to throw a shawl over her chemise and race to the stairs in the entry hall. A retinue of men gathered at the foot of the stairs, appearing more wretched and damp for their exposure to the evening's unpleasant weather, but Lady Beatrice had eyes only for Lord Montagu.

How strange it was now that she'd once thought him so odd, so incomprehensible. How could an earl possibly be a sentient, oversized sandwich? It was beyond absurd. Every time she broached the subject of the earl's curious visage in polite society, she'd been rebuffed, the topic considered too vulgar for genteel discourse. The *ton* knew that Lord Montagu was the spitting image of his father, although she had longed to spy *that* family portrait in the sandwich-man's halls. Every conversational foray had been met with the same circuity: that his manners were most refined, his air was the result of good breeding, and his was a most generous nature. No one spoke ill of him.

"Gentlemen, my Lord," she said by way of greeting.

Lord Montagu performed a quick bow. "You'll have to forgive us for our sudden and somewhat abused appearance this early hour, Lady Wellington. Our morning angling expedition has yielded us quite the slippery fish, as it were."

Warmth and gratitude swept her core for his prior insistence of handling this matter personally. Her sex restricted her ability to be her own agent in her pursuit of her father's murderer, and the limitation chafed her. Yet, despite her initial vehemence when she believed Montagu responsible for Papa's murder and the sudden notice of sale for Sawthorn Manor, the earl had been quick to assist.

She blushed as she thought of how she first sought him out, to demand his return of Papa's possessions and the deed to her childhood estate. She had been ice and rock to him at their first audience. *Despite your affected assurances, Lord Montagu, your name was reported on*

Papa's dying breath. From my own inquiries, were you or were you not one of the last men to meet with him the evening he was beaten so terribly? You should know that he died badly, succumbing to his wounds by morning. Oh, how she burned with embarrassment to think of what she'd said then. *Lord Montagu, my visit is strictly a courtesy from one peer of the realm to another. I am watching you. If you are the responsible party, I will discover the evil deeds you've committed and I will have justice.*

As the earl towered in her hall arguing with the old man, undoubtedly Papa's murderer and Montagu's blackmailer, she was struck by how dashing a sandwich he made. How even this late and despite the weather, his bread looked so white, unblemished and invitingly soft, and his protruding lettuce leaf, so fresh. She wanted very much to lean into his soft gluten exterior and take strength from him, knowing that Papa's murderer was finally caught. It was over.

When she finally turned her attention from the earl and fully assessed the murderer, her mouth gaped. "*Uncle Louis*?"

The constable tensed. "You know this man, Lady?"

"Of course, I do." Beatrice could hardly believe it. "This is my uncle, Louis, brother to my father. Although I have not seen him for many years. Undoubtedly, this... is he."

The rotted teeth, soot-stained face, and gruff, disheveled manner was difficult to reconcile with the older kindly gentleman who had once smiled sweetly at her and bought her lavish dolls and bonbons.

"He had a terrible falling out with Papa some years ago. Only after much pressing, Papa told us that his brother had devolved to a vile creature. He didn't want his debauchery to reach the ears of polite society and ruin his chances of marriage for me and my sisters."

"Debauchery? Vile creature?" Uncle Louis hocked and spat. "That bastard cheated me out of my birthright! My inheritance! He *wronged* me. Threw me out of our ancestral home and left me to die friendless in the world. But did that stop Henry from doing the same? No. Everyone knew he held the same vices as me: drink, cards, and whores up to his eyeballs. But to act so high and mighty? And leave me with nothing? I swore I'd gut him like a hog for slaughter and leave him to bleed out in the street like the animal he was."

Lady Wellington braced herself against the wave of lightheadedness from that image, but otherwise remained stoic.

The sandwich earl tightened his grip on the man's arm. "Sir, you will watch your tongue. We're in the presence of a lady."

"Don't think I've forgotten you, either!" Uncle Louis snapped at him. "I would have gotten away with my revenge if it weren't for you! I should have known a witness statement in the newspaper was a setup. 'Spied details of the fleeing assailant,' my arse. I'm sure to have *you* to thank for that bit of deviousness."

"You are mistaken, dear Uncle. That bit of the plot was my own device. Lord Montagu was only so kind to see it executed. I think you'll concede that deviousness is a family trait." Lady Wellington wrapped her shawl more tightly around her shoulders and turned toward the stairwell. "But I think that we all have heard enough and that the hour is very late. Please allow me, my lord, to retire for the night. I suddenly find myself most fatigued."

•

Lord Montagu delayed until well into the afternoon the following week before returning to call again on Lady Wellington. Upon his arrival, the footman waved him into the parlor room that smelled very much of *her*. "Forgive us, my lord. The lady was not expecting you to call this afternoon. She will join you presently."

Lord Montagu nodded, distracted. *Blast it.* He should have sent a bloody card. How embarrassing would it have been to arrive to strange looks from the staff and the house empty? Why did this simple protocol not occur to him while he drove himself mad this last fortnight, both keeping himself away and devising strategies to meet? *Dammit, man,* a card. Was he a complete imbecile?

He sighed and rubbed the back of his crust. He was not at all himself. The image of her disarray had plagued him since their last audience. Her chemise and shawl had done little to hide her intoxicating form. He had but to close his eyes for the barest moment for it to spring back in vivid detail. The gauzy white under-linen over magnificent breasts, the curve of her hip against the fabric, and—most salacious of all—the subtle peek of calf. The memory stirred his lettuce and melted the slice of Swiss deep inside him. It dribbled down against his thick, hard slab of ham until he throbbed at attention. How he wanted to follow that mouth-watering flesh further north to explore all the wondrous hills and valleys of her topography.

His mad reveries of that night always concluded with the sharp resolve on her face, her head held high, stiff-backed in the face of her father's murderer. He could not reflect upon the night's events without admiring Lady Wellington for her cleverness and her strength of character to see this through to the end. Few women would have led such detailed inquiries and pursued justice so fiercely for a man who was by all accounts not the most dutiful nor loving Papa. Montagu previously had his doubts regarding her part of the plan when she laid it out before him. *You forget, sir, how we women do battle.* She held the folded newspaper aloft. *You may go trudging through every sewer and every house of ill-repute in search of a man you may never find, but I would much rather have* him *come to us.*

He shook his head in awe of her. He had never known her like. She had successfully lured out the fox and managed the trick so elegantly. As she'd turned to excuse herself for the evening, he'd been struck by two realizations; he had never admired a woman so much in his life, and he never wanted her to walk away from him again.

Lady Wellington's gentle step announced her arrival several moments before she physically entered the room. In her black chenille gown with the fetching dark lace at the neck and elbows, she seemed diminished since they'd last met. The fire from her cheeks had banked, her skin having paled, and her face was drawn.

Lord Montagu stood and bowed. "I trust, lady, that you are well."

"Forgive me, my lord." She bobbed a curtsy. "I did not expect your call. I'm afraid you will find that I do not make the best company these days. Please, sit." She gestured to the green damask settee and settled herself on the matched pair before him. "Oh, I suppose that I am well enough. As well as can be expected from this frightful weather."

He frowned at the sadness that so clearly marked her features. "But something is definitely amiss."

"Oh? I take it that you have not been following the papers, then?" She smiled wanly at him and offered the folded newspaper on the settee beside to him. "Do not think me ungrateful for the pleasure of your company today, sir. Perhaps it will do me some good. I merely find myself surprised I should have any visitors today now that word has spread."

The headline read in bold, *Louis of Wellington Arrested on Charges of Fratricide, Intentions to Commit Murder, Conspiracy, and Theft.*

Lord Montagu blinked at the article and internally swore.

"I admit it rather smarts to have the same weapon I used against Uncle Louis applied to me as well. Perhaps I deserve it." She pouted in bemusement, and her lips were enough to steal his attention in spite of their soured look. "Sometimes I like to think myself cleverer than I am. You can imagine my dismay to realize how the news of Uncle Louis' confessions would break. Despite all my efforts to secure both mine and my sisters' future happiness, we are now tainted by association to his crimes. No good family will want any of my sisters as a wife now." She lowered her gaze as tears gathered in her eyes.

The sight of those translucent pearls sliding down her cheeks cut him like a knife to the gut.

She blinked back the tears and smiled at him. "Such an ingrate you must think me! If it weren't for your assistance, we would have not regained the deed to Sawthorn that Papa had gambled with, and everything would have been well and truly lost. Perhaps I should count myself most lucky that we are well and truly without family or friends. I would have had no chance at inheriting if a long-lost cousin fell from the woodwork. As the eldest, I must now be the one responsible for all of their futures."

"You're not without friends." Lord Montagu dismissed that concern. Had he not proven himself a friend already? "You don't have to shoulder this burden alone. You may yet still marry."

"You are exceedingly kind, sir. I am grateful for your kindness, but even I am forced to admit that chance is very likely fled." Her smile turned wry. "Perhaps country life might treat us all more gently."

Lord Montagu stilled. The most exquisite pain tightened at his core. "You are… leaving."

"I'm afraid that we must. It's what my sisters and I were busying ourselves with just as you arrived." She smoothed her hands over the skirt of her dress. "I am glad you've come. We expect to be on the road home tomorrow, but I would be grieved not to have had the chance to well and truly thank you." Her eyes met his and burned once more with fire and intensity. "I was neither kind nor polite at our first introduction, but you listened to me, considered my insight thoughtfully as if I were an equal, and trusted me to play my hand when the time came. I know that partly you were motivated to discover the identity of your blackmailer, but still. Words cannot express what that meant to me. Truly, you have proved a credit to your reputation. I will always remember what you have done for us."

Her countenance flared to life in his mind, as did the sight of her slim form moving away from him. How it galled him. Blast it, here she was doing it again. Trying to depart from him, and this time not for an evening but for the rest of their lives. It would not do, dammit. It would not do at all.

He straightened on the settee, resolved. "So will you not offer me some recompense for these actions for which you are so grateful?"

She stared at him, startled. "Of course, I would. I would give you anything I could within my power. But what could I give you that you could not get yourself?" The gears behind her eyes turned. "If it's capital you seek, I really won't know what Sawthorn is capable of providing until we arrive, but I will send word to your secretary—"

He took her hand and the action silenced her. He spoke softly. "My dear Beatrice. It's not your capital I want, nor your gratitude, nor your farewells, but your heart." He stroked the back of her hand before moving it to his chest. "Do you not feel how my artichoke heart beats for you?"

Lady Wellington gaped. "What—what are you doing?"

The sandwich lord pulled in her hands until they sunk into the whiteness of his bread. "I offer you myself, a share of my possessions and a part of my soul. I love you. Marry me."

"You—you can't mean this."

"I do. Most ardently."

"But there have been no signs, no subtle flirtations, no secret caresses, no indications of any of this!"

His grip on her hand loosened, and his brows furrowed in consideration. Eventually, he said, "Quite right. I've neglected the process most terribly. I will repent, starting now."

"That's not what I—"

•

Lady Beatrice could not have been more shocked as he leaned in to kiss her, and not only because he didn't have a mouth and she had previously assumed his mouth-area was a little down and to the right. She could not accept what was happening. How could she? Even if she could overlook how nonsensical his offer was, she was not a person who got what she wanted most deeply. She could not afford to think such happiness was a possibility for someone like *her*.

Her mother had swallowed love's lies. Her parents' happiness didn't last for long, and Mama lamented on her deathbed what a fool she had been, to be so blinded by something as fleeting as love. Beatrice swore to her mother that she would not make the same mistake.

She struggled halfheartedly to resist his touch, but he was more skilled than she expected for a man without a mouth. He adeptly stoked the fires of passion, and soon she melted into his kiss, losing herself in the intimacy, repaying his caresses in kind. She cupped the approximate location of where she estimated his cheek would be, and he leaned into her touch, as if he were as hungry for her as she was for him.

His soft sandwich form curved around her body, pulling her close. His bread was every bit as plush and comforting as she'd imagined. Delicate sensations thrummed beneath her breast. Part of her knew it was wrong. To have a living sandwich in her arms, and to want him so all the same. To want more of him. She longed to run her fingers across his lettuce leaf, to tweak the seeds nestled in his tomato slices. She wanted to pry open his pillowy exterior and spy his naked core, to greet the parts of him she'd dreamed of late at night. And though she blushed to think about it, she wanted to wrap her fingers around his pink meat and slide it along her tongue.

So she did. She dropped to her knees and lapped him up. He gasped at her boldness, the use of her teeth upon him, or the shock of having such sensitive parts of him so brazenly explored. Under her careful machinations, he shuddered a release within few moments.

With the taste of him thick on her tongue, he pulled her up to kiss her more fiercely than before. Her skirts rose under frantic attention. She burned in excitement for this sandwich man, *her* sandwich man. As a girl growing up, she'd learned from the stables the basic mechanics of lovemaking. But with a sandwich? How did one love one so thoroughly with both heart and body?

But she needn't have worried. The earl knew this business well enough.

When she made her own gasps of pleasure, she cried out. "L-lord Montagu!"

"*Please*," he whispered huskily in her ear. "Please call me Hamothy, my love. All my closest friends do."

"Oh, *Hamothy*." His name was a gentle exhalation on her swollen lips.

"Tell me yes," he grunted between his own passionate gasps. "Tell me quickly."

Who knew the love between a lady and a sandwich could reach such heights of ecstasy? She'd never allowed her heart to open for this kind of love before. A relationship with him would not be the same as her parents' doomed marriage. And dear Lord, how she loved him. There was no other way for her to respond. "Yes! Oh, yes!"

She expected to feel embarrassed several moments later, when all clothing had been righted, hair smoothed back into place, and the earl's spilled condiments dabbed up from her fine settee and the corner of her mouth, but she didn't. It had felt *right*. All of it. More than right. Now, she wanted more. She reached for him and he reclaimed her hand.

They were still gazing adoringly at each other when Beatrice's sisters called from down the hall. She cleared her throat and called back, "Over here!"

All six of them gathered in the doorway, their eyes as round as dinner plates. Whether they were shocked by the appearance of Beatrice's sandwich lord or the fact that her hand was gently fingering his crust, it was impossible to know. She'd save those explanations for another time. For now, she merely beamed at them. "Sisters, I have the most wondrous news!"

One Small Snack for Man

Kara Race-Moore

"Hello, Earthlings! Welcome back to another episode of *Cooking on Mars*." Dr. FitzSimmons smiled brightly for the camera as he stood in the Mars One communal kitchen area. A cutting board, knives, dishes and ingredients were all laid out on the counter for that episode's dish.

"I'm Dr. Calvin FitzSimmons," he introduced himself needlessly, as if he was an ordinary cooking show host, instead of one of the Original Seven. "Many of you know me as First Step," he continued, "for my *small* role in the first human mission to Mars." The photo of his famous red footprint, the first step a human had taken on Mars, now decorated the walls of classrooms and dormitories around the world.

He smiled at the camera with false modesty. The intrepid explorer was no stranger to the spotlight and knew exactly how to stand to show off his lanky frame and perfectly combed red hair to his best advantage. Being chosen to be part of the first group of humans on Mars had required being intelligent, resilient, creative—and able to look good in press releases.

"Here on *Cooking on Mars,* we show you how, in between collecting data on planetary life cycles and testing theories of physics, we manage to make delicious meals when the nearest grocery store is fifty million miles away." Before he had left Earth, First Step had trained with an acting coach to let his Irish lilt be just strong enough to identify him as #TheIrishOne, but moderate enough for any English speaker to understand him easily. Talking like some rich toff had, he reflected, been worth the price to move him forward in the selection process, even if his grandfather had endlessly mocked him for it.

"Last time, we made a delicious tabouli salad, showing the expanded capacity of the hydroponic garden. Today, we're veering back into meat eater's territory as I make a ham sandwich. This will be no Kubrickian concoction of paste and cardboard; some of the ingredients were produced right here on Mars, while others made an incredible journey to be part of today's meal."

A squat loaf of bread sat on a cutting board in front of him. "The first sandwich in space was corned beef, smuggled on board during the Gemini 3 mission by John Young. This pioneer of space flight was then severely reprimanded by both NASA and the United States Congress for the damage floating crumbs could have caused." He chuckled. "Quite the little tempest in a teapot, that was. Still, they had a point about the dangers of mixing crumbs and delicate machinery while in micro-gravity." Being willing to break rules, First Step thought, was part of space exploration, something all astronauts intrinsically grasped, and bureaucrats never could.

First Step picked up a bread knife to begin cutting the loaf. "For a long time, only flatbreads such as tortilla wraps were allowed on the space ships and space stations, since they were much less likely to crumble, and dense spreads like peanut butter were used for filling, since, again, they were less likely to break apart in a reduced-gravity environment." He cut a slice from the loaf and began slicing another. Crumbs scattered across the cutting board, like the inevitable Martian dust tracked into the airlock.

"Here on Mars, even with only one third of Earth's gravity, we don't have to worry about floating crumbs, but we use the 'Wilkerson-Process' to make bread. This uses carbon dioxide instead of yeast, controlling the rising process in a low-gravity environment, and we don't have to worry about shipping the yeast from Earth, which, poor thing, does *not* travel well." He smiled as he finished cutting the second slice.

"The flour was made from a mix of wholegrain wheat and spirulina, both grown by our very talented Dr. Sakai in the hydroponics garden, and together these ingredients produce a flour that provides a needed source of fiber and protein. Our specialized oven bakes the bread at a low temperature, which takes longer but is well worth it to be able to enjoy the smell of fresh baked bread for the first time since we left Earth." He pulled in a deep breath and sighed. "I can tell you, it was just *heaven* when we baked that first loaf here." His smile hid his thoughts of how dry that first attempt had been. It may have smelled delicious, but it had been dry as the desert outside. They were still working out the kinks of retaining moisture. Placing both slices of bread flat on the board, he moved the rest of the loaf aside.

"Next, the spread," he said, picking up a small jar. "Back in Ireland, butter would be the more likely choice, but here we've been experimenting with mayonnaise recipes. Mayonnaise has a relatively short shelf life, and wouldn't last the trip from Earth to Mars, so we've used our own recipe. The egg powder and milk powder are too vital for our breakfast dishes, so we used a vegan recipe." He grinned at the camera. "We scoured the internet—and a big shout out to Yingyue for her recipe from her blog, AtomicVeganPunkGirl!" He dipped a knife in the jar and carefully began to spread it on the two slices of bread. "You want to be careful and not overdo it or go over the edge. You want to spread it evenly, up and down, like following the lines of a football pitch, just enough for a thin coating. There!" He flourished the knife as he finished applying the mayonnaise.

He screwed the lid back on the jar and turned to the joint of meat on a platter in front of him, which sat incongruously in the ultra-modern kitchen. "Until now the closest we've had to fresh meat has been the Petri-Pork and Better Bovine cultures we've grown in the lab here." His mouth stretched wide in his much-practiced commercial smile. "The cultured meat is cloned tissues of meat originally from Earth, generously provided by Future Foods Inc., food from tomorrow to be eaten today,"— he smoothly slipped in the tag line without gagging—"and while it takes up much less space and resources than a full-grown cow, it comes in a pre-ground state, and doesn't exactly slice." First Step thought back, slightly nauseated, to all the chili, "meat loaf," and burritos they'd eaten to use up the ground meat they'd had on hand.

"Today, we have a ham-on-the-bone that was boiled here, the meat itself from a successful experiment in cryogenics, frozen on Earth and shipped here, where it was unfrozen, as fresh as if straight from a butcher's shop." The large haunch of ham looked deceptively ordinary and slightly out of place. First Step did not mention just how much money this cryogenics experiment had cost, not wanting to scare off potential new investors in the Mars colony.

He wasn't sure how he felt about the bourgeoning cryogenics program. That was very likely going to be the future of space travel for live cargo, not just fresh food, and the thought of someday traveling like a frozen popsicle was unnerving, to say the least.

"I'll just carve off a few pieces here," he said. "And place them there, just enough to fill the inside." He deposited them carefully on one piece of bread, a bubble of joy rising in his chest at the sight of a real slice of meat on actual loaf bread. "The rest of this ham is going to be used in many, many meals. Be sure to tune in when the bone goes into my Granny Martha's recipe for split pea soup! Making as many homestyle meals as possible has been an important part of this mission—it helps keep us sane." He gave the camera a not-quite-reassuring grin.

He turned to the waiting tomato and head of lettuce and gestured as if showing off prized jewels. "Experiments with plants have been conducted since the earliest days of Earth-orbiting capsules and space stations. Hydroponic grown tomatoes and lettuce were already available on the good ship *Pegasus* that brought us here to Mars, and the garden was one of the first sections assembled here.

Our garden is a vital part of Mars One, for the oxygen it provides, the carbon dioxide the plants absorb, the fresh food produced, and the sight of something *green*,"—he stressed the word with no irony—"in a world that is red, red, and more red. The hydroponics garden is everyone's favorite place to unwind, recharge, and take a deep breath of homemade oxygen. There we can enjoy the sight of green and water, two things we have in short supply here on the Red Planet."

"Speaking of red, we next have the tomato." He used the sharp little kitchen knife to cut into the vibrant tomato, slicing off several dripping-wet wedges. "These provide a bit of moisture to the sandwich, especially important here on a desert planet." Watery red drops puddled on the cutting board. So much water in one little slice of red; he resisted the urge to pick one up and suck down the juices, instead placing the wedges of tomato on the slices of ham.

He turned to the lettuce with a broad smile and tore off two leaves. "I'll just be using two broad leaves, here and here," he said, carefully positioning the rough sheets of greenery on top of the rest of the ingredients. "Now these, you do want them to be overlapping the bread a bit, so they stick out. This way you get a little bit of the green. I grew up on a farm, you know, and green was everywhere.

We want the green to be as visible in as many things as possible." He carefully re-positioned the leaves, shifting them slightly to be in just the right place. "And, of course, where there is ham, there is cheese, and that, my friends, is straight from Earth.

We are not at the level of making fresh cheese here, as Mars One is still a small habitat, but as we continue to expand, we have plans to reach the point where we can support a self-sustaining farm, and Phase IV of humans on Mars includes having live pigmy goats shipped from Earth."

A thin yellow square of processed cheese waited on the table. "American cheese," he said, peeling back the plastic, releasing the dairy product to the processed air of Mars for the first time since it had been packaged on Earth. "Hermetically sealed, carefully preserved, this cheese is well-suited for the journey from Earth to Mars—truly the pioneer product of the dairy industry."

The American cheese had been the result of a long, protracted debate over what type of cheese to ship to Mars. First Step had argued for Irish Swiss and had been contacted by an Irish company that was more than happy to have him be their spokesperson, but they had demanded too high a cut in the bidding process. Numerous French companies, of course, wanted to send cheese to Mars, but balked at the required sterilization processes. An Italian company had tried to get their Provolone to be the official Martian cheese, but with no Italian astronauts currently part of the mission, there had been no angle for their brand and the Provolone that they had suggested didn't have enough utility for the variety of Martian meals. And a Russian company had been pushing hard for Dr. Mikhalova to be seen eating their cheese on Mars. Not unlike the multiple companies bidding to be the one used to provide the rockets, rovers, and safety equipment—every corporation wanted to see their products and brand displayed prominently on Mars.

Lifted between his thumb and forefinger, the slice of cheese rose from the safety of its plastic wrap and landed on the bed of the Martian ham sandwich, with no sign of the aggressive competition over its very presence.

First Step then picked up the second slice of bread and placed it with surgical precision on top of everything else. "Now, my grandfather taught me that bread was never meant to be triangular. That you want to cut a sandwich in two rectangular halves like a good field, and I've always kept to his habit." He cut down, separating the sandwich into two perfect rectangular halves.

"And there we have a Martian ham sandwich." He bit into one half, and munched and swallowed with obvious delight. "Thanks for joining me, and, as always, our kitchens may be millions of miles apart, but we should all enjoy the simple pleasures of a simple meal, no matter what else is going on. *Sláinte*!"

Wrappers and Crusts

Frances Boyle

Shadows of motion I'm trying to record
with a blunt pencil, a sketch I dash
off too quickly, the seconds sandwiched
in. I shade the background: that wall with the ivy,
old maples, one moving point, the weight
of stones piled tight for a crowbar to lever.

I can't count on luck, throw dice, pull the lever.
I doodle in circles, like the grooves on old records.
If it weren't for the stories, could I stand the wait?
I read of passionate friends like Lillian and Dash,
how thirty years' strength wound together like ivy
their love and their struggles, cold coffee and sandwiches.

I juggle quite glibly, but I'm what gets sandwiched
twixt rocks and hard places. Is there something to lever
me out? I'd climb but my hands might find poison ivy.
Every day is the same, there's a skip in this record.
Could I be my own hero with attitude dashing?
Old burdens and new, could I bear the weight?

Wrappers and Crusts

I've been driving all night, too anxious to wait,
the car's full of wrappers and crusts of ham sandwich.
Reading my maps by the light of the dash,
I hum fifty ways Paul says he could leave 'er.
The late-shift DJ spinning all those hit records
carries me far from walls covered with ivy.

I've seen people I love full of tubes and IVs:
the words must be squeezed out, they really can't wait.
Find a way to mark each so it stands clear on the record.
Hire a town crier, skywriter or a student with sandwich
boards – whatever the tools, just use them to lever
open the floodgates, don't fear cold water will dash.

Our own history is code – dash, dash, dot; dot, dot, dash.
The door to the playground is hidden with ivy.
I know that a balance is just one kind of lever.
"Let me down, Farmer Brown" begs the kid with least weight.
The story most real is told through bites of ham sandwich
and I often forget what I most want to record.

If you imagine the lever's strong enough for your weight
climb the brambles and ivy just to bring me that sandwich.
Lope a hundred-yard dash, and set your own record.

Bedeviled Ham

Robert Perret

"You can see yourselves out," I said, snapping my newspaper up in front of my face in a futile effort to end the conversation.

"Please, Mr. Graves." Dottie LaMarche tugged at the fold of the newsprint with one dainty finger. The resulting funnel poured my eyes right into her cleavage as she leaned over my desk like a pinup. The way she had slunk in like a silver screen ingenue was the first sign they were playing games.

"This is a serious business," I groused. "You're wasting my time."

"We are serious," Nate LaMarche said, plunking down a brick of bills wrapped in a brown band. "Count it."

If the pile was real, he'd just set the ante at five thousand, a sweet plum that made me like him less. Where Dottie had gone all sticky red lips and smoky eyes, Nate looked like an assistant bank manager on vacation, pale and round like a mole rat. He was throwing that wad like a punch, trying to put me in my place.

"That's real swell, kid," I said, snapping the newspaper back up, "but I don't aim to be the laughing stock of my profession."

"You are a legend," Dottie cooed. "That's why we came to you. They don't make detectives like Mack Graves anymore. The Lost Dagger of Shangri La, The Knight's Chalice, The Doomsday Formula. This is just like that."

"I don't care how eccentric you can afford to be, a ham sandwich doesn't hold a candle to any of those."

"This isn't just a ham sandwich," Nate whined. "It's the ham sandwich that killed Aaron Peals!"

"The Sultan of Song was killed by a bottomless bank account and a lack of impulse control."

"Fine, then it was his last meal. When Sarge Simmons had it sealed in a lucite cube, it became a valuable artifact. The most valuable artifact in rock and roll history."

"If you say so." I snorted.

"The Sterling Auction House says so. Here's what they appraised it at the last time they tried to get me to put it on the block."

Nate pushed a piece of paper—so thick it was on its way to being a blanket—across my desk. It was flecked with silver and the letterhead was deeply embossed. Everyday schmoes didn't even know that stationery like this existed. The figure inscribed thereon was remarkable.

"If you don't believe me, give them a call," Nate huffed.

"Okay, kid, I'll look around on a few conditions. This is a cash deal. My name never appears anywhere near this, and I don't hear the words 'ham sandwich' again or I walk. Let's just call it the artifact."

"Sure thing, Mr. Graves!" Nate panted.

"Leave your address and I'll be over presently."

After they departed, I took a couple slugs of whiskey to acclimate myself to the situation. The dame had been right that they didn't make gumshoes like me anymore, but that was because the modern world didn't need doors kicked in and ne'er-do-wells dangled from balconies. Things had changed and left lantern-jawed Mack Graves behind. What they pinned a medal on my chest for in my heyday would have gotten me thrown behind bars now. Over the years, the calls had slowed to a trickle, and what few came in were mostly looking for talking heads for a historical film, or an endorsement for the latest detective thriller. I was nearly the last of my generation, a museum piece occasionally hauled out of storage to add a dash of verisimilitude to their nostalgia. I didn't fancy fading away into a sepia-toned montage. I meant to go out on one last marquis case, they kind that would land me on the front page again. But a goddamn ham sandwich? That kind of epitaph I didn't need. At least it was action, and a sorely needed payday.

The LaMarches lived out in a part of town that hadn't even existed a few years ago. Now there were beige mansions as far as the eye could see, each exactly like the next. It was no wonder the gold addresses were displayed so prominently. I pulled my faithful LTD into their driveway and went to knock on the door. Before I had the chance, Dottie had thrown the door open, wearing a sheer strip of fabric that might technically have passed as a housecoat. She held a pair of amber drinks.

"A sidecar, Mr. Graves?"

"Even I haven't drank that in twenty years," I said.

"It would be a shame to let it go to waste," she said, pressing up against me.

"Is Mr. LaMarche here?"

"He's in his office, working." She pouted. "I won't see him again until the Nikkei closes."

"The Nikkei?"

"He leverages foreign options during after-hours trading or somesuch. All I know is he disappears into his trading room and leaves me all alone."

"Where was the artifact taken from, Mrs. LaMarche?"

She sighed. "This way."

The living room had all the charm of a hotel event center, but at the back of the house Dottie opened a door onto a real eyesore of neon lights, mannequins in sequined jumpsuits, and a legion of guitars hung like wallpaper.

"Aaron Peals probably never had this kind of collection of Aaron Peals memorabilia," I quipped.

"It is a real mania for Nate," she said, already on to the second sidecar.

"You don't mind all this?"

"I can't complain. I don't want for anything, and I'd rather Nate have this hobby than a mistress."

"Nothing else was taken?"

"Nope. Nate has everything in here cataloged and photographed a dozen different ways."

She walked me over to a glass case that had a circle expertly cut out of it.

"The cops aren't looking into this?"

"The insurance company is willing to write a check, which makes it case closed as far as the cops are concerned. Nate wants the ham sandwich—I mean, artifact."

"Who else wants this artifact?"

"There's only a couple of collectors at his level. You need beaucoup bucks to keep up, and Aaron Peals is getting pretty ancient."

"Any of these collectors been snooping around recently?"

"No, Nate keeps his collection locked up tight. He thinks it creates an air of mystery. The other guys know what he has, but only because they are paying such close attention to the auctions and estate sales."

"Who has access to this room?"

"Basically nobody. Even I had to be granted special permission for today."

"How does that work?"

"See all the cameras and sensors everywhere?" She gestured to the corners of the room. "This is a so-called smart house. Everything computer-controlled by Nate."

"Do you have footage of the theft then?"

"Nothing useful. It was a lone man in full Aaron Peals regalia. He was a lunatic or he was mocking Nate or both."

"I'd like to see that footage."

"I'll ask Nate to send it to you."

"Wait, if there are cameras all over this place, doesn't that mean your husband would have seen anything that happened between us?"

"Yeah." She sighed, draining the last of the second glass.

I couldn't get back to the safety of my office quick enough, but I shouldn't have been in such a hurry. When I arrived, I found Sarge Simmons with his rhinestone cowboy boots propped up on my desk.

"Evening, Mr. Graves." He tipped his pristine white hat to me. "Do you know who I am?"

"Of course. Mr. Simmons, rock manager extraordinaire, or raconteur, depending on who you ask. I must say you are looking surprising hale and hearty."

"Don't that beat all," Simmons said. "You are thinking of my pappy, although I obviously dress the part. My name is Jimmy." He stuck out his hand, revealing five rings across five digits. Reluctantly, I shook.

"I'm accustomed to doing business from that side of the desk," I said.

"Shoot, let's not worry about the formalities," Jimmy said. "I can see you are a real no-nonsense desperado, so let's get down to brass tacks. I want the ham sandwich."

"I can recommend Marvin's Delicatessen right down the block," I said.

Jimmy gestured, and the door closed hard. I turned to see that two more men were standing behind me.

"We both know that's not the ham sandwich I'm talking about."

"I don't know anything about any ham sandwiches," I said.

Jimmy snapped his fingers, and his goons seized my arms, pressing me hard into my own desk.

"Don't get cute with me," Jimmy said. "I know you were just at LaMarche's place with her."

I just grunted as the goons wrenched my arms in their sockets.

"You don't even know what you've stumbled into do you? Well let me clue you in, Mr. Graves. That sweet-smellin' slip of a thing who was wrapping herself all around your dusty bones is none other than Ali Sudan."

"Is that supposed to mean something to me?"

"She's the Mata Hari of the Pealean world. She's been playing the long con on LaMarche. How could anyone believe a woman like that would be with him?"

"So you think LaMarche's wife is some kind of secret agent who has spent years trying to steal a ham sandwich? The guy is worth millions, hundreds of millions."

"The ham sandwich is worth more," Jimmy said.

"Well I don't have it. I've never even laid eyes on it."

"Ali Sudan picked you for a reason."

"If she is all you say she is, she probably thought I'd make a good patsy."

Jimmy considered for a minute. "No, that's not it. That's not her style."

Suddenly, there were police sirens in the air. Jimmy and his thugs disappeared, and if it weren't for the throbbing pain in my shoulders I would have almost believed they had been figments of my imagination. My office was lit up in red and blue from the lights down on the street. A moment later, there were three uniforms standing in my doorway.

"Mr. Graves? We need you to come down to the station and answer a few questions."

"About what?" I groused.

"The murder of Nate LaMarche."

"I just saw the guy."

"That's why you are coming downtown."

In my day, interrogation rooms were concrete boxes with metal furniture bolted to the floor. The place they took me was nicer than my own office. The chair I was plopped in had seventeen different levers to adjust the lumbar support, there was a carbonated water cooler in the corner, and there was a video intercom so the perp could call the desk. Outside the window was a manicured garden, with lush willows gently swaying in the breeze. I was beginning to reconsider a life of crime.

A few minutes later, the detective came in, with a dark blue pinstripe suit and a regulation ponytail. At least she'd spent some time walking a beat, because for all her polish she didn't have an ounce of jewelry on. In a scuffle a perp doesn't hesitate to yank out an earring or turn a necklace into a garotte.

"Mr. Graves, my name is Detective Reyes. Thank you for coming in to speak with us."

"Your pals didn't give me much of a choice."

"Your reputation precedes you, obviously, so let's handle this like professionals." She powered on a computer tablet to take notes. "Why were you at the LaMarche residence earlier?"

"Mr. and Mrs. LaMarche contracted me to locate a missing item for them."

"The ham sandwich."

I squirmed in my luxury chair. "It's a cultural artifact worth more than you or I will ever see."

"Can you provide a copy of that contract?"

"What? No, I'm old school. Handshake deals, you know."

"Per state code you are required to maintain certain documentation."

"Okay, so write me a ticket for being a lousy bookkeeper. I was told I was being hauled in here for a murder?"

She tapped at her tablet and a flat screen monitor on the far wall came to life. It showed footage of when I arrived at the house. After a brief interruption it then showed me scuttling back out to my car. I had to admit the footage didn't cast me in a good light.

"Tell me what happened while you were inside the house," she said.

"Don't you have it on tape? The guy has cameras in every corner."

"What we have on tape is you looking awfully friendly with Dottie LaMarche on the way in and then fleeing the premises about half an hour later."

"The lady is half my age, if that. I don't like to admit it, but I'm not exactly the Lothario I once was."

"When was the last time you saw Nathan LaMarche?"

"At my office about an hour before this. I don't have fancy cameras, but I'm sure their cellphones were jibber-jabbering away the whole time and you can track that, can't you?"

"So you assert that you did not see Mr. LaMarche while you were inside the house?"

"That's right."

"Did you hear him? Was there any sign of him?"

"Mrs. LaMarche said he was all locked up in his trading room and wouldn't be out for hours."

"So she showed you the Aaron Peals room."

"Damndest thing I ever saw."

"And the ham sandwich display?"

"I only took a gander at it. I'm sure your techs have a report on the thing a mile long. From what I could tell someone took a glass cutter and scooped the artifact out. Isn't there a video of it?"

"That's right, a costumed individual went right in and out without so much as looking at anything else in the room."

"That's weird, right? Each and every knick-knack in there has got to be worth five figures, easy."

"It tells me the place had been cased. Are you sure that you did not have a prior relationship with Mrs. LaMarche?"

"I'm flattered you would think so little of me."

"We have algorithms looking for your face on the earlier security footage. Am I going to find anything?"

"I swear to you there is nothing to that angle. I first met both of them this morning at the same time at my office."

"Did Mr. LaMarche seem frightened while he was at your office?"

"No, if anything he was pissy."

"Pissy?"

"You know, he's a dweeb, and somebody took his precious dweeb treasure away. He was pissy."

"Sounds like you didn't like him."

"His money was green."

"Money?"

"Yeah, that's right, the money. There's a five-k brick in my desk drawer. Should have his fingerprints all over it. There's your contract."

"There wasn't any cash in your office."

"What?"

"My pals took a look around while they were there."

"You have a warrant for that?"

"We have a dead husband and a missing wife. The paperwork will land where it needs to."

"Son of a bitch," I said. "Jimmy Simmons."

"Sarge Simmons' son?"

"Yeah, he was in my office right before the cops showed up. Was trying to shake me down for the artifact."

"Why would Jimmy Simmons believe you have the ham sandwich?"

"I don't know. He was watching Mrs. LaMarche I guess. The whole thing had a real creepy vibe to it. If she was fooling around with someone, Jimmy would be a good place to start looking."

"If they were conspiring together, why would he believe that you have the ham sandwich?"

"I didn't even want this case. You think this is how I want my career to end? Why is this artifact such a big deal anyway?"

"I can't discuss an ongoing investigation. Certainly not with a suspect."

"But there is a reason?"

A wry grin flashed across Reyes' face for just an instant. She made a non-committal wave. "Thanks for the tip on Jimmy Simmons. Don't leave town."

"That's it? Are you going to get my cash back?"

"This situation is exactly why you need paper trails, Mr. Graves."

"Am I still a suspect?"

"Officially, yes. Unofficially, I've studied you my whole life, Mr. Graves, and I'm a pretty good judge of character to boot. Mack Graves doesn't O.D. a pencil-pushing dweeb with digitalis in his soy latte. Besides, I just received notice that Dottie LaMarche boarded a plane to Hong Kong. I've said too much already, but we've got enough dots to connect this picture."

•

A couple of weeks later, a delivery boy came shuffling into my office with a bag of food.

"You got the wrong address, friend. Chinese just burns a hole in my stomach these days."

The boy just left the sack on the table and bowed slightly before disappearing.

"Hey! Come back here!" I yelled at the slamming door. I knew better than most that there were few free lunches in life, so I dumped the bag out, hoping there might be some rice and steamed vegetables I could do away with. Instead, there was a parcel wrapped in newspaper. According to the headline, some Triad boss had taken over a genetics lab. It seemed he had acquired the perfectly preserved DNA of legendary singer Aaron Peals and he meant to create a clone. "That would be the ultimate Pealean collectible," the man was quoted as saying. I was afraid I already knew what was inside the parcel. I untied it and found a note in impeccable cursive.

"After all the trouble I put you through, I thought you deserved an artifact of your own. Bon appetit!" The missive was sealed with the sticky red lipstick I remembered so well. Beneath that, lying on my desk like a smoking gun, was a goddamn ham sandwich.

Feral Lunchbreak

Chris Sumberg

Revved-up psycho chewing
ham 'n' gristle sandwich,
mouth and jowls jouncing:
Boing-boing boing-Boing-BOING!

Ham Amongst Friends

Chris Sumberg

Edsel DeSoto and her cat Toto
were eating a sandwich of ham.
They gnawed on each side
until Toto cried:
"You're biting me, dear little ma'am!"

That Thin Fuzzy Line Between Ham Sandwiches and Bio-Terrorism

Eric Potter

Dormitory C, where I live, is at all times a brisk 17 degrees Celsius and is the coolest dormitory, which is why Charlotte likes to come here. I should clarify: Dorm C has a standard temperature that is several degrees lower than the other dormitories in the compound. It's not that those of us who live here aren't *cool*; that's just not what I meant. We're not cool, though. People here tend to think of us as the human analogues of what we study, and what we study is fungus. Mould, more specifically. Ours is really a legitimate and elegant science, but it's just not nearly as sexy as astrophysics, or engineering, or even geology. This is absolutely the only place on Earth where fucking *geologists* are cooler than astrobiologists. They study rocks and dirt. The geologists, I mean. Rocks and dirt. My team works with stuff that's alive—not only alive, but alive in *space*—and yet the geologists always treat us like dweebs.

This guy Roy Crawford—he's not even a PhD or anything—just *Mr.* Roy Crawford the rock specialist, he comes up to me and Dave at last month's Site Community

Singles Mixer (or SCSM for short—pronounced like *Schism)* and gives me a noogie. A fucking *noogie*! What kind of asshole grown man gives another man a noogie at all, let alone at a social event? Roy is an absolute cock. It's really not important to the story, but he is. He's an absolute cock. And the thing is, we really don't get any contact with the outside world here. There is an exceptionally limited pool of available—let alone dateable—women in the compound, and Roy fucking noogied me in front of all of them. He's a total goddamed cock.

Whatever. Anyway, so Charlotte tends to come to Dorm C because the AC's always amped up in here to prevent the growth of any spores that might remain on our clothing when we leave the lab or the impact site. Most of the others here are too nervous to talk to her, but I talk to her sometimes. Her hair is the colour of marigolds, and she smells like something you'd put on waffles. I'm kind of the alpha in my team, you see.

The most intriguing thing about Charlotte is that she's private sector. She studied ethics at Oxford or Harvard or something, and she was sent here as part of an outsider think-tank to determine what we ought and ought not to do with whatever we find at the impact site. It's pretty standard I guess, but I can't wait to show her my work. Oh, and if only Roy knew what I've got in store for her. He's probably over there showing her boring mineral ratios or some crap. A woman like Charlotte isn't interested in geologists.

We found out last week that she would be coming around to each team to conduct interviews. She would want to know what we were working on, they said, and what theories we had regarding the meteorite's origins, the properties of our specimens, and what we hoped to accomplish overall. Dave is absolutely scared to death of her.

"What's so scary about a sexy woman?" I asked.

Dave frowned and said, "Sex has nothing to do with it. She'll ask us about what we're doing with our specimens." We were eating lunch in the lab, and Dave was unwrapping another of his revolting cooked ham and cheddar cheese sandwiches. He brings the same sandwich every day in the same kind of brown paper bag, and I'm convinced he chews every bite the same number of times. Dave is a creature of habit.

"And we'll tell her, won't we?" I said. "Come on, Dave. We're two brilliant, young-ish scientists who, despite specializing in mycology, are actually at the forefront of humanity's greatest discovery. Think about it, Dave, *anything* we do with our specimens constitutes groundbreaking science. We could shove a specimen jar right up our own *asses*, and the effects would still constitute new scientific knowledge. That is objectively badass, Dave. And as luck would have it, we do happen to be sitting on a little something rather sensational, don't we? You are a brilliant *astro*mycologist at the cutting edge of science as we know it. That's the sort of thing that gets high schools named after you! If that doesn't get at least a few women in bed with you then nothing on Earth will."

Dave wobbled his hotdog-shaped legs, barely shifting the muss on his frumpy corduroys, and his naturally moist face fogged the bottoms of his glasses while he chewed. "I suppose that doesn't sound so bad. When you put it that way."

Dave's a good guy. But obviously I hold no hope for him getting past awkward greeting-type hand gestures with a girl like Charlotte. Being honest, he's really not an evolutionary competitor against anyone. He's a genius, don't get me wrong. But he's the kind of guy where you could go right up and knock on his door, pick out your ears with a Q-tip right in front of him, and shove the waxy mess into his breast pocket, and he'd just give a high little laugh like you're his lover and you gave him a tickle. Dave could discover a cure for breast cancer that happened also to be a deliriously effective aphrodisiac, and he'd still never get so much as a tug on his trousers. He is, therefore, an absolutely ideal roommate.

"I'm still not sure we should tell her anything," Dave said. "Colonel Marsters was incredibly explicit when he said —"

"I know what the Colonel said. So we don't go into absolutely every single detail of the project. We can still highlight the big points, and perhaps casually mention the fact that we're planning a little soirée in a couple of weeks, her presence at which would be very, very welcome. Check our fermenting vessels, by the way, I thought I heard them gurgling a bit more than normal this morning." Dave went, still chewing on his sandwich, to the back room.

I should explain: Dave and I have more than one project in the works at the moment. As I was planning on mentioning to Charlotte, the collective biology teams are throwing a compound-wide party at the end of the month, and Dave and I are supplying the drinks. Alcohol is closely regulated on the premises, and very little of it is ever allocated for the purposes of getting smashed, so getting hold of some decent hooch takes a bit of creativity: we order grain and hops with the help of the kitchen staff, and every piece of lab equipment we could ever ask for is already here, fully sterilized, at our disposal. All it takes after that is for someone to harvest and cultivate some decent brewing yeast, and Dave and I happen to be two of the world's most prolific leading experts on all things mouldy, yeasty, or fungal. Child's play. By next Friday, we will have five carboys, each filled with 40 gallons of the finest beer science can produce, and a working still, which we will use to make vodka from grain and purloined botanicals. We've been working on distilling the hard stuff for a while, so no trouble there, but beer takes at least a couple of weeks to ferment, so we're on something of a tight schedule, having only added the yeast yesterday.

There was no change in our sample specimens, so we decided to disinfect and leave the lab for the afternoon. We walked up the metal staircase to the well-air-conditioned, tent-like walls of Dorm C, where I was both delighted and appalled to see Charlotte—apparently deep into a conversation with geo-idiot *Roy Crawford.* And wouldn't you know it, the clownish prick was indeed talking about mineral ratios, some sort of blah-blah bullshit, the meteorite most likely came from the Sigma Orionis system, yadda yadda, what a cock. Charlotte looked up and saw us coming.

"Dr. Morley, Dr. Pearlman, just who I was looking for," she said. Dave's eyes widened.

"Ah, Dr. Young, it's so lovely to see you," I said, and turning then to Roy, "I hope *Mr.* Crawford isn't bothering you."

"On the contrary." She smiled. "I'm learning a great deal about extra-terrestrial mineral formations. It's fascinating."

"Hey Allen, hey Dave," Roy piped in. "Did you both make sure to wash your hands before you came up here?"

Now I was just going to go red-faced and retort with something like "Fuck you, Roy," or "Shove it, Roy, you're the physical manifestation of pink eye," but Dave spoke first.

"Actually Roy, come to think of it, I'd observed during last month's SCSM that you have been exhibiting what looked to me to be a small polypous mass on the lower right half of your nose, the colour and shape of which are tantalizingly similar to that of an extremely rare nasal Conidiobolomycosis, which could be possible for a man of your age in this climate. Would it be a terrible imposition for me to perhaps draw a sample? It could genuinely help my resear—"

"Listen here, you badger-faced wimp," Roy shouted, advancing on Dave.

"Please, gentlemen," Charlotte stretched her arm into Roy's path. "Mr. Crawford, it's been a pleasure talking to you, but do you think you might give me a few moments with

Drs. Morley and Pearlman?" She smiled brightly at Roy, whose expression instantly melted.

"Sure, uh, of course," he said, backing up. "Whatever, mould-nerds." Roy walked out of the room rubbing his nose.

I said it before: Dave is a veritable genius, if perhaps an accidental one. I'm not entirely sure whether Dave was trying to burn Roy or if he genuinely did notice a rare subcutaneous fungal infection on Roy's nose, but either way, colour me impressed. Especially if Roy actually is host to nasal Conidiobolomycosis. I mean, that could be just one more thing to get our names into some peer-reviewed journals. Not that some rare nasal fungus holds any sort of candle to what we've found, though. Nasal fungus is just neat.

"So what can I—we, what can we do for you, Dr. Young?" I said. "And might I add, yellow is most definitely your colour." She was wearing a yellow blouse above slim khaki pants. Women appreciate when you notice these sorts of things.

"Thank you, Dr. Morley," she said, smiling at the both of us. "I was hoping to get a chance to tour your lab before we conduct our interview. Colonel Marsters seems to think that you two have found something quite impressive."

I grinned at Dave, though he remained silent and deer-eyed.

"As it happens, Charlotte, I think you will find our research to be among the most important scientific discoveries of the—"

A wet boom erupted, echoing down the hallway from which Dave and I had recently come. A breathy rush, like the sound of a river, followed for quite some time, almost as loud as the initial boom had been.

"What the hell was that?" cried Charlotte.

Dave was already running in the direction of the lab.

An attack? Sabotage? Terrorists? Gas leak? In that kind of pandemonium, the brain tends to assume the worst. What had happened down there?

•

"Beer."

"I'm sorry, what was that?"

"...It was beer."

"I'm afraid I must be misunderstanding you, Dr. Morley," Colonel Marsters' hot breath was now my entire oxygen supply. "Because I thought you just told me that both you and Dr. Pearlman had been left in charge of half-a-ton of the most scientifically important material in our lifetimes, as well as a state-of-the-art scientific facility, provided by the taxpayers, stocked with hundreds of thousands of dollars' worth of equipment, and you two fuck-nuts were brewing yourselves two hundred gallons of goddamned *beer* in there like a couple of high school virgins!"

Colonel Marsters' anger was, I suppose, reasonably justified. Everything he'd said had been true, but being entirely fair, I didn't know what high school Marsters went to, but at mine the virgins were never the people who blew up the science lab as a result of running an illicit brewery, and besides, nothing terribly important got damaged. The samples we'd been running were still in their sealed refrigerator units, the meteorite sample itself was stored safely in a walk-in freezer whose security features rivalled those of most bank vaults, and nearly all the taxpayers' lab equipment was fully intact. It was all just now incredibly sticky and yeast-scented.

"And you two taint-hairs are damn well going to make it all un-sticky!" The Colonel's shouting seemed to be somewhat upsetting Charlotte, who was sitting in a chair in the corner. "That laboratory had better be squared away and smelling like baby wipes in a hospital by breakfast time tomorrow, or I will have you both wiped from this world like shit from an asshole, do you understand me?"

Colonel Marsters reamed us out like that for a while. Dave perspired the whole time and his face looked like something you'd order from a seafood restaurant and then send back. I don't assume I looked much better. Eventually, Charlotte pulled Marsters out into the hallway and came back alone two or three minutes later.

"I do not envy you two right now," she said, sitting down in front of us. She took off her glasses briefly to collect her thoughts, replaced them, and looked back at Dave and I with the knowing smirk of a dealer at a casino. Damn, the woman was breathtaking. "But I expect that your little beer incident may be one day remembered as a funny footnote," she continued. "From what I've been able to surmise, there has been a rather important discovery made at this impact site."

Dave mumbled, "I'm... I'm not sure how much we can... we're supposed to..."

"I'm a representative of the United Nations," interrupted Charlotte, "and I'm empowered by an international authority to determine the nature of the work being done at the impact site, and whether or not the circumstances here warrant... intervention."

Oh boy do I love a powerful woman. And Charlotte—pardon me, *Dr. Young*—was laying down the law. It wasn't clear exactly what Charlotte knew, but her powers (on paper at least) clearly exceeded those of Colonel Marsters.

The woman wanted to know what Dave and I had been working on, and I always aimed to impress.

"Well, what would you like to know?" Dave clearly perceived the confidence, which had disappeared in the presence of the screaming colonel, now returning to my voice, and he widened his eyes, trying to signal caution. I knew what I was doing.

"Well, Dr. Morley"—Charlotte was smiling—"Why don't you start from the beginning."

I obliged.

Don't worry though, I didn't tell her everything. I told her about the context first: how the GSC had received reports of a particularly large meteorite strike in the Alberta Badlands earlier this year, the properties of which were initially deemed to be "unusual." Then, when pale fuzz began to cover the meteorite's surface, Colonel Marsters was put in charge of containment, and the government issued small, highly specialized teams to study both the meteorite and the site upon which it first made contact. Initial theories suggested that the impact occurred within a particularly dense patch of subterranean moss, or a related subset of fungal cultures whose proliferation was encouraged by both the heat of the meteorite and the new mixture of topsoil. The fuzz was at that time considered a nuisance—an environmental contaminant that needed to be identified and then eliminated so that real science could be done on the space rock with unusual properties. That was where Dave and I came in. We were a glorified cleanup crew, the scientific equivalent of a healthy dab of anti-fungal foot cream. But not for long. Believe me, between Dave and me, we have a working knowledge of every single species and subspecies of fungus, every culture of mould, and an intimate understanding of every one of their properties. When it became clear that we had discovered a new species of fungus, Colonel Marsters and the brass were less than intrigued. However, when we discovered that this new species of moss was genetically distinct, in its entirety, from every other known species on Earth, the reaction was somewhat more enthusiastic.

"Aliens," Charlotte said, wide-eyed. "So you two are the first people in history to confirm the existence of extra-terrestrial life."

I felt I'd need reconstructive surgery if I grinned any wider. Even Dave was smiling, despite himself. I mean, she said it, Dave and I had made perhaps the most important scientific discovery in human history.

"Jesus," Charlotte breathed. "I knew that the nature of the discovery had something to do with extra-terrestrials, but I had figured there were just some fossilized remains or something. You honestly have a living species of alien mould growing in your lab?"

"Perhaps you'd care to come and see it some evening?" I said.

"I will certainly need to examine the specimens," she said. "But I will have to put in a request for a team of my own scientists to obtain a sample to do independent research. This is big."

Dave suddenly looked worried.

Charlotte snapped back to a clinical focus. "What properties have you observed the mould exhibiting?"

"None," Dave said. "Nothing yet, that is."

"Well nothing out of the ordinary, anyway," I corrected. Dave was looking at his shoes. "It's pale blue, you might mistake it for kitchen mould. It's dormant so far, when contained, and metabolizes glutinous and carbohydrate solutions quite efficiently, but it's not the first fungus to do so. We'll have to expose it to more diverse—"

Colonel Marsters strode loudly back into the room.

"That'll be enough for today, Dr. Young. I trust you've gotten all you need from these gentlemen."

Charlotte looked annoyed for a moment but composed herself. "Thank you, Colonel," she said. "I most certainly have." Then, as she got up to leave the room, she turned and said, "I'll be in touch with you both again shortly. We have quite a few things to discuss, I should think."

When the door closed, Colonel Marsters was back on top of us.

"What did you tell her, scumbags?"

"N-Nothing!" I stammered. "Or, well, nothing important! Just the context, the details."

"What details would those be, exactly?"

"Just about the mould, sir, just—"

The colonel rubbed his face. "Well that's just wonderful. You just told the UN representative that we have an alien species growing in our basement. All you dumb-fucks had to do was tell the woman that you hadn't yet conducted research sufficient to provide conclusive results. You could have shown her a sample of some weird stupid fuzz with some unpronounceable name, mentioned some fungi gibberish, and she would have walked away with nothing more than perhaps some mild nausea. Jesus Christ, you two have caused me a shit-stack of trouble today."

The colonel paced for a moment, and Dave and I slumped in our chairs. What were we supposed to have told her? We hadn't done anything wrong, and we hadn't quite told her *everything* either.

"I want you both to listen to me very carefully," Marsters said, sitting back down. "In a moment, I'm going to ask you both if you told her anything—anything at all—about the conversation we had when you first came to us with the discovery. About the task I assigned you both to do. I'm going to ask you that question, and if either of you shit-stains gives even the slightest impression you're lying to me, I will have both your skulls for decorative paperweights. Do you understand me?"

"Y-Yes sir," we both said, a bit too loud.

"Did you two worthless little nerds tell Dr. Young *anything* about the objective to which you were assigned?"

"No, we didn't," Dave almost yelled. "We just told her we discovered it, we don't even know exactly what it does yet. We didn't, we didn't tell her anything, I swear."

The colonel looked at me, and I shook my head quickly, pointing at Dave. "Like he says," I stammered.

Marsters seemed satisfied. "Good. Now, you will both leave immediately and get that lab cleaned up. And then you will do your jobs and keep your ugly mouths shut from now on. Do we have an understanding?"

We sure did.

•

"I still don't get it," Dave said, flushing industrial lemony bleach-water down the maintenance drain. "Why would the beer have gone off like this? The yeast was only added two days ago. It couldn't have produced enough carbon dioxide to cause an explosion like this."

Dave and I had done a thorough mopping. The lab was no longer sticky, but a defiant yeasty smell still lingered, seemingly on every object. There was a lot more to do, but it was well past lunchtime, so we decided to stop. As we walked to the fridge, all I could really think about was getting back to our work in order to prepare for Charlotte's next visit. I wanted to have something new to show her, something to stun both her and the scientific community at large. It wasn't enough to have simply found alien life; Dave and I needed to have *contributed* somehow to the discovery. Furthered humanity's understanding. "It could have been the equipment," I said.

"No," said Dave, unwrapping yet another brown-bagged ham sandwich. "The beer was fizzing when we got down there. It had already fermented to the point of producing both alcohol and carbonation."

"I can never understand why you always eat those things," I said, looking at Dave's ham sandwich. "And always the same ones. Don't you ever get tired of ham?"

Dave shrugged.

"Besides, there's a bigger picture here to pay attention to, Dave," I said. "Charlotte has likely already informed the international scientific community of our findings. We might *already* be famous. We need to get back to work as soon as humanly possible, we've got to have something new to—"

Dave looked suddenly crazed. He stuffed his whole partially-eaten sandwich into his pants pocket, reaching for a pen like a crazy person, and ran wordlessly to the main lab where we kept our frozen samples.

•

"Holy Christ," I said, "look at that stuff go."

"It's the same with the glucose mixtures as with the botanicals," breathed Dave. He stared down through his fogged glasses. "Enough with the biologicals, let's try some synthetics."

I ran to get some mineral and petroleum solutions, my heart racing. I've said it before, and I'll say it again: Dave is a genius. He'd figured it out when I'd used the words *humanly* possible. What about things that weren't humanly possible? What about *other-worldly* things?

It took only moments for the samples to metabolize the synthetic solutions as well. I can't even begin to describe the excitement Dave and I both felt at that moment—this was unlike anything any human being had ever encountered.

"It's the sheer speed of it that miffs me," I said. "Even at room temperature, once this stuff is activated, the reaction time is mind-boggling."

"Yes, and this makes it highly unstable," replied Dave. "Just imagine it, we must have accidentally gotten a few micrograms of the stuff into our carboys, and it only took a couple of hours to over-complete a process which, using Earthly yeasts, takes weeks. God only knows what this fungus could be capable of."

•

We told Colonel Marsters about our discovery.

"It's quite an enigma, sir," I began. "It's visually very similar to your standard Penicillium—something you might find growing on some old vegetables, for instance—but its properties are like nothing we've ever seen before. In simple terms, it is a highly programmable, multi-taxonomic species of fungus which, when activated, is seemingly capable of metabolizing any arrangement of both organic and synthetic matter at a prodigious rate."

"The beer, for example," continued Dave. "We believe that a small amount of it was inadvertently activated and mixed into the carboys, where it adopted the properties of the yeast and metabolized the carbohydrates in the grain. Sir, it did in a couple of hours what takes high quality brewing yeast two weeks to accomplish. It is highly potent and, when added to an active mixture, highly and unstably energetic."

"Unless of course you keep it inactive and at low temperatures," I added. "Our frozen samples seem perfectly inert."

Colonel Marsters was thrilled, and spoke to us urgently, smiling.

"Well done, boys, well done," he said. "You'll both do your country proud. From now on, I want you both to report everything you find directly to me. Have a report on my desk by the end of the week with whatever concepts you may have regarding our little project. Remember, think as big as possible. We need to explore every conceivable possibility, both conventional and unconventional. Most importantly, inform absolutely no one about anything you find, and show no one what you're working on, and *especially* do not inform Dr. Young of any aspect of our project whatsoever, understood?"

We both nodded, eager to keep the Colonel in an even-tempered, complimentary mood.

"Keep up the good work, Doctors."

Marsters even saluted us. Dave and I were both glowing when we left his office.

When we arrived back at Dormitory C, Charlotte was once again there waiting for us, this time thankfully without Roy Crawford.

"I'd hoped to have a word with you gentlemen," she said. Her tone was still confident, but somehow her body language seemed more reserved than before. It was a pretty safe bet that Marsters was using every ounce of power he could to keep her out of the loop, and it was an even better bet that she knew there were things we weren't telling her.

"I've uh, got to get to the lab," Dave said. He looked at me as he slunk down the stairs. I knew the sort of look he was giving me. But of course I was going to stay. This was a golden opportunity! A newly vulnerable Charlotte was now asking to speak to one of the men responsible for humanity's greatest discovery, and I was fully planning on indulging her.

"Pardon my partner's rudeness," I said. "Please, have a seat."

"Actually Dr. Morley, I was hoping to—"

"Please, call me Alan."

"Pardon me, Alan, I was hoping to take you up on your offer to take a tour of your lab." She smiled, almost shyly, and placed her hand softly on my knee. "I would be fascinated to see your specimens. I mean, I never thought

I'd get the chance to see real live alien beings in my lifetime."

Well there I was in quite a pickle. If you are perhaps less than familiar with the life of mycologists, it is difficult for me to express just how rarely it is that a beautiful, powerful woman takes any interest at all in your work—I mean, we spend our days growing and studying fungi in cold, damp laboratories, which I'm told is a less than ideal context for pitching woo—and Charlotte was not only interested, she was practically begging me to let her see my lab! I mean, discovering alien life was one thing, but this was glorious. On the other hand, we had been directly instructed not to do precisely this, mere moments before, by a wild-eyed colonel who I'm pretty sure doesn't even remove his gun belt to shower. I had to be smooth about this.

"Oh my dear Charlotte, I would love nothing more than to show you our lab," I said, doing well so far. "But unfortunately you'll have to give me another day or so. You see, Dave and I are in just a bit of hot water with the *man* right about now, what with our beer project exploding"—women love a bad boy—"so I wouldn't dream of bringing you down there without first tidying the place up properly. I respect you too much, Charlotte."

Her eyebrows raised, but she did not reply immediately. I felt a connection between us. I was an important man now, a man even with a certain degree of mystery, and Charlotte—beautiful, brilliant, slender Charlotte—was trying to solve me. I was now in the business of seizing opportunities.

"I'll tell you what," I said, reaching into my back pocket. "I know it's awfully hot during these Prairie summer nights. I've actually been in the J-Dormitories a few times myself, and I understand you might find yourself a bit too hot and sticky for a good night's sleep." Charlotte's eyes were flashing the same way the Engineering girls' do when you ask them to dance at a compound mixer. I had her eating out of the palm of my hand. "So I'd like you to have this." I handed her my spare key card. "If at any point at all you feel like you need to cool off, maybe just shoot the breeze, as it were, I'd be very happy for you to come by. Day or night." I winked.

Charlotte looked down at my proffered key card for a moment or two as if grappling with the idea. She was a professional woman, after all. Finally, she straightened her back and put her hand on mine, accepting the key card and grazing my hand softly with hers.

"That's very sweet of you, Alan," she said, smiling. "I really appreciate your thoughtfulness." She put the key card gingerly in her green leather messenger bag. "Well," she said, getting up, "I'd better get going. I'm sure you and

Dr. Pearlman have a lot of work to do. And let me know when you've tidied the place up. I'm very eager to see what you've got going on down there."

Oh yes, that was most definitely coy wordplay. I am a legend.

Dave, however, was less enthusiastic. It's possible that Dave is asexual, though more likely he's just an anal-retentive personality who needs everything to be just so in order to feel okay. As for me, I like to go with the flow. For example, who knows, maybe I'll have a late-night visitor? The thought was thoroughly energizing, and Dave and I had one of our most productive days since arriving at the compound. The mould from the meteorite samples proved even more effective than we had anticipated previously: in one experiment a small, appropriately dosed portion of the mould successfully metabolized pure kerosene, degrading it before our eyes. The same was true of a five-kilogram ingot of stainless steel, which melted away as though we'd exposed it to mercury or acid, except the whole process only took seconds. When the mould had fully metabolized each substance, it stopped. It was only interested in the substances it had been programmed to consume. We produced more than a few concept notes to present to the Colonel and went to bed late, having lost all sense of time out of excitement.

I slept heavily, exhausted by the fullness of the previous two days' events, re-energizing myself for what more there was to come; the Colonel had some very big plans indeed.

I woke up in the dark to a heavy kick from beneath my cot. Charlotte was standing over me, glaring like a drunken fiend. In her hands were Dave's and my concept notes for the mould.

"You fucking *monsters*," she snarled.

"Wha—but..." I was only just pushing past the sleep she'd brought me out of.

"Both of you, and Marsters, you're both fucking sick. You're animals, how could you possibly—"

"Whoa, calm down sweetheart," I said.

In retrospect, those four words had been poorly chosen. Charlotte punched me right in the mouth, and I nearly lost consciousness. But before she could bludgeon me any further, Dave—poor, feckless Dave—walked into the room still wearing his faded baby blue pajamas. She rounded on him.

"This fucking ass-clown I could see getting up to something like this," she yelled, gesturing to me, "but I'm so much more shocked that you could even begin to *consider* something like this! You're supposed to be dorky, well-meaning scientists, not... not biological arms manufacturers!"

Those words hit home.

It wasn't like it was our idea. We'd been given direct orders, and in no uncertain terms. You've seen how Colonel Marsters can be. We'd be heroes, he'd told us.

"*How do you think we're going to guarantee the safety of our project?*" he'd said to us when we stuttered in vague protest. "*This is how we guarantee the security of our nation, and even perhaps the security of these new forms of life.*"

"We weren't trying to actually *build* any weapons." I whimpered. "And we had our orders."

"But why *weapons?*" She shouted. "If your notes here are in any way accurate, this stuff has nearly unlimited potential—it could clear oil spills in a matter of hours, it could rid the Pacific ocean of plastic, it could eliminate the need for landfills, it could completely revolutionize the way we recycle, it might even hold a cure for cancer!" She was actually trembling, she was so clearly disgusted and deeply, profoundly angry.

"It can still do those things, can't it?" Dave asked.

"Not if you two deliver any of this to Marsters!" Charlotte screamed. "The things you've thought of in here..." Charlotte was pale, swatting at the pages we'd written. "I hadn't even begun to *think* about this stuff—*life*, God damn it, newly discovered *alien life*—as a weapon until I looked in your notebooks. Any one of these concepts—this mould could wipe out entire forests! It could destroy an entire nation's oil reserves, it could be used to slaughter millions!"

Charlotte was right, of course. We just hadn't been thinking about it that way. We were academics, after all. We tend to think entirely in theoretical terms. It wasn't until just then I think that either of us had even considered the real application of our work as a distinct possibility.

"Every great force in this world must be used for the peace and security of mankind," Colonel Marsters had told us. *"Just think of the opportunity we've been given. Canada has never really been known for its military might, I hardly need tell you. But with this... the heavens have opened up and sent us a tool to rival, or exceed, even the atomic bomb. Imagine a weapon, as innocuous as a bit of mouldy bread, that could be programmed to consume whatever we tell it to. Imagine a pathogen with absolutely no cure because nothing on Earth has ever come into contact with it before. It would be undetectable, unstoppable, and unlimited in its capacity. If you can unlock the true power of this substance, gentlemen, you will be greater even than Oppenheimer. Canada—the world—will owe you an unending, hero's debt."*

The man had been incredibly convincing. Charlotte, however, apparently disagreed.

She just stood there for a moment, breathing heavily, still clutching our papers, and with a sudden flash in her eyes, she jerked towards the staircase. She flew down the hallway and flung our notebooks back into the laboratory, flicked a zippo lighter out of her pocket, tossed it inside the huge automatic door, and ran. Dave and I would have run too, but we didn't really understand what she'd done until after she ran through the door and when an absolutely skull-cracking boom sent us both flailing to our asses.

•

They later asked Dave and I for our full names and occupations, for the record. "Dr. Alan Robert Morley," I'd said. "I worked in the compound as a mycologist. My primary duty, after having co-discovered the extra-terrestrial species of fungus, was to determine the feasibility of its weaponization."

Charlotte had been arrested and court-martialed, having committed several felonies, not least of which was blowing up government property and injuring over a dozen people in the process.

"Describe the impact of Dr. Charlotte Young's actions on your laboratory," they said.

"It was reduced to rubble," I'd replied. Apparently, Charlotte had been so horrified by the weapons Dave and I had theorized that she had emptied out our refrigerated samples and released the valves on every tank of flammable gas in the lab before coming up to accost us in our beds.

"And the original meteorite?"

"...It's gone too."

Apparently, she performed incredibly well under pressure. Charlotte had, I'd been told, used leftover demolition charges from the excavation crews to disintegrate the relatively small meteorite. There was absolutely nothing left to salvage.

That was true of our careers as well.

With no surviving evidence whatsoever of Dave's and my discovery, it was as if the whole thing had never happened at all. The whole situation was deemed classified, and the only two people who knew about the fungus were Charlotte and Colonel Marsters. Neither of them was in any way inclined to talk.

•

When we were released, no longer the two most important scientists in recent human history, Dave and I decided to take a Greyhound back to Toronto, where we thought we might be able to apply for our old jobs on the Dairy Board. We had nothing with us anymore except a couple of dirty (but non-exploded) outfits that had survived due to the heavy industrial dormitory laundry hampers. We were smelly, jobless, and now legally required to stay in the country until the whole mess had been sorted out. Neither of us really cared; we were still sore from our catastrophic plunge from grace.

"Charlotte wasn't really all that good looking, when you get down to it," I said, drawing with my fingers on the sweat-fogged bus windows.

"I still don't quite get it," Dave said, slumped in his rigid bus seat. "They said every *trace* of it had burned up. I mean, we hadn't gotten far enough in our research to have a good understanding of its reproduction techniques, but it must have been flinging spores everywhere. The beer wasn't even close to where we kept the samples. How else could enough of it have gotten in there to cause fermentation?"

"Oh, come off it, Dave. Can't you see that none of it matters anymore? Nobody's ever going to believe that the two of us discovered, and nearly weaponized, an alien species of fungus."

"But they would if we were just allowed back into the site for an hour or two," Dave said with more feeling than usual. "It *must* be there. Spores must have proliferated enough to at least extract and cultivate a new sample of it. How else can you explain the beer?"

"Enough of that Dave, I mean it. It's unhealthy to dwell on such things. Let's just move on with our lives. For Christ's sake there must be a rest stop coming soon, I'm famished."

"Here," Dave said, reaching into his pants pocket. "I've —" Dave's voice cracked and his whole body went rigid.

"What is it you've got there?" I pulled his hand from his pocket. "Is that *another* one of your stupid ham and cheese sandwiches? Jesus, Dave. And you've been keeping it in your pocket too, on a bus? In this heat? Look at it, it's as mouldy as a..."

Dave glared at me, wide-eyed, and it suddenly made sense. Dave hadn't brought a ham sandwich with him. This was the same sandwich he'd had two days ago in the lab.

He'd always had a ham sandwich in the lab.

"Oh Dave," I said, as calmly as possible, "A few days ago when we were eating lunch and I asked you to check the carboys, did you by any chance bring your sandwich with you?"

Dave slowly nodded his head, his eyes still somehow both wide and dim.

Well that explained the beer.

"It must be able to sustain itself on my ham sandwiches without becoming unstable," Dave breathed. "It's still here... I've... I've got..."

Dave, in fact, had the sole sample of the first, and only, alien species ever discovered, now thriving in a half-eaten sandwich he'd kept stuffed in his trousers. Indeed, Dave's ham sandwich was, at that moment, the single most important, most unfathomably dangerous object on the *entire planet*. And there we were, rolling through Saskatchewan in a sweaty Greyhound bus.

•

This story has already gone on too long, so I won't drag you through some sort of surprise ending. Dave tripped when he got off the bus and the sandwich rolled into a cornfield. You know, the stuff most of Saskatchewan is covered in. I wish I could tell you that we contacted the appropriate authorities and contained the incident, but I mean, who even are the appropriate authorities in the event of an alien fungal outbreak in a Saskatchewan cornfield? Neither of us are currently proud of it, but here it is: Dave and I, after a moment, just got back on the bus.

At first it seemed like everything might have been okay. That is, the Greyhound trip from D'arcy, Saskatchewan to Toronto, Ontario was as uneventful as it sounds. But when we got to Toronto, it was only a couple of hours before the news started picking up our little mishap. Not that we were given credit immediately, though. It seemed instead that a mysterious fungus was consuming most of Central Canada and this was, you know, unusual. Fire trucks gathered, pesticides were dropped from airplanes, deities were prayed to, and in the end both Charlotte and Marsters corroborated by ratting Dave and me out. We were found by Interpol three days later, trying to board a plane to Yellowknife.

The crazy thing, though, is that nobody actually connected the event with the meteorite strike until we told them. I guess nobody pays attention to that stuff. And in the end, what's the difference, really? A meteorite here, a ham sandwich there. Hell, if the damn meteorite had stuck only a few hundred kilometers to the East, Dave and I might be in an entirely different position today.

As it happens, the part of the prison both Dave and I currently occupy—a deep Fed prison nobody's supposed to know about—is called Dormitory C. Honestly, it's not all that bad. We still have taxpayer-provided lab equipment, and we still answer to a short-tempered militant with a cliché Joss Whedon name (Reynolds). Furthermore, you may be pleased to know that Charlotte still hangs out in Dorm C (deep Fed prisons are co-ed; thanks *liberals),* and, oh boy, she does *not* care for me at all. But in the end, none of us have been left out of humanity's greatest discovery. Incidentally, Canada now occupies a firm, albeit fuzzy, seat of bio-military world power. Now we can all just sit here (in our respective detention facilities) and enjoy the fact that the true story of humanity's First Contact involves a Canadian guy named Dave who accidentally dropped a contaminated ham sandwich, filled with a weird alien fungus, in a cornfield in Saskatchewan.

Disconnect

Kristin Procter

There is so much to lose in loving.
Even your favourite lunch place
can change their toppings, unannounced,
slide sliced tomato
with its rubbery flesh
and its beady eyes
onto the previously perfect ham sandwich
you order every Friday afternoon.
It's as if they don't know you at all.
With such disappointment in the world,
it's a wonder anyone opens their heart.

Tavern Ham

Lawrence Berry

Ed opened the Matchstick Bar in the center of a long lazy turn where the asphalt hummed with a steady flow of vehicles. There were a few very small towns close by contributing a trickle of customers. His business relied on mostly anonymous, one-time guests leaving Denver and heading in the general direction of the Gulf of Mexico.

His contractor specialized in building log homes and the Matchstick Bar looked like a mountain lodge grown seedy with time. The bar occupied the front of the building, with a kitchen behind, and Ed's small apartment at the end of the structure. The surrounding countryside was semi-arid prairie and carried no trees with the exception of scrub oak, growing in dense, brushy groves like islands in an endless pale green sea. When the winter wind howled, the Matchstick howled with it, beams twisting, floorboards rattling.

Ed listened to the wind ripping around the Matchstick, sincerely hoping his new sign didn't get torn away. He was offering a free ham sandwich with every pitcher of brew, desperate to lure some drinking people in.

Since they'd built the interstate, traffic wasn't a tenth of what it had been. Business couldn't get much worse. Maybe a couple dozen people would see the sign and decide *hey, I could use a brew and a ham sandwich*.

Lucy had just finished polishing glasses when the man entered. He was tall, broad-shouldered, in a Cattleman's duster and a wide Stetson hat. Long hair fell down to his shoulders in tangles, and he had bright eyes in a sullen face.

"Anywhere you like," Ed said. "I bet you came in for a ham sandwich?"

"I did." The man strode down the long front of the walnut bar and took a seat at the end by the picture window, stars showing in the deep-blue twilight. He put his back to the glass as if he hated something out there, maybe the approach of a cold winter's nightfall.

"Gotta have a pitcher if you want the tavern ham for free."

"Whatever's on tap."

Ed thought about running down his list of brews, new and improved now that he was close to starving, only to think better of it when the stranger put his weird scarlet eyes on Ed, watching his hands as they went under the bar for a pitcher and a glass.

Ed was too old these days to run back and forth, putting up beers and waiting on tables, so he had to keep Lucy happy. They had an agreement that he'd pour only at the waitress's station and she'd bring down the beer, hopefully with enough charm to earn a tip.

After an assessing glance, Ed selected Miller High Life (always smooth, never bitter), leaving an inch of creamy foam at the top. Lucy put the alcohol on a platter, and Ed went back to the kitchen. Nothing but the best for his customers—Boar's Head ham, sliced and ready on a serving plate, thick slabs of rustic, homemade bread, lettuce, tomato, and an industrial-sized jar of mayo. Ed made the man a sandwich fit for his size. When it was done, he carried it out to Lucy's station. She added chips, pickles, and a colored toothpick through the middle to hold the sandwich together.

While she brought it to the customer, Ed wiped down the station, remembering that he had to keep up with the spills or stand in beer all night. The stranger said something in a mumble Ed couldn't make out, and Lucy laughed, a tinkle of music, and patted him on the shoulder.

The moon rising behind the stranger showed a platinum sliver above the eastern hills. The stranger drank the glass down and took a bite of sandwich with wolfish teeth. As he ate, the moonlight gilded his back and the bar on both sides. He shivered violently. The draft brought in a little cold, but not enough to explain those shudders.

Lucy came back, tapping the bar top to irritate Ed. When she was irritable, she made herself irritating.

"What did this one say to you?"

"He told me I was good enough to eat."

"I can't say that's mannerly."

"A lady hears worse, believe me."

They both looked down at the stranger, who was putting his big, meaty paw on the rest of the sandwich, shoving it toward a hairy mouth.

The stranger's sharp, pinpoint eyes rested on Lucy as if she was some kind of delicacy.

"The man's dry, Ed," Lucy said, in a constrained voice, more than a little freaked out. That was Lucy's favorite expression. Freaked out.

"He must have inhaled that beer," Ed said, automatically drawing off another pitcher, another perfect inch of foam on top. He put it at Lucy's station and she looked at Ed, then down at the stranger. Something about the man scared her.

Of the two of them, Lucy was the bad-ass. He was an old man with a bum left arm and arthritis. He felt for her, being scared and needful of a decent tip. He decided to be friendly, see if his good nature could make things more cheerful.

"I'd say a second round calls for another ham sandwich." It didn't. The sign made that clear. But what the hell. Lucy had stayed with him when most would have quit.

He went back to make the meal, hearing Lucy's boot heels kicking slowly down the bar. She was taking her time, thinking about delivering the beer, and Lucy was not much of a thinker. Ed glanced at the stranger, who was bathed in the sterling glow of the rising moon, and damned if the man didn't look a foot taller, and wider, too. A big bear of a man. The sterile, sharp glow put his face and hands in shadow, but his gleaming eyes watched Ed carefully, and his ears seemed to twitch under his Stetson, listening to Ed walk back to the kitchen.

Ed leaned against the butcher-block table, wondering what the hell to do. The stranger was becoming more unnerving by the minute, horrifying even, while Lucy brought him beer and Ed himself did the man favors. A lot had happened in the last quarter decade. He'd been robbed seventeen times. Three times he'd pulled the shotgun and twice he'd killed himself a robber. Ed told himself that he needed to firm up. This was no time to go weak in the knees.

The sandwich practically made itself. He was so practiced, having gone to a cold kitchen and cold cuts years before to save dinero. He brought it out and put it at Lucy's station, but Lucy wasn't there. Ed looked down the bar and the man had her next to him, a thick arm wrapped around her shoulders.

The stranger said something that sounded like *bring it*, his words thick and deep.

Ed walked down the groove he'd worn in the oak floor, carrying brews and whiskey for thousands of thirsty folks. Close up, the beard covered the man's face, his heavy nose prominent as a snout. His eyes seemed red and bright as the moon painting this end of the bar. The smell of the man rankled Ed's stumpy old nose. He stank worse than a nest of raccoons.

Ed slid the sandwich over and the stranger took it in his free hand, devouring half of the thick makings in one bite.

Ed watched him chew, quick and economical as an animal, glancing at Lucy's ghastly face. The man's long dirty nails were an inch from her throat.

There was a time when he would have gone back for the shotgun and put the stranger out, but those days had passed. Lucy saw Ed's indecision and quivered with fear. He wanted to wink at her, to tell her that he'd find a way to do the necessary thing, but the stranger scared the starch out of him. He could feel his legs shake.

The entry door opened, and Ed automatically turned. "Howdy! If you're drinking, you get a ham sandwich on us!"

"I'm drinking," the man said. He carried a duffel over one shoulder, wearing a Winchester hunting jacket with a padded shoulder. The occasional hunter made his way into the Matchstick, tracking deer, fox, coyotes, and raccoons along the river bottom west on Titan Road.

"Got a name?"

"I'm Austin." He was as tall as the weird stranger, but not so heavy and not nearly as wild. Both his jacket and his pants were cargos, with lots of pockets stuffed full of things, everything buttoned and tied down. Ed liked him. You keep bar, you like some people, the rest you simply serve without relating to them more than you have to. People talk. You hear every story in the world nine times and become an expert on the nuances of betrayal, grief, and unfaithfulness. To keep from judging, every new person becomes an atom in the one person you relate to, the universal stranger far from home.

Austin decided on Heineken. Two bucks more a pitcher, but Austin had class. All the while Ed wrestled with what was going on and what he should say. Giving the man a warning seemed in order if he could figure out a sly way to do it.

As he poured, he gestured to Lucy to come down and get the pitcher.

His gesture surprised the stranger and Lucy twisted free, boot heels clicking as she came to help.

Austin moved to let her pass and went halfway down the bar, putting the duffel on the stool beside him. The stranger stared at the duffel, then switched to watch Ed's hands work the beer. A man gets a load of buckshot with his Pabst Blue Ribbon, he remembers to watch the bartender and what he does with his hands.

Lucy got a tray and Ed put the pitcher on it, smiling at the one inch of curling foam. Fried with fear or not, he could pour a fine pitcher.

"I'll just get your sandwich."

Lucy brought the beer to Austin, who said something, his voice too deep for Ed to catch. Criminy! He was going deaf on top of all the rest of his malfunctions.

Hunting was hungry work. Ed made Austin a ham sandwich fit for a king. He brought it out and put it at Lucy's station. Her eyes were wide, but she put a tray under the sandwich, adding a toothpick, pickles, and Lay's chips. Lucy nodded to the end of the bar. "That's one's dry. I'll get this one."

"What did Austin say to you?"

"That I should stay to his left," Lucy whispered, Ed just catching the words.

Ed thought about the importance of staying on Austin's left, pouring another Miller High Life. The stretch of the bar between Austin and the stranger was maybe twelve feet, close enough for a handgun if he had one in that huge duffel.

The stranger watched him pour, watched Lucy slide the pitcher toward Austin, coming in from the left, staying clear of the two men. He made his move, launching himself over the bar with the agility of a mountain lion.

Austin stepped back off the stool and swung a shortened over-and-under from his coat, velcro ties tearing free, firing at the stranger from the hip.

Ed expected a swarm of pellets but saw instead a whirling, expanding, flash of silver dimes punching into the stranger's chest dead on the heart. Austin gently moved Lucy aside and the man slid down the side of the bar, pooling on the floor.

"Dear God, what is it?" Lucy said. But she must have known.

Ed could make out the deformations of face, snout, jaws, forehead, and hair, the longer, heavier body, the claws where hands had been. And it was changing as he watched, the features shifting back toward humanity.

"I've been following this one since he killed a restaurant full of people in Canada. I'm after him for the bounty. Better step back. Don't get any of his blood on you. I'll haul him out, put him in my truck, and we'll mop up with bleach."

Austin guided Lucy a couple steps away, as she didn't take instruction from anyone, Ed himself frozen in place at the tap, one hand on the Heineken handle.

Austin opened another cargo pocket and took out two thick blocks of cash in bank wrappers. He put them on the bar. "For your trouble."

It had been a long time since Ed had more than just enough. The sight of the money made him giddy. Lucy wasn't shy. She took hers in an unsteady hand. They'd have some mess to clean up sure enough, but Austin was taking the body and that was the important thing. His advertisement sure as hell had worked! It had brought him some badly needed business. Ed laughed to himself, mostly out of relief that the stranger hadn't ripped the two of them into small pieces.

"That sandwich you promised me?" Austin asked. "After we tidy up?"

Ed took the cash and put it under the bar, by the shotgun he'd been too terrorized to pull. "Yes?"

"Can I have that to go?"

He-Ham

Virva Peikko

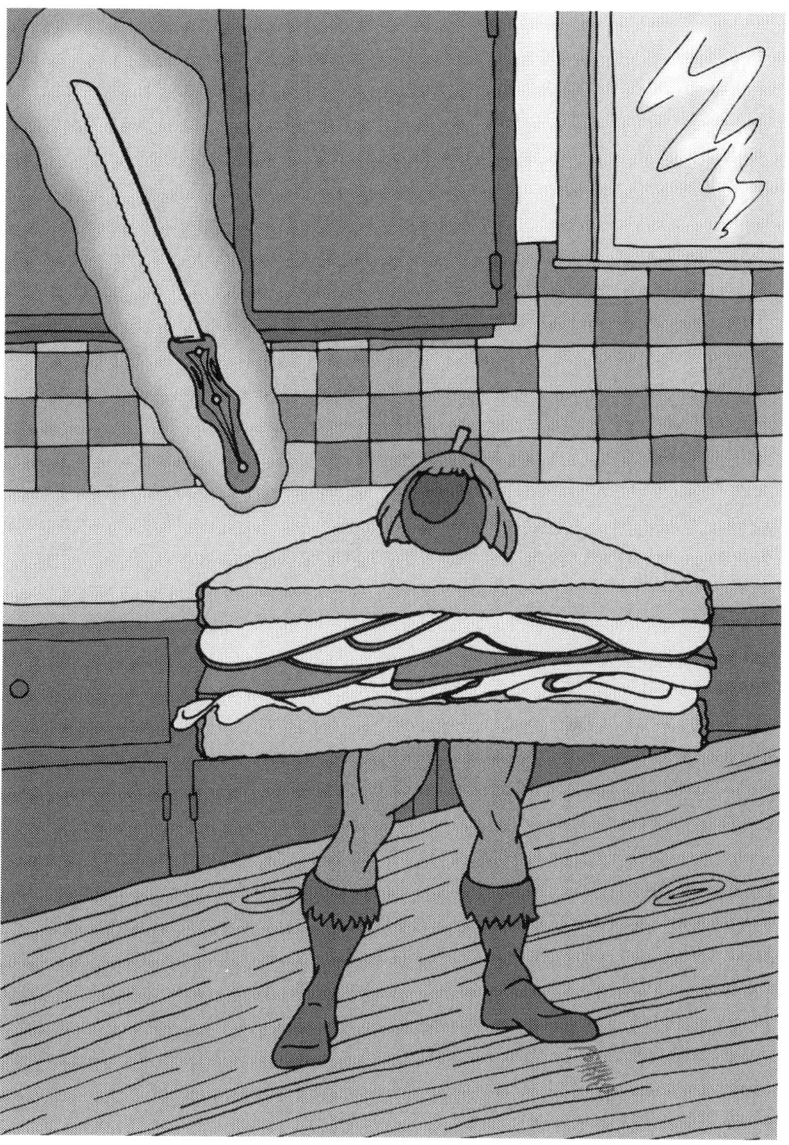

Little Bone-Brittle

Regina Kenney

It happened again that morning. My mom and I just got back from another boring trip to the grocery store where she, as always, refused my excellent suggestions on what to eat that week. I ran in first with my two bags of groceries, threw them on the counter, then raced to the living room to catch the end of Ninja Fighters, and there she sat.

She was in her nightgown, with her head hung low, sitting in the dining room at the table, mouth slightly open, staring across the room at an empty chair.

Seeing her startled me, and I gave a loud yelp. She snapped from her daze and slowly looked at me. "Edmund. You didn't finish your meal."

My mom came into the room and gave a quick sigh of relief when she saw her. "Mrs. Grundy, are you... are you ok?"

"I spent all day cooking, and Edmund won't finish his meal," Mrs. Grundy replied and stuck her bony finger out towards me, exposing the red and blue veins stemming from under her arm.

"Oh no, Mrs. Grundy. That's not your son Edmund. That's my youngest, Robbie. Remember?"

Mrs. Grundy pursed her lips and stared at me. She squinted her eyes as if to say that she knew I really was Edmund and how dare I let her dinner go cold.

"C'mon, I'll walk you home." My mom motioned with her hands for her to stand. "Robbie, unload the rest of the groceries from the car."

The old woman looked up towards the ceiling and her face relaxed. When she looked back at us, her eyes were bright and cheery. "Oh, Elizabeth, of course. I am so sorry. I must've gotten confused when getting the paper this morning..."

"It's no problem. These things happen." My mom carefully helped her up out of the chair.

"Oh, this must be such a disruption in your house, I really do apologise. Robbie, I hope I didn't scare you. These houses just start to look all the same to me..." she said and started to the door with my Mom helping her.

Mrs. Grundy lived two doors down from us. It started about four months ago when she began to let herself into our house and wander around. My mom said that she and her husband used to live here years ago with their son but had moved to the smaller house on the block when their son passed away. They didn't want to leave the town, but the house reminded them too much of Edmund. My mom loved Mrs. Grundy; the two would have afternoon tea every so often. When we first moved in, Mrs. Grundy came by right away with an apple pie. Over the years, my mom had given her a house key just in case I was ever locked out when I came home from school.

"She just gets confused sometimes," my mom explained while scooping out mash potatoes onto my plate. Meatloaf. Again. I started to whine about the meal, and my mom gave me a stern look. "Eat it. We don't waste food in this family. You should be happy to even have dinner, there are starving children in Africa who have nothing to eat."

I stared at the plate and moved my fork around the lumps of potatoes and peas.

"And don't play with your food. Or else no trick-or-treating tonight." At this, I started shovelling the food into my mouth. I had worked all week on my spaceman costume, and Jimmy was coming over at 7 p.m. dressed as a werewolf to go out into the neighbourhood.

"Oh, before I forget, remember to go trick-or-treating at Mrs. Grundy's house tonight. She said she barely got any trick-or-treaters last year."

I gave a frustrated sigh. Mrs. Grundy's house was creepy. There was a long hedge leading up to the porch, and it always smelled like cats and liquorice. Bobby Clint told us that it was one of those houses that didn't give out candy but gave out healthy things, so we all avoided it. After dinner, I put on my blue long johns and the cardboard space-vest I had made from an old storage box. My mom found a football helmet in our garage and drew little rocket ships on the side so I could breathe when exploring new planets. She also bought me a space gun at the Dollar Store. Jimmy rang our door at 6:30 p.m.

"Bang! Bang!" I jumped out from behind the stair and pointed my space gun at Jimmy.

"Werewolf defence shields!" Jimmy yelled and blocked my attack. Jimmy's parents couldn't afford a costume, so he had his mother's eyeliner marked around his face to represent fur. He had stuffed scraps of pelts from his uncle's taxidermy shop in the holes of his shirt.

We ran around the living room, ducking behind couches and shooting at each other.

"Na-uh!" I screamed, "Werewolves can't have guns, they're allergic to silver!"

Jimmy attempted a roundhouse kick in the air and screamed back, "Guns aren't made of silver, the bullets are!" I dodged his attack.

"How do you load the gun then?" I said and threw a pillow towards him.

"Scientist captured me to give me radioactive powers and a silver antidote! Pew! Pew!" He caught the pillow and started firing.

My mom yelled at us to settle down, so we sat at the kitchen table and went over our plan. Jimmy was the best artist in school and had drawn a map of our street and the cul-de-sac at the end. We went over the most important houses, and the big blue house at the corner had a star next to it because they gave out whole cans of soda pop.

"You boys look adorable." My mom snapped photos of us. "OK, remember to only go to the houses on our street, and stick together."

We shuffled outside. It looked like both the nightmare world and the magic kingdom had opened their gates. We could see a princess with a mermaid walking up to the house across the street. Some teenagers in devil masks ran by us, howling, while a group of angels and superheroes passed us to knock on my door. We ran to the corner to the big blue house and then were off to the yellow house across the street, which always gave out whole chocolate bars. We skipped Mr. Jefferson's house (raisins and toothbrushes every year) and then headed to the cul-de-sac, where the houses were close together and easy to run to.

On our way back, with our bags bursting, it had gotten dark. We passed Mrs. Grundy's house, and I stopped outside.

"Oh wait, we have to go here," I said, and Jimmy looked up at the house.

"I'm not going up there," he said. I looked down the street, and all the other houses had children running up and down. But Mrs. Grundy's house looked as though no one was home.

"C'mon, my mom said we have to." I knew if I didn't go, Mrs. Grundy would mention it to my mom, then it would be no TV for a week.

"I'll wait here, you can go up," Jimmy said and started rifling through his candy bag.

I looked at the house and started up the hedged pathway. The grass had not been cut in ages, and the acrid smell reached me as soon as I neared the porch. Mrs. Grundy had hung a skeleton on the door that had turned yellow from years of use. I knocked on the door.

There was a long pause, and I was about to turn around when the door started to open. Mrs. Grundy stood there in her nightdress, hunched over.

"How lovely. A trick-or-treater! And let me look at you, what are you dressed as?" Mrs. Grundy peered at me through her red glasses.

"I'm a spaceman," I said.

"Oh, of course you are. Look how handsome you look." She grabbed a plate behind her. "And here is your treat."

She dropped a sandwich, wrapped in plastic, in my bag.

"Are you going to eat it?" she asked.

"What?" I looked up at her. Her eyes seemed to have changed. They had a thin glaze over them, and she looked intently focused on me.

"Are you going to eat the ham sandwich I made for you?" Her fists tightened on the tray, and her smile dropped.

"Uh... yes," I said.

"You remember what happened the last time you didn't eat the sandwich I made you, don't you?" Her eyes were intense, and her frown started to grow longer. "You had to stay in that house, didn't you?"

I glanced back at Jimmy, who was fiddling with his fur pelts. I didn't know what she was talking about, but I just wanted to run. "I am going to eat it. Thank you."

"Good boy." And at last she turned and shut the door.

"What'd you get?" Jimmy asked as I neared the curb. He had resumed examining the candy in his bag. "A ham sandwich," I said, and Jimmy burst out laughing. "That's what Bobby said she gave out last year! That lady is nuts.

Are you going to eat it?" We started to walk the two doors to my house.

"Of course not," I stammered, and as we got to my front yard, I chucked the wrapped sandwich into the bushes outside my house. My mom went through my Halloween candy every year when I got back, and I knew she'd make me eat it if she found it. She said that she didn't have a lot to eat growing up and that was why she never let me waste food.

We headed to my front door debating over what was the best costume we had seen. Obviously, it was Tina Miller's shark costume. My mom let us choose five pieces of candy to eat while we watched cartoons, then Jimmy's parents came at 9 p.m. to pick him up.

That night, after I brushed my teeth and got into my pyjamas, I went upstairs to my room, got into bed, and felt under my pillow. I had stashed two chocolate bars and one lollipop there, and they were still safe. I tore open the coconut chocolate one and popped the whole mini-bar in my mouth. I lay back in bed, happy and full of sweets.

The night started to fade. I was tired from running around the neighbourhood. I lay in my bed thinking of how funny Jimmy looked with his rabbit fur poking from the top of his pants and wondering if pizza was going to be served tomorrow at school. I had been so excited about my costume all month that I felt a weird emptiness that Halloween was now over. The next holiday was Thanksgiving, which was alright I guess, but then after that it was Christmas... My eyes started to close, and I fell asleep.

I woke up hearing a creak on the stair. My door was slightly open, and I stared at it. The house was dark. And the branches of the oak tree outside my window gently tapped the frame. I waited. I wanted to jump up and close the door, but then I heard another loud creak. Something was moving very slowly up the stairs.

I grabbed my covers and pulled them tight as I stared at the door. My breathing sounded loud, so I tried to hold my breath. Something heavy had stepped on the final landing at the top of the stairs and let out a small gasp. My arms stiffened, holding my covers. I tried to yell for my mom, but no sound came out. I was still staring at the door when it started to move. The hinges gave a soft squeak, and the door slowly opened wider.

The sudden jolt of fear allowed me to move again, but all I did was pull the covers over my head and switch to the fetal position. I could feel my door creak open and something moving around my room. I tried to hold my breath because my breathing became so loud and the heat filled the space under the covers. Then I felt the bed move from a weight placed at the edge of the mattress. I crouched, shivering. I waited for what felt like fifteen minutes. Then I got up the courage to peak outside my covers. I wanted to bolt for the door, but my legs felt like jelly.

I pulled the covers just over my nose, and there sat saw Mrs. Grundy, sitting at the edge of my bed. She was staring at me, with her hands folded on her lap.

My fingers tightened and lowered my covers just below my chin. Her face was hardened, and I could smell milk and peppermint on her breath. She was in her nightgown. Her mouth was slightly open, and her eyes stared at me without blinking.

"How was it?" she asked.

"Huh?" I stammered. Startled at the sudden noise.

"My ham sandwich." She stared and stuck out a pointy tongue to wet her dry, cracking mouth. "Did you like the way it tasted?"

The old woman started to lean closer to me, and her wide eyes seemed to have yellow cracks.

"Um... yes. Thank you," I managed to say after a long pause.

"Do you know what happens to little boys who lie?" Saliva started to form at the edge of her mouth.

"I am not lying. I ate it." I could feel my hands start to shake.

"That's a good little boy, then." She didn't move. She kept her intense stare. "Then you deserve a bedtime story. Because good little boys who don't lie deserve stories." She moved closer, and I could see the hairs from her chin.

In a hushed tone, she began, "Once upon a time there was little boy who lived on a crooked street. His name was Little Bone-Brittle because he never ate what his mommy told him to, and so he was skinny and frail. All the kids would throw stones at Little Bone-Brittle and he cried every night because he had no friends. There was a kind, beautiful woman who lived on his street who saw Little Bone-Brittle crying when he walked home from school every day. The beautiful woman used to have a son, but her son turned out to be a wicked liar, so he had to be punished. She took pity on Little Bone-Brittle. One day she gave the boy a ham sandwich so he could grow fat and make friends. But Little Bone-Brittle was a naughty boy, and he threw the beautiful woman's sandwich up against her house. The next day, when he came back from school, he found that his mummy had gone away. Deep away. Below the forest. And the sheriff could never find her except a few teeth that were left at the home in the bathroom sink. Good night."

And with that, the old woman stood up and silently left my room.

I sat up straight in bed and stared at the door. Seconds, minutes, maybe hours went by, and I stared at the door. I hadn't heard her go down the stairs, so I thought she might come back into my room. My eyes started to get heavy, but I listened, half asleep, waiting.

I heard the magpie chirping outside and knew it must be morning. I had fallen asleep sitting up, and my fists were still clenched. As soon as I opened my eyes and saw that it was light out, I jumped out of my bed and raced downstairs. I ran outside and started looking in the bushes in our front yard. And there it still was. My ham sandwich. Still wrapped. I tore it open and started eating it as fast as I could. The bread was stale, and the mayo tasted warm and sour, but I didn't stop. I ate the whole sandwich.

At school, I couldn't concentrate all day. I kept thinking about Little Bone-Brittle and ham sandwiches and my stomach had a sharp pain. During spelling hour, I asked Mrs. Schaum if I could go to the bathroom, and as soon as I got to the stall I started retching in the toilet. Finally, the end of the day came, and I raced home from school and burst through the door. My mom was boiling water on the stove, and I gave a huge sigh of relief. I ran up to her and gave her a hug.

She hugged back. "Oh that's awfully sweet, how was your day at school?"

"Good." I breathed. My heart was still pounding from the run home.

"Oh, mind the oven, honey, I'm making Mrs. Grundy's tea."

I froze. And slowly turned to see Mrs. Grundy sitting at our dining room table.

"Oh hello, Robbie! My you are getting so big for your age!" She smiled sweetly, and her eyes were alight and warm. My mom brought her the tea. "And how did you like trick-or-treating last night? You made a very handsome spaceman!"

"It was good," I managed to get out and just stared at her. She started to talk to my mom about the harvest festival next week. I sat at the kitchen table and looked at her. She looked so different today then she had last night.

"Oh, Elizabeth, I have to say, your lawn looked so neat this morning. The bushes out front looked trimmed and clean." Mrs. Grundy gave a quick look at me, and my mouth fell open. "I was worried there would be wrappers from the neighbour kids' candy, but it looked spic and span."

My mom changed the subject to Thanksgiving and started chatting about what relatives would be coming up from the city. After about an hour, Mrs. Grundy stood up and said, "Well, this has been simply lovely, but the TV repair man is coming over at 4 p.m., and I want to clean up a bit." She stood up and put on her shawl.

"Thank you so much for dropping in, Mrs. Grundy, come by anytime." My mom smiled and stood up to walk her to the door.

"Oh, and I forgot to tell you." Mrs. Grundy stopped midway through the door and turned around. "I swear I am losing my mind sometimes. Just as I was putting away the Halloween decorations this morning, I found a whole bag of Halloween treats from last year—remember I told you, I didn't get many trick-or-treaters—at the bottom of my holiday storage bin. I don't know what to do with them."

"Oh, those don't go bad. If you like, I can send Robbie over tonight to fetch the bag. He'd love to eat them." My mom smiled.

"Good. He can come over at 7 p.m. to pick them up." Mrs. Grundy turned and looked at me. "See you tonight…" A thick smile spread across her face. Then she turned and left.

All of Us Atoms

Josh Lefkowitz

Atoms crashed into a bang
many miles and moons ago
so that I could be here, writing now
to tell you about a sandwich just now

that was also made of a million atoms,
ham atoms, swiss cheese atoms,
ciabatta atoms all carby and crusted,
which I had for second lunch just now,

which pushed aside for a couple moments
the atoms that make me feel not-enough,
the heavy, miserable, furious atoms
I'm lucky enough to inherit by blood –

Why lucky? Because – I think it's true –
Even the blues are better than absence
of blue, or any other color –
A cry of despair in the woods still shakes

the trees, still wakes the robin

who flutters and flees his nest, streaking
across the sky, now spied by a woman
and man, who embraces his picnic partner

in an act of love – which led to me,
and you. So happy or sad or
bored, digesting a sandwich or two, I try
to remember we matter. I try. I do.

Hook and Grinder

David F. Shultz

first published in The Horror Zine, February 2008

They're going to kill you today, said the voice inside his head.

Cold metal underneath stuck to Albert's naked flesh, pinched and cut into his pink flesh. A smell of rust and defecation hung in the air, so strong he could taste it. His muscles were stiff. There wasn't room to stretch inside the crate.

Slivers of light pierced through the grating. On the other side, a shadowy figure moved with an unnatural, lurching gait. Each footfall reverberated through the metal floor and sent shivers down Albert's spine. The enslavers were grotesque creatures with oddly shaped bodies, gangly stretched-out limbs, folds covering grey flesh, heads that towered high above. He didn't know for what hideous purpose they had brought him here, only that they didn't care about his suffering, or maybe they enjoyed it. Albert held his breath as the footsteps quieted into the distance.

"Pssssst," a voice whispered from a neighbouring cell.

"Shhhh!"

"What're you scared of?"

"What do you think?" Albert had vivid memories of unruly captives tortured into submission. The enslavers seemed to delight in the process, erupting into fits of hissing and wheezing sounds as they snapped bones, jabbed with metal prongs, or forced struggling faces into buckets of waste water. Afterwards, limp bodies were dragged like brushes across the metal floor, painting the floors with swaths of blood.

"Albert? Is that you?"

"Yeah. Who are you?"

"It's Erik."

Albert was silent.

"Erik," the voice repeated. "VP of processing division."

"I'm sorry, who?"

"Oh, geez. They warned us this might happen."

"What?"

"Trauma-induced retrograde amnesia. Memory loss, Erik. Do you know why you're here?"

Every moment he could remember was the same, tortured inside this prison, nothing left from before the abduction. Albert suspected the aliens had taken his memory along with his freedom.

"No," Albert answered finally. "I don't know."

"They're auditing us for moral externalities."

"Huh?"

"Listen, Albert. I don't think I have time to explain everything. But they're gonna kill us today, and then everything's gonna be okay."

"What? They're gonna kill us?"

"Yes," Erik said. "Any time now. And all you have to do is let them do it."

A panel swivelled open below and Albert dropped, crashing onto an open metal platform. *Clang*. Erik landed a few feet away. Albert squinted, blinded by searing light.

A silhouette towered above them, moving silently and methodically. Albert froze in terror. In one of the creature's long-fingered hands it gripped a metal hook. It raised the hook overhead, then brought it swiftly down. The point burrowed deep into Erik's back, hooking under the shoulder blade.

The creature pressed a red button, and Erik was hoisted up on a rickety chain. His dangling body joined dozens of other victims, each suspended by hooks in their backs, all of them sliding along a ceiling conveyor, wriggling helplessly.

"Don't worry, Albert," Erik called down from the meathook. "It'll be over soon."

The creature reached for another hook.

This was it. Albert charged forward and tackled the enslaver, knocking it flat on its back. The hook clattered to the ground, and Albert grabbed it. He slashed, tearing through the rubbery flesh of the creature's neck. Blood spurted from the gaping wound and spilled between clutching, corpselike fingers. The creature writhed on the floor and looked up at Albert with yellow eyes. Then it was still.

"What are you doing?" Erik shouted from above.

"I'm gonna kill every single one of those things," Albert said, fingers clamped on the handle of the hook.

The conveyor pulled Erik into a dark opening in the wall, and he disappeared into shadow.

"No," Erik shouted from the darkness. "Albert, please, you have to let them take you!"

"Like hell I do," Albert muttered. He scanned the room, then stepped through the only exit. The adjoining room was massive. Splatters of blood traced along the floor, dripped down from bodies dangling high above. In the middle of the room was a large tubular machine. Albert watched in horror as the conveyor lowered a wriggling human body into the device. There was a sickening sound as the machine struggled with flesh and bone, like a blender. From a spout on the bottom, pinkish-red paste oozed onto a conveyor.

The bloodied hook rose out from the top of the machine, absent a body. Another hook moved to take its place, dangling a fresh victim. Erik was next in line.

"Albert," Erik yelled out as his feet lowered into the machine. "What are you doing down there? You've got to go in the grinder!"

"Are you insane?"

Erik was lowered into the machine, and the top erupted with flecks of blood and chips of bone. The same sickly paste squirted out onto the conveyor below. The bloodied hook rose, and Erik was gone.

Albert took off running. He darted through an exit into a long hallway. He sprinted across, footsteps echoing on metal. As he neared the other end, he stopped in his tracks. Three of the enslavers were rounding the corner. Albert spun to run back the other way, but three more of them appeared, blocking the hall on the other end. He was surrounded. Time slowed as his vision darted back and forth between the approaching creatures. Then he saw his escape. Small circular windows were spread along the wall, like portholes, just large enough for his body. Albert darted to the closest one and peered out, and his heart sank. The ground lay more than a hundred feet below. A barren landscape, red rocks that extended for miles, like the surface of Mars.

Albert glanced back at the steadily approaching aliens.

"I'm not gonna give you the pleasure," he said, and crawled through the window. Maybe he couldn't escape with his life, but he'd be damned if he'd let these hellish creatures take it. Albert plummeted to the rocks below. He closed his eyes, felt nothing but rushing wind, and braced for impact.

Darkness.

"That one won't count," a voice said.

"You can't be serious. He died, didn't he?"

Albert blinked awake as voices argued around him.

"Well, yes, he died. But not in the product line."

"Where does it say he has to die in the product line?"

Albert shook his head, hoping to throw off the disorientation. He was reclined in a comfortable chair. The room was clean, sterile looking, with teal walls. Some kind of laboratory or medical room. One of the two arguing men wore a lab coat and held a clipboard. The other wore an expensive-looking suit. Albert recognized the suited man. It was Erik.

"We need to account for every product," clipboard man said. "If he doesn't die in the product line, then it doesn't count."

"Then why'd you let him die outside? Whose fault is that?"

"Excuse me," Albert said, "can someone please tell me what is going on?"

The two men stopped and looked at Albert.

"Good to see you're awake," clipboard man said. "I understand you are experiencing amnesia?"

"Yeah. And my head hurts." Erik moved to rub his head, and his fingers ran up against a tangle of wires. There was an array of electrodes attached to his scalp. "What in God's name is going on?"

"All of those symptoms should clear up soon," the man said, and extended his hand. "I'm Doctor Rahim."

Albert shook.

"I'm afraid what Erik has told you is correct," Rahim said. "The last one won't count."

"Last one?" Albert raised an eyebrow. "Won't count for what?"

"For the audit," Rahim said.

Erik shrugged.

"We must determine if management is willing to pay all the costs associated with operation," Rahim explained.

"In the case of your meat processing facility, we are most concerned with the cost imposed on the animals in your production line. We are running neural simulations to determine if you and the rest of management are willing to pay the moral costs of your business model."

"So all of that torture—"

"—was a simulation of your production line, modified suitably to your vantage point."

Albert gripped his face. His head was spinning.

"How long was I in there for?"

"About three seconds," Rahim answered

"Three seconds?" Albert screamed. "It felt like years."

"There's an accelerated perception of time," Rahim explained. "It would take too long otherwise."

"Albert," Erik said. "We're almost done here. Let's just finish up so we can get back to doing business."

"You mean you want me to go back to that hellhole?"

"Just a few more times."

"And if I refuse?"

"It's your choice," Rahim said. "You can quit any time you like."

"But you can't quit now," Erik yelled. "They'll close down the company!"

"That's right," Rahim said. "If management is not willing to pay the cost of negative externalities, the company will be graded as economically inefficient."

"We have hundreds of employees, Albert. You want to put them all out of a job?"

Albert remembered the company he ran and the employees who counted on him. People with families to support. "How many more times do we need to do it?" Albert asked.

"Just once per animal," Erik said, "divided between management. It won't take more than a few hours."

"How many simulations is that for each of us?" Albert asked.

Rahim checked his clipboard. "About sixty thousand."

"Sixty thousand?"

"It's just a few hours," Erik said. "You'll be back in time for dinner."

"I don't think I can do it."

"You have what it takes," Erik said. "That's why you're in management—you understand the meaning of sacrifice!"

"I don't know."

"It gets easier, Albert. See for yourself. Just go one more time. It'll only take three seconds."

Albert thought about the thousands and thousands of loyal customers, who, without Albert's company, would have to find alternatives for their sliced ham. Prices would skyrocket. No more sliced ham in school lunchboxes, so many disappointed children, so many lunches ruined! Albert was proud of his company, he was proud of how successful they had been under his leadership, and he was proud of his product. It was time to show what he was made of.

•

They're going to kill you today, said the voice inside his head.

Cold Slices, Hot Bodies

R.D. Sullivan

If Ben had thought for a moment that the line, "Would you like to come up for a cup of coffee?" could have Amber hot to get into his apartment, he might have bothered to clean up a bit. And buy coffee. Now that it was out there, he wasn't sure how to deflect. Or if he even could.

What a stupid question anyway. It was so cliché. So scripted. What had he been thinking?

But thinking wasn't what he'd been doing, at least not with his head. In all honesty, he'd panicked. There she'd been, staring at him in the back of the taxi, face full of anticipation, and he didn't know for what. A kiss? Less? For him to get out of the car and disappear from her life forever?

What a pig he'd be if it were the last and he went in for the first. So the question. A fumble. "Would you like to come up for a cup of coffee?"

"I'd love that."

So quick, that answer. She didn't hesitate. Amber was not panicking.

Yet his panic only increased with her yes as he desperately struggled to find a way to back out. If tomorrow wasn't Sunday, he could say he had an early meeting. Then, she'd never talk to him again for such a weak rejection.

Hadn't she said she was allergic to cats? Too bad he didn't have one.

Hell. It had been going so well, too. A few drinks, mini-golf, a nice dinner at a not-too-fancy noodle joint. Their connection had been immediate, conversation easy and laughs many. She'd held his hand while waiting for the taxi. He'd put a hand on her back, helping her in.

And those moon eyes the whole ride here. Him by the door, her in the middle.

"What?" she asked.

The panic must have been written on his face, the way he'd drifted off into it. He smiled sheepishly and ran fingers through his shaggy black hair. "I lied. I don't have any coffee."

Amber laughed and scooted a bit closer. Her thigh pressed into his, warm and electric. "You never said you did."

"Doesn't asking someone to come up for coffee imply there's coffee?"

"Tea, then?"

"I'm not really a tea guy, either."

"I'll find something." Amber found his hand and intertwined her fingers into his.

"Also," he continued, "maybe it's a little messy. I didn't really expect company."

"Is the garbage overflowing? Take out boxes so old something will bite you if you stick a hand in?"

"No?"

"How long has it been since your sheets have been washed?"

"Um... Four days."

"Good!" she said brightly. "I'm in, then."

She'd asked about his bedsheets. That was a good sign. Wasn't that a good sign? Even as he returned her smile, a nervous tension blossomed in his stomach. He really liked this woman. He wanted to see her again, not just have one fun date and then be that guy who pushed too hard before she was ready.

But if he was being honest, he couldn't wait to get her up to his apartment.

•

Amber scoffed after stepping through his front door. She had been very close to backing out when he'd said it was messy, but this? The place just looked lightly lived in. A water glass on the table. A plate and skillet stacked in the sink. Mail on the counter, shoes and socks kicked off and left in front of the couch. Messy would have been a couch covered in laundry, pizza boxes on the counter, and that sharp, musky smell dude apartments got when they didn't clean often enough.

This place was just plain nice. Framed art, decent furnishings, clean carpet. Unless his bedroom was an unmitigated nightmare, she wasn't sure what he'd been worried about.

"Can I offer you… a glass of water, I guess?" Again that sheepish smile, that cute little embarrassed shrug. She wanted to drag him to the living room, fling their clothes about so the place was properly messy, and do things that would make him keep the couch forever out of fond memory. Her date seemed a little more reserved, however, and she wanted to respect that.

"That would be nice. And I'm a bit hungry. What do you have to eat?"

"Make yourself at home, I'll see what I can find," he said, and stuck his head in the fridge. Amber hooked her purse on the back of a chair and sat at the dining table while he rooted around. "Bad news. I've got cheese singles, a little bit of almond milk, condiments, and some lunch meat."

"Bread?"

He thought for a moment. "Yes! Just bought bread."

"What kind of lunch meat?"

"Ham."

"A ham sandwich it is." And then, because she couldn't help herself, "Do you have a pickle you could add to my meat?"

The way he froze in the fridge thrilled her. Ben cleared his throat. "No pickles in the fridge."

In the fridge, he'd specified. God he was cute. What a night it would be if he wanted it as bad as she did.

"I'll survive pickle-less for a while, then."

He came up out of the fridge with an armful of goods and set it all on the counter behind him. When he got a plate, she hopped up next to it, watching him lick his lips, wanting to be the one to lick them.

"Mayo?" he asked.

"Sure. I'm not picky. Ben," she said, brushing his thigh with the toe of one high heel, "I'm going to ask you something and you can say no, okay? I don't want to move too fast because I really had fun tonight, I don't want to scare you away. It's just..." She trailed off and bit her lip.

"Just what?" he asked, his voice husky and quiet.

Amber moved her foot until she was massaging the inside of his thigh, up and down, from her perch on the kitchen counter. "Just, I thought maybe I could check out your pickle while you make me a sandwich."

His laugh was quick but not unkind. "I don't even know how you made that sound sexy. That should not sound sexy."

She could tell from the bulge in his pants that her toes brushed that he wasn't entirely opposed to the idea, but he hadn't said yes yet. "Is that a no, then? I don't want to be too aggressive."

"That is definitely not a no." His hands were flat on the granite, pressing hard. Everything in his stance was taut, rigid. "It's just..."

When he wouldn't meet her eye, clearly hesitant, she dropped her foot from his thigh. God, she hoped she hadn't screwed this up already.

"Just what?" she asked.

Ben dropped his head and laughed softly. When he looked back up at her, his cheeks were red.

"Just that it's, you know, the kitchen. Wouldn't you rather..." He shot a meaningful look towards the hallway, presumably towards his bedroom.

Amber toyed with a button on his shirt. "I don't know. I thought it might be hot." When he hesitated still, she hopped off the counter. "Don't worry about it."

She tried to keep the disappointment off her face as she leaned in to give him a quick kiss, but Ben surprised her by weaving a hand into her hair, holding her in place. He let her guide the action, matched her intensity, met her tongue with his.

She grinned when he broke it off, his lips pressed together as if to savor the ghost of her passion still lingering there.

"Maybe," he said.

"Maybe's not enough." She kissed him lightly again.

"I want you so bad," he said against her lips.

"Then let me."

Ben swallowed hard. "Yes."

"Yes?"

"Yes."

She kissed him, kissed him again, lightly at first, then deeper as she pulled his head into it. His hands came up to touch her, explore her, but she pushed them back down and pulled away.

"Nope," she said. "You've got a sandwich to make."

"Seriously?"

"Seriously. Consider it tax for not actually owning a coffeepot." Amber dropped to her knees between him and the counter, trailing a hand down his torso and over his thigh as she went.

"You're not giving me much reason to get this sandwich done in a hurry."

"Well," she said, smiling up at him, "we can't move on to other things until that sandwich is made. You don't want the night to end with just this, do you?"

•

Amber pulled his zipper down as he reached for the bread. Her hand freed him from his slacks as he laid out two slices on the plate. When she took him in her mouth, he grunted in pleasure. His eyes closed, and he set the mayonnaise and butter knife back on the counter.

His hesitation clearly hadn't gone farther south than his beating heart.

"Jesus," he said.

She started slow, and it was delicious. One hand gripped the base of his shaft while the other cupped and massaged his sac. As she moved back and forth, her tongue wriggled and flicked every inch, explored the ridge of his head, licked his tip. The hand holding him worked up and down in unison with her mouth, driving him wild.

This was really happening. This hot, funny, sexy woman was between his legs, right now, and she had been right—it was definitely hot. He wanted to yank her up, lead her to the bedroom and return the favor.

But no. Nothing else until the sandwich was made, she'd ruled. It was deliciously evil.

As if reading his thoughts, she chuckled, him deep in her mouth, and he groaned with the sensation of it. Then, he picked up the butter knife and got back to work.

It was hard to concentrate. Even harder to keep his hips steady. They wanted to meet her thrusts, but he thought accidentally knocking her head into the cupboard door would end the night prematurely. The condiments were on. The meat layered on nice and thick. He was unwrapping the cheese singles when that warm lightness started to spread across his lower belly, and he hissed through his teeth.

"Slow down," he said. His fingers fumbled at the plastic around the cheese, but it was useless. Dropping the still-wrapped slice, he put both palms back on the counter. "Amber, please, stop."

Her mouth came away and her hands stilled. Brow furrowed, she looked up at him from where she knelt.

"Is everything okay? Was it too much? I can..."

Ben chuckled even as his knuckles were white on the counter. "Everything is fantastic, but if you keep going like that, it's going to be a disappointing night for both of us."

When she picked up on what he was saying, she cracked a wicked grin. Raising one eyebrow, she gave a little twist and pull with her hand. "Is my sandwich done?"

"Cheese. Only cheese left, but... oh god... I can't get it unwrapped with you doing that."

Amber shrugged and slid her hand back and forth a couple more times. "Better hurry then." Yet she didn't put him back in her mouth, just worked his length slowly with her hand, head resting against the counter. It was still distracting, but it let him back off from the edge. And let him get the damn cheese slices unwrapped.

"Done!" he cried, slamming the top slice onto the sandwich.

As she stood, the one hand stayed wrapped around him, working him still, even as she looked at her sandwich. "Ooh," she purred. "Looks perfect."

He captured her mouth with his, tasting her, tasting himself on her lips. This time she didn't push his hands away as they began to explore. He ran them over her hips, her ass, her waist, to her breasts. Never breaking off the kiss, he massaged through the fabric for a moment before reaching around behind her.

As he unzipped her dress, she let go of him to start unbuttoning his shirt. Together they tugged and wriggled and tossed until they were before each other, naked, hands exploring and massaging, pinching and rubbing. While she returned to stroking him, his head dipped and he took her nipples in mouth in turn. Amber pulled his head tight against her chest and moaned through closed lips, fingers tightening on his dick.

"Bedroom?" he asked and licked the nipple he'd just let go of.

Her chuckle was throaty and deep. "Here," she said as though commanding it. Whatever lingering resistance he felt fell away as he took in the gorgeous woman before him. With one arm he slid the plate and condiments aside and lifted her bare ass to the counter.

•

Before she could even gasp at the cold granite on her skin, he was between her legs, nuzzling into her folds and flicking out with his tongue. She lay back, welcoming the cool stone, letting him slide her towards the edge and prop her legs over his shoulders. While he got to work, she trailed her own fingers in slow circles around her nipples.

Amber closed her eyes and enjoyed his worship of her sex. He suckled, licked, and probed while she moaned and wriggled. Her hands pinched and rubbed at her nipples, legs twitched and tightening as he brushed her clit again and again, flicking it with the tip of his tongue at every pass.

It started as it always did, merely a warm tickle in her lower half, a sensation she strove to grab, to cling to. In response to her increased moans, he got more aggressive between her legs, targeting her clit, sucking on it, torturing it with his tongue. The sensation spread across her belly and down into her thighs. She put a hand between her legs to clutch at his hair while her breath caught in her throat. Intense was the wave she rode, and Amber stayed on its edge for as long as she could. When it finally broke, she cried out, back arching on the granite as the world narrowed to that singular sensation exploding between her legs.

Ben slowed his attentions and when Amber finally opened her eyes again, he grinned, clearly proud of himself.

"Holy wow that was amazing." Letting him pull her to sitting, she rose into his kiss, Ben seeming hungry for her mouth. "Condom?" she asked against his lips.

"Hold on. Bedroom."

Amber shook her head. "My purse, then. Zip it open next to my cell phone." She smacked his ass as he hopped away, biting her lip and admiring the figure he struck. Tall.

Lean. Just enough around the midsection to really grab onto if she wanted.

He was back in a flash. The foil tore between his teeth but then he paused. "Would you rather move to the couch? Someplace more comfortable?"

"Not unless you want to. The kitchen is proving a whole lot of fun." She spun the plate with the ham sandwich and grinned at him.

"Nope. Just thought offering was the chivalrous thing to do." As he spoke, he rolled the rubber down. Once it was in place, he lifted her off the counter and set her feet on the floor, then drove her back into its edge with the ferocity of his kiss. She pushed back just as hard with a laugh and worked him with her hand, savoring his groans.

"Ready?" she asked.

"Oh god yes, I've been ready since the taxi."

"Like this." She broke away and turned, putting her back to him, and bent over.

•

Ben ran a hand down her back as she gripped the edge of the counter, stepping up until her luscious ass was against him. She pressed back, his erection rubbing between her legs. With one hand, she guided him into her. He pressed until he met friction, pulled back, and pushed forwards again until he slid all the way in. Under his hands, Amber's body gave a shudder and she made the cutest, smallest moan in the back of her throat.

He leaned over her as he began to thrust, kissing and licking and biting at her back. With one hand, he searched out a breast, but when he reached between her legs with the other, he found her fingers already there. She rocked in time with him, bracing against the counter and meeting his thrusts, her moans growing more intense. He, too, was slowly losing himself. Standing upright, he grabbed her shoulder and hip, and picked up his pace.

Amber stopped meeting his thrusts now, letting him move how he needed, along for the ride. His body screamed that he was so close, so very close, but he fought to stave it off. Her cries were increasing as well and if he could just wait...

Suddenly she gasped and danced under his hands, panting and moaning with her orgasm. He let go, thrusting hard and deep, and cried out himself. Buried inside of her, he gave, both hands on her hips, still thrusting ever farther forwards, lost to the pleasure of it.

It was her laughter that pulled him back. He collapsed on top of her, laughing as well, and they both sank to the floor.

"I, uh..." Ben started. She just laughed again and snuggled into the crook of his arm.

"Oh my god, that was great. And here I was terrified I was going to be too aggressive and scare you off."

"Ha! I was so worried in the car that if I kissed you, you'd slap me and never talk to me again. I still can't believe you made me make a sandwich, though."

"Oh! The sandwich!" Amber was on her feet before he could stop her, sliding the plate off the counter. She sat against the cabinet and gave him a hand up. "The sandwich was the best part. Now we have snacks." One triangle half came his way and Ben couldn't deny how good it looked right then. "Fuel," she added. "For the next round."

"Ambitious," he said, giving an approving nod. She held her half out like a toast and he tapped his against it. They both bit, and both moaned with delight. "I take it all back," he said. "You're right. The sandwich was a brilliant move."

Café Zeno

Tom Fugalli

A ham sandwich
can be divided in half
and the resulting halves
divided in half
ad infinitum.

A ham sandwich divided ad infinitum
will result in either
an infinite number of pieces of some size
or
an infinite number of pieces of no size.

If the ham sandwich divided ad infinitum
results in an infinite number of pieces
of some size
then the sum of the pieces will be
a ham sandwich of infinite size.

If the ham sandwich divided ad infinitum
results in an infinite number of pieces
of no size

then the sum of the pieces will be
a ham sandwich of no size.

Therefore
ham sandwiches are
infinitely large
or
they do not exist.

Still Dawn

Die Booth

Nothing reminds Steph of being a kid more than butties with the crusts cut off. She picks a finger sandwich off the frilled glass cake-stand in front of her and inspects it. Cucumber and cream cheese, delicately sliced into the sort of size that makes her wonder if there's even a full round of bread in total on her plate. The most expensive bread, per slice, in the world: Afternoon Tea. It tastes decent enough, but the mini cupcakes and strictly single glass of Prosecco are better. Afternoon Tea for one, at eleven in the morning. She'd meant it to be self-indulgent: a farewell-for-the-weekend kind of treat from a city with places that actually serve things like finger sandwiches. Only, now it just feels sort of depressing.

It's not true. Something reminds Steph even more of being a kid. And it frightens her silent.

It's unsettling how returning to Grebley can feel like dying and coming home, all at once. The station is like some freaky bubble in time, exactly as Steph remembers it, right down to the graffiti she memorised on too many hours spent waiting for delayed trains and rail replacement buses. 'We all deserve to love and be loved'.

It's still there in faded marker pen, dated '94 and flanked with a cluster of decidedly less sentimental and more lurid declarations. She suspects that this is likely an omen for the rest of the town. How can a place not change, when she's changed so much? It's as if it was lying in wait for her all these years, biding its time until the inevitable day she'd get the call and ping, magnetised, back. Most adults probably feel like this, returning to the shrunken site of their childhood, like killers to a crime scene. Except, Steph thinks, it's probably worse for her when everyone here thought she was a little boy growing up.

Hell, even she'd thought it.

"Hi. Hiya, I wonder if you can tell me which way Constance Road is, please?" Steph knows full well where Constance Road is, but she suddenly has this unsettling feeling that she doesn't exist, so it's any excuse to interact with a human. The guy behind the vented glass window looks about bored enough to fake his own death, but he perks up a bit when she speaks to him. "Just out the main entrance there, love, and take a left and straight on. That's Constance Road there at the end." He smiles, amicably.

"Thanks. Oh and—where's your toilets?"

"Ladies is through that door on the left."

"Thank you." It's all good. It's okay. Everything is in order and she hasn't somehow stepped back in time by coming here. She goes straight out of the front door. She doesn't really need to pee, and if the station guy is watching and wondering why she asked and then never went, it's his own perv problem.

Outside is appropriately grey, a pestering mist of drizzle sneaking up everyone's umbrellas. Steph pops her collar—speckles of damp already clinging to the faux fur lining—and wishes she'd brought a brolly anyway. Her hair'll be ruined: it's always been stubbornly straight and now her carefully tonged curls are probably going to drop out from the rain. She tucks the length of it down the back of her jacket, tries to pull her neck into her collar as far as it'll go, like a sea anemone drawing in its tentacles. She thinks again of crust-less butties. Crisp butties. Dawn.

Dawn is the only thing she misses about this town. Their mums were mates and so they were plonked together at an early age, but it worked out fine. She'd go knocking round Dawn's house every weekend to play out, building flying pirate ships in the trees and turning the Tarmac to lava. She remembers it all more clearly than she can picture last month: the days lasted a week each and it was always sunny. At lunchtime, they'd go back indoors and Dawn's mum Vera would make them crisp butties. Cheese and onion was both their favourite. But Steph always hated crusts.

"Crusts make you hair curl," Dawn recited, the first time, sagely, as Steph pulled the edges off her foamy white bread, her lip curled in distaste.

"Curls are for girls." That was an accepted fact, too. She deposited her crusts onto Dawn's plate. After that, it became ritual.

Steph pats her damp hair down with shaking hands. It's nearly six now, later than she normally eats dinner. She has to go to the café on Constance Road, so she may as well get food there. Dawn might not be there: she has no clue if she even works at the place anymore. It might be closed for the day already. But, knowing Vera died, Steph has to visit.

She could do this walk with her eyes closed. Her feet are trained to these streets, and it's all too easy to fall back into step. The sun is fading, but there's no sunset. The grey is just getting darker. When she turns onto Constance Road, the light is so low that the shop windows look like fairy lights strung along the length of it. Everywhere is slowing. Shutting up for the day. People hurry past with their heads bowed to the weather. They don't give her a second glance. Why was she worried about returning? Steph frowns at her reflection in the betting shop window. She's worried people won't recognise her. She's worried they will.

The café has a different sign compared to when Steph last saw it. 'Vera's', painted in a curly red script next to a cheery picture of an over-spilling cup and saucer set at angles that are probably intended as jaunty and energetic but look to Steph like they're in the process of being dropped. Frozen, a moment before the crash. The lights inside are still on and a sign reads 'Open', with the logo of Grebley 133 Radio. The sprung bell dings as Steph pushes the door wide and the woman sitting at one of the tables looks up sharply from her plate, like she's been caught doing something she shouldn't. Steph's insides rush. There's no mistaking.

"Hey. Caught me having my tea." Her chair makes a too-loud noise against the floor as Dawn stands and wipes her hands on her apron.

"No worries, sorry—I thought you were still open."

"Just about to close—no, it's okay." Steph pauses as Dawn waves a hand. She's still swallowing a mouthful: Steph glances at the plate, some irrational part of her expecting to see crisps. But it's just a regular ham sandwich, mustard smearing the white plate. When she looks back at Dawn, Dawn is looking at her oddly, head tilted. "Do I know you? I swear I recognise you from somewhere. Did you go to school 'round here?"

She left because it was easier, and lord knows Steph deserved something to be easy in her life. Then it was just too simple to let go and not to look back. Dawn hasn't changed. She looks just the same, sounds just the same. The echoes of the sixteen-year-old who Steph waved goodbye ring loud and clear through Dawn's whole vessel. And Steph—she feels the same. "I—yeah. I did. We did." A hot-cold, dreadful feeling swallows her skin as she sees the flickering instant that recognition kindles. "Hi Dawn. So sorry to hear about your mum."

"Oh my god." She says it slowly and Steph can't quite read the emotion behind it. But she hopes. "How long has it been?"

"Twenty-two years."

"Oh my god." Dawn repeats. She draws 'god' out, long. Her palms retrace their path across her apron, smoothing. "Twenty-two years. You just got in?"

"Uh huh."

"You must be starving!"

Steph blinks at her. The electric lights suddenly feel too bright, artificial like this is a movie set, and she has to fight the urge to giggle because of how Dawn just worded that, as if Steph hadn't eaten in two decades. Like she'd been away from home for that long. She nods. "Yeah, I... could eat. I mean, I was gonna get some food here, if you were still open."

"Crap." Clicking her tongue, Dawn hurries past, to the door. Turns the lock, and the sign to 'Closed'. "Lock-in in a café? Not quite the same as the pub, mind. What can I get you?"

"Just a buttie would be good. I mean, obviously, I'm paying..."

"Don't be daft." A wave of her hand. "Cheese and onion crisps, right?"

The noise Steph makes is mostly a laugh, but sort of a sob. "Whatever you're having is fine."

"Not a veggie then?"

"Nah."

Dawn cocks her head. "You change your name?"

"Steph," Steph says. Dawn nods, looks pleased, and Steph is struck by a sudden wonder. "Did you change yours?"

"Nah. Still Dawn."

Still Dawn. Steph watches her, pottering around behind the big glass-fronted deli counter, buttering bread, placing the ham. The same meal they've always shared, except now it's ham, like grown-ups, sliced diagonally instead of cut into squares. The same, but different. She works quickly, arranging the plate just out of Steph's line of vision, picking up her own half-finished dinner on her way back to the table.

"So,"—Dawn sets the plates down, takes the seat opposite Steph and rests her elbows on the white table-top, smiling her time-travelling smile—"welcome back to the arsehole of the universe."

"Grebley isn't the arsehole of the universe," Steph says, softly. "Arseholes are useful. Grebley's like, the coccyx of the universe."

She hadn't realised how much she's missed Dawn's laugh. Dawn tucks her hair behind her ears and says, "Well, fill me in, then. What you been up to?"

Steph thinks. There's a lot of ground to cover. She looks down at the plate in front of her. Next to the salad and the crisps and the neatly-triangled round of ham sandwiches is an extra set of crusts.

Mist-taken Lunch

Harris Bor

What guilt accompanied that bite
The dreaded pig
Sliced and sandwiched too close to the veggie stuff
For me to notice

The gulp and recognition
Provoke images of oblivion
Impurity causing the corrosion
Of my passably kosher soul

In freeze-frame
The rabbi's finger wags, he whispers that
There's no greater trespass
Than half-blind absent-mindedness

I remind the constricting gullet
Of Nietzsche's death of God
But nothing it seems can dislodge the food
Powerless against memories of ancient rules
About chewing cud and cloven hooves
Like molten rock exerting their subterranean influence

And through the geyser's steam I dream
Of the half-baked ham-thin promises
Of the forever not-yet end-times
When the forbidden will be permitted
And the permitted, forgotten
Then, as the prophet says
We shall beat our spears and swords
Into knives and forks and tuck in, smiling

Alimentary Mistake

Jayant Avva

There were two of us in the ship. Feinberg was our pilot, and he had a PhD in nanoengineering. I had a PhD in particle physics. We had aced the physical tests and undergone training regimens that were adapted from NASA astronaut training. Our ship had been shrunk roughly a millimetre in length, with us inside. The nanotech team had delivered as promised.

"The control system entered a limit cycle when you piloted it, didn't it?" Feinberg said.

I nodded. "I had to disable autopilot to get it back on track."

"The last limit for full operation in 250 was one hour," Feinberg said. "Anyone test it further than that?"

250 Pascal-seconds is the viscosity of peanut butter, or shortening, and the craft could operate for an hour submerged in the same. I shook my head, but the question was rhetorical. We were aware that most of the checklist questions during takeoff were multiple checks against something minor going wrong. In this specific case, it was a precaution against the highly probable but unwelcome scenario of being ingested by an animal or human. We

were banking on the speed and the strength of the ship. It could escape closing jaws in a flap of a hummingbird's wings. It could withstand pressures that were a thousand times those exerted by an alligator's jaws. All in all, the craft insulated us from all dangers that we could envision at that size.

What we had overestimated was the structural integrity of the walls of the room in which we were having our first trial run. Rooms, containers and spaces are often the least studied of variables, since they occupy the background. This overestimation would soon intertwine our fate with a ham sandwich.

Feinberg operated the craft in the motion that he had practiced so many times with a simulator, and which we had observed ad nauseam. It was textbook perfect, and yet the ship leaped forward, throwing us back in our chairs.

"Rats!" Feinberg yelled.

"We're headed for the wall, Harry," I said.

"This didn't happen in training." Feinberg worked the steering wheel.

"The MATLAB update popup in your bottom right may be the issue," I said, eyeing my replica of the controls monitor.

Feinberg didn't respond, as he tried reversing the motion of the craft. We shot into and through the wall, in spite of Feinberg's best attempts.

Feinberg maneuvered the craft with increasing appreciation of how much he had to scale down his touch and made a wide 180-degree turn. None of us had trained for such precision.

"Jesus!"

We saw a row of sharp teeth in front of our ship. Feinberg yanked the steering to the right, barely clear of the canines. My monitor had a zoomed-out version, which was a replication of the average human visual field.

"Poodle incoming!" I said.

"Thanks, Jake," Feinberg said, as we shot away from a King Kong–sized poodle, who was shaking her head vigorously and appeared to have eyed us. "Just a little more of a heads up, next time."

"Sorry," I said. "Next challenge—we're headed for Eduardo."

We had flown several yards outward by this time, toward the street that lined the research building. Our simulation runs were still a work in progress, and we weren't prepared for dodgeball with such precision. We saw a mix of flesh tones and brown fill our monitor.

Eduardo, one of the lawn maintenance crew, was blocking our current trajectory.

"Decelerate, you piece of shit," I shouted, as we tried to prevent forward motion, using their computers.

We decelerated, but not enough. We shot into something solid and yet soft. The ship was embedded in one of three slices of ham between two slices of wheat bread, generous dollops of mayonnaise, and a couple of tragic lettuce leaves. We had crashed in a ham sandwich that Eduardo was having for lunch. Eduardo took a bite, his mouth closing over not just his delicious sandwich, but also our state-of-the-art, Elon-Musk-eat-your-heart-out, ship.

This was damned inconvenient. We hadn't finished training maneuvering inside bodies yet. It was part of our training, to be sure, since we had worried about being swallowed by a whole host of beings. We hadn't reckoned that we would be inside the oesophagus of a man during our alpha test, though.

If we fired the thrusters now, it would be like a tiny bullet shot right out of Eduardo's insides. Feinberg, in spite of our predicament at that point in time, appeared to regain some measure of equanimity. He focused on the controls and visuals. We were inside a bolus travelling down Eduardo's throat, competing with the downward momentum of an unknown mass pushing our craft, which we guessed was part of that bolus.

We exited the bolus.

"That's bolus number one," Feinberg said. "Hold on to your hat, we'll have more company."

Sure enough, as I scanned the monitor, I saw a roughly spherical mass approaching us from a distance. If we exited the way we entered, we would have to play dodgeball or fly through the boli.

"Should we exit from the other end?" I wondered aloud.

"Not unless we want to kill Eduardo."

He was right. Given the number of variables in play, going deeper into Eduardo's alimentary canal would spell sure death for him. So, we would have to exit the way we entered, timing it so that we flew out when Eduardo opened his mouth.

Bolus number two smashed us from above.

"We're going through them," Feinberg announced. "Hold tight."

A soft bolus wouldn't change our momentum much, so long as we travelled at a higher velocity in the opposite direction. We tore clear of the chunk of ham and bread and flew further up. Bolus three smashed us next. We continued our trajectory, reaching the higher end of

Eduardo's throat. Just a few more moments, and we would be home free.

"AUTOPILOT ENGAGED!" sounded over the speakers, accompanied by a beeping sound.

"What the hell!" Feinberg said, scrambling to regain manual control, but the craft was already turning.

"It's the same control problem as before," I said.

Feinberg turned pale. His fingers flew past multiple screens and dialog boxes, struggling to get the ship to respond. There was a beep as he clicked something, then a sound like a million bees buzzing at the same time.

•

Later, while compiling the incident report, the ground crew described to us what happened next. The ship regained normal size. Eduardo's chest exploded as the nose of the craft tore through his rib cage. His right arm, ham sandwich in hand, was thrown aside, torn off the shoulder joint. His head and neck were nowhere to be seen, and recovered later from the branches of a tree, a few yards behind where the craft regained normal size. The lower portion of Eduardo was crushed beneath the craft's weight, and the fuselage was now decorated with his blood and guts. The materials analysis team recovered the ham sandwich.

We stared gloomily through the blood-soaked windshields. The alpha test had been a *de jure* success, and a *de facto* failure. Eduardo's death cast a shadow that would hover for a long time. The unspoken and perhaps callous thought that hung in the air like a Damocles sword was about money. Would the ensuing investigation place a possibly permanent pause on our project's funding?

Argument Over the Lack of Ham in a Ham Sandwich

Derek Kannemeyer

"That little bit's a bit too little!"
complained the customer, annoyed.
"I was not a little nettled
to find I bit upon a void."
The vendor of said bit of victual—
a ham sandwich—his name was Lloyd—
smirking, and not a bit unsettled—
to goad the guy, for he enjoyed
seeing folks sputter and spray spittle
while strangling on an adenoid—
and quite a lot—it's jot and tittle,
in fact, of what got Lloyd employed—
surveyed the thrust plate, stated, "It'll
have to do—your bite destroyed
most of the evidence. Which was brittle."
"This restaurant I will avoid!"
returned the customer. "Regret'll
be your lot! And not a little!"
But Lloyd just stood there, noncommittal—
patient, yet stern, like Sigmund Freud—

till bit by bit his bile was bottled;
belt was buckled; bill was settled—
until (less bitter, but still nettled;
blotting his chin of lettuce spittle)
he'd added a three per cent remittal—
as tip—oh, what a lot annoyed!

Words of the Lost

Tim Brown

The priest trudged up the rocky hill, catching the reflection of thousands of stars and planets and the pale-gray clouds of the galaxy. Twice per cycle, he would make the climb towards the machine's elaborate cathedral housing, crafted of rare metals and gems. With a long sinewy tendril, he pushed open the wide doors leading into chamber after chamber, each bathed in colors of the ultraviolet spectrum.

The final chamber barely contained the machine. Wires streaked across the front of the thing, multicolored and winding between one another, creating a large netting. A few pistons chugged away on each side, their purpose lost to time. The priest looked at the emerald screen in the dead center, brushing a few stray wires to the side.

SCANNING AND TRANSLATION: IN PROGRESS

It had never said anything else, but it needed to be checked all the same. Just beneath the screen, enclosed in a glass booth and sealed off from the outside world, stood a small metallic rectangle. Wires had been soldered to all sides of it now. The machine had become desperate to recover any information from the metal object. It had devoted itself to this cause since the priesthood built it untold generations ago.

Though the priest could not understand the symbols emblazoned on the front of the thing lost for untold ages, he often traced them in his spare time. He kept his drawings of these symbols in a binder, admiring how his work had become cleaner and more identical over time. A long straight line with a small notch at the top, drifting left. A dot next to the bottom of the first line. Then an oval, vertically oriented. The last two characters confused the priest the most. One looked like the first line, though instead of one notch the line on top was longer, perpendicular to the connecting line. The final character was another line with an oval cut in half and attached to the right side.

•

Loose chunks of mauve rock crumbled beneath his feet as he slipped back down the hill towards his home. A smattering of protesters shouted all sorts of things at him, none of them pleasant. He had grown used to the, accepting their hurled insults as just a part of his calling. The angry masses twitched as they followed his slow crawl across the rocks towards his house.

Standing there, greeting him eagerly at the door, was his offspring, chosen at random from the pool at the orphanage.

"Hello, Father," he said, "did it finish yet?"

It was a running joke. The priest would come home, tell him that it might tomorrow with a chuckle, and then they would sit down for nourishment. Lifting the hot stone in the middle of the hut, he produced the same green pile as last cycle and all the cycles before in an oversized ladle. The priest had eaten last cycle, and common law mandated that it was his adoptee's turn to re-nourish. He squatted down on the dirt floor next to the stone and watched his son consume.

"What will happen if it gets translated?" he said between bites.

"We find the wisdom of a civilization which has been dead for millions of generations."

His son slurped again at the pile of slush. "If this is as important to us as you say, then why are there so many protesters?"

The priest shifted forwards slightly. "There are people that believe that this is a waste of time and resources, both of which could be better spent on other things like improving quality of life and feeding the less fortunate."

"Do you think they're right, Dad?"

"I don't think so. Studying the wisdom of ancient civilizations can have great benefit. We can learn from the past, learn from the mistakes they made and apply them to our lives."

"But we could apply the energy spent by that... thing to directly benefit those people. Isn't that a better cause?"

The priest watched his son ingest the last few morsels in his bowl. "This was my choice. I can't say one way or another whether this is a good use of resources. I just know that this is what my duty is. To check on the machine, repair it if necessary. Just like you will have your own duty in time." He replaced the ladle beneath the warm rock. "Now rinse up, it's almost time for rest."

•

Stars shone brighter than before when the priest left his house again to check on the machine. His son lay in a puddle, soaking up what radiation he could from the stars overhead.

The barriers were packed to overflowing as he passed. The people gave shouts and cries of how hungry they were, how little time they had left on this asteroid unless that machine was dismantled, one writhing pile of animosity.

He didn't see the rock until it was too late. It hurtled towards him, exploding in a purple haze as it impacted just above his eye. He reeled, scrambled up the steps surrounded in a mist of hurled rocks and insults. Once inside the safety of the church, he mopped up the blue fluid oozing from the cut. The security team would be there soon, detecting the pain he had felt.

Despite the wound, his job still needed to be done. The priest bulled through the six chambers, flinging the doors open. He had hardly spared one look at the chugging machine before he turned around and started back towards his home.

A violent crash at the first set of double doors jolted him. The entire cathedral began to shake and quiver. A handful of guards spilled out onto the multicolored tile, perspiring and sporting azure splotches on their uniforms.

"They killed three of our men. We're all that's left. Sal'Zaboth ran as soon as the rocks started flying, the coward." The others peeked through the windows, giving no more than fleeting glances.

"It will be all right," the priest said, placing an appendage around the nearest guard. "This is a place of peace, there will be no violence within these walls."

A rock struck the window, sending webs throughout the glass. The guard peering through fell to the floor, began to shake. The priest stood him up. "What is your name, son?"

"Twi'Enboth,"

"Gather the rest of your men, Twi'Enboth, we will barricade the doors and take refuge in the final chamber. Can you do this for me, Twi'Enboth?"

"Yes, priest."

"Good, let us go forth and do the machine's work."

After sealing each of the doors behind them, they scattered pews and tables behind the thresholds, posing an insurmountable barrier behind each. The four of them crowded together behind the final barricade as the machine clicked and hummed. While the guards were checking their weapons, Twi'Enboth noticed the priest's mandibles twitching in a rapid prayer.

Outside came shouting, pounding. Twi'Enboth watched the blood drip from the priest's forehead, heard the crash of the first barrier and the shouts of people as they mounted the furniture, making their way towards the next obstacle. He could hear the individual crashes of stones against the windows and the glass, each blow extracting some of the magic of the place, some of the mystique it carried. With each barrier demolished, the priest's chant grew more urgent. He was the stream of words that came from him, becoming one with the prayer.

In a single thrust a shaft of violent light forced its way through the final door.

•

Ding.

The sound cut through the conflict, stopped the priest's chants. They all crowded around the machine's screen in the respite.

TRANSLATION COMPLETE. SHOWING ALL RECOVERED DATA FROM THE DEVICE.

Twi'Enboth stared at the glowing monitor. The pistons had stopped churning, and text flickered across the screen. Beside the screen, a thin slip of paper was ejected with a copy of the text. The four of them stood over it. "What are we looking at?"

The priest stood there, contemplating the repeating lines, the same thing over and over. "We are looking at the last words of a species dead for eons. We are looking through time, at the faces of Gods." The angry mob had become pacified, staring in towards the unknown mess of wires and bodies. The priest stood, pushed open the door as the crowd stood around him.

"Hear me! The machine has finished translating what was lost to time. Today we have stepped back thousands of generations, into another pocket of a reality which is not our own. Today we see what wisdom our predecessors have written. Listen and I will tell you! The translation is complete, the machine no longer needs to function. Energy will be restored, though what gift is that compared to the speech of the dead passed on to us? Sit, children, and I will tell you."

The guards joined the mob as the priest unfurled the slip, holding it to the light. He began to read.

"Gramma's Ham Sandwich Recipe. Ingredients: two slices of sourdough bread, two ounces deli ham, one leaf of lettuce, one slice tomato, one slice of cheddar cheese, mayonnaise. Spread the mayonnaise on both slices of bread. Layer the lettuce first, followed by ham, tomato, and cheese. Slice diagonally and serve."

The crowd sat there.

"What's *may-yo-naze*?" one of them asked.

"The words of Gods have been written eons ago. Perhaps this '*may-yo-naze*' was a religious artifact, lost to time." The priest stepped down from the platform, sat alongside the quiet crowd. "We may never know what this passage means, not entirely. We may spend our lives studying it to no avail. The concept of a 'recipe' confuses me as much as it does yourselves. I want everyone to mull it over. Let us draw meaning from 'Gramma's Ham Sandwich Recipe' and think about how we can apply it to our everyday lives. It is what our ancient friends would have wanted."

The people obeyed. Plaques were hung over entrances as each family took a mantra and brought it to their living. With the duties of the machine finished, it was cheerfully dismantled, its parts smelted and reused to build new machines, ones with selfless purposes. The priest walked the line of houses beneath the milky sky. Across the way, his son and another child were arguing over a bowl of nourishment, each of them claiming that they hadn't eaten longer than the other. The priest squatted down between the two and took the bowl from them.

"Children," he said, "there is a portion of the scripture which applies here. Can you tell me what it is?" When they both looked at him with blank expressions, he continued; "'Slice diagonally and serve.' The act of turning one into two. Get a bowl from our home, son." When he returned, the priest took the bowls and swept half of the contents into the other. "There," the priest said, handing the bowls to the children. "'Slice diagonally and serve.' Each gets his own, in time." He stood again, continued to walk into the calm portion of their asteroid, noting with a bittersweet twinge how their world had become both larger and smaller.

The rocks turned from purple to a deep crimson as he walked alongside the dancing suns.

Oh, Comely

Shannon Green

Longing plain on his face, he stared across the diner.

A thing of beauty wove between the tables towards him with a sensual strut. Perfectly pink flesh dressed in shades of green and brown, as if trying to hide in the greenery, some sort of camouflaging to blend into the background of this crowded bar. He saw her anyway. The waiter smiled as he set the sandwich before the seated man.

"Thank you," the man said as he lifted the sandwich and inspected the neat stack: bread, lettuce, tomato, ham, mustard, and bread; the fries on the side an afterthought, as was the beer he had ordered to slake his thirst. This would be the true bliss at the end his long day of work, a ham sandwich, perfectly crafted by artisans who termed themselves "short order cooks".

He picked up the tower of ingredients, feeling the slightest toasting on the bread, and inhaled deeply. The mingled scents of the components forming a perfect whole, he bit into the ham sandwich and knew a moment of unequaled bliss as he realized that the ham was apple glazed.

Rearrangements

Justin A. Burnett

As the last guest slams the door behind her, someone laughs. I spin around. I could've sworn everyone left. A man... what's his name? Julian. Julian is draped beautifully across the sofa with the carelessness of a discarded condom.

"Nice, man," he says. "The idea was brilliant. You just had trouble with the presentation."

"The presentation?" I say.

"And the mayonnaise was a problem."

"The mayonnaise?"

"Well, not mayonnaise, per se. Mayo itself is never a problem. The quantity, however"—Julian gestures vaguely over to the plastic tubs stacked in the corners of the living room—"is unnatural. Besides, some of it appears to have gone bad."

How could this have happened? I planned everything. No detail escaped my judicious scrutiny. And it all went so well, at least up to the most vital moment. Julian laughs again. I must seem ridiculous. I straighten my tie and shrug casually. "Nothing ventured, nothing gained," I say, composing my voice to eclipse my embarrassment.

"Are you gay?" Julian asks.

"Pardon?" I say, ambling absently to the liquor cabinet by the door.

"Are you gay? It's a reasonable question. When you meet someone at a gay bar and they ask you on a date, you tend to assume they're gay. Given this date's... ahem... originality, I feel I have a right to reexamine my basic assumptions."

"No," I say, attempting to steady my hand as I pour a scotch, "at least I don't think so."

"Well, what was this about then? I wasn't the only man invited, as I'm sure you're aware, and everyone seemed equally surprised by their... counterparts."

I throw back the scotch and immediately pour another. Julian tries to lean into my field of vision. I turn away. I can't bear to look at him.

"It was nothing explicitly... sexual," I mutter, allowing the sentence to die in ambiguity.

"What was it, then?"

"Rearrangements," I say, and fall silent.

I wish he would just go. He'll never understand. Explanations will only make me more ridiculous. More vulnerable.

"Pickles," he says.

"Come again?"

"The jars. You have pickles as well, I see. Lots of them. Bags of bread too. And I smell ham. Your apartment is a sandwich factory."

Sandwich. That degrading word. That cookie cutter wielded by the intellect, like all words, to maim and disfigure the objects of the world. Sandwich. Julian laughs again. It appears he finds himself amusing. He says "sandwich," and imagines an object held between two hands, bitten into, kneaded by a tongue still cold from beer while the Dallas Cowboys score on the television. "Sandwich," as if that were all to the story; as if everything is a given totality, indifferent to its parts, immune to alterations and new, exciting relationships; as if a "sandwich" isn't a composition, no less grand than Mozart's *Requiem*, every bit as sublime as the Sistine chapel, nuanced and rich like *Faust* or *The Brothers Karamazov*.

"You don't get out much, do you?" he says. His voice hints at derision but doesn't fully achieve it. Something else blocks the way. Sympathy?

I turn and force my stare to turn cold.

"No offense, man. You could've fooled me, you know. You were something else at the bar. So self-possessed, refined, almost arrogant. I didn't tag you as a shut-in. And I'm generally pretty good at tags."

I smile. I can't help it. It's the same old story. Yes, I'm quite impressive, I suppose. I have an education, along with some money and the manners included in the package deal of a semi-charmed upbringing. But when they get to know me...

"I confess," I say, staring into the scotch, "people often find me to be... not quite what they expect."

"I'll say."

"You are free to go," I say with a gesture towards the door.

"Of course I am. No one else seemed to require directions."

"Yet you stay."

"Call me curious."

I sigh, still staring into the scotch. Curious. It's been a long time since anyone bothered to be curious. Suddenly, I remember my manners.

"I apologize, Julian. I seem to have forgotten myself. May I offer you a drink?"

"Hey, you remembered my name! Pretty impressive, given the sizable crowd you managed to accumulate. That must've taken a lot of work, organizing them all. Whiskey, please. Whatever you got."

I pour a Disaronno. Julian politely accepts the drink as I collapse in the armchair across from him. The excitement returns, slowly at first, and far from the afternoon's frenzy of anticipation, but something about a sympathetic ear... well... if I can't have a willing participant, I'm happy to settle for a listener. Who knows, besides, what rearrangements the wily dark has in store?

"Man, this is good stuff."

"What are you curious about, Julian?"

"First, I suppose, the sandwich materials. We can get to the juicy stuff after."

Before I begin, I lean close to Julian. His eyes never falter. His features remain locked, paralyzed in solid confidence. Why isn't he afraid? Everyone else was afraid. I could learn to love a man like this.

"You must know from the start, Julian, that I despise words. Every event I'm about to relate will be butchered by the words I employ to describe it. It's an unfortunate obstacle, but I suppose there's no way around it...

"It begins with the ham sandwich. I used to be like everyone else. I used to be what you would call 'normal,' a word that really means mindless, blind, slavish, robotic, etc. The stream of cookie cutter adjectives never ends. All definitions are stuck in circularities, even my own. I used to think a ham sandwich is a ham sandwich and that's that. It didn't occur to me to go on. I never picked the scab. I never even realized it was an option...

"My father didn't drink. My mother did, and my father stayed angry about it. He adored Mother, however, and wouldn't dream of expressing anything short of adoration to her. In our little family of three, the only people left to take the brunt of Father's fury were me and himself. We took turns. He would settle into an apathetic depression until my studious and unathletic nature reached a pitch he could no longer ignore. I'd take my stripes with dignity, and he'd lumber back into his introspective cave. This cyclic process ultimately drove me into myself, I suppose. I left the family bosom a replica of the man I hate...

"College didn't improve things, naturally. I hadn't learned how to leave the fear behind with the old man. I carried it along like a blindfold. Accordingly, I remained in the dark. I lived alone in an apartment a few miles from campus. I owned a car but preferred to walk. I spent most of my life walking. I spoke in class, of course, and my words seemed to impress everyone. Outside, however, I preferred not to share them. I was still afraid, I suppose, of being the studious, intellectual child my father despised, as if every pair of strange eyes merely hid his own...

"I graduated early with honors and accolades. Rather than suffer the humiliation of a return to my family, I went straight to work. I secured a position at the university. I was going to teach mathematics. I decided to drive to work to celebrate my first day. That's when I finally awakened...

"Initially, I awakened in a hospital bed. An accident, they said. Severe head injuries. Hemorrhaging. I remained in half-sleep for a month. There's not much to recall during this period, outside the endless bedside exchange of nurses for neurosurgeons, sponge baths and presumed relatives I didn't recognize...

"I was disabled, they said. Permanently. My father took pity on me, I suppose, or saw an opportunity to wash his hands of the past. He volunteered a lavish sustenance to accompany me to either his funeral or mine, whichever held the shortest number in the queue...

"I was happy to reinforce my habitual solitude. Only something had changed. It begins, as I've mentioned, with the ham sandwich. One morning, I made one, just as I always had. My father hated sandwiches. They were too bourgeoisie for his palette, I suppose. So naturally, I adored them...

"Have you ever looked beyond the unity of a ham sandwich? Have you cared to dive past the object and into the sea of relations? My first ham sandwich after leaving the hospital bloomed in magic between the buds of my tongue and the conductive saliva. A piece of ham in relation to the sweet tang of mayo. That honeyed moisture paraded to the fore on the shoulders of a sour suggestion. The harmony of both ham and mayo, electrified by the pale-green thunder of pickles. And the bread, the often-neglected bread! More than a finger pad. It is the soft medium of the sandwich's sea change, a course along which the elements mingle and depart, rearranging to form new emphases, metamorphosing by rearrangements of associations, like a palette of paints stirred by the brush. Like the seasons, autumn churning summer with a breeze and freezing the water dry. Like spring, lifting the ocean and dousing the parched winter. Like life itself...

"As you can see, I fall apart in my attempted description of this revelation. It is the words, Julian, not my thoughts, that are ineffectual. The words. They hide these things, the malleable underbelly of objects. The word 'sandwich' bars you from the fluidity of its nature. It's a matter of ontology. Language is an ontological system—a crude, barbarous thing imposed like a blind surgeon's scalpel over the perfect corpus of the natural world. How can I describe it to you? I realized, in short, that the ham sandwich was a conglomeration of discrete elements entirely altered by their relationship with other elements. And I realized this was a metaphor for everything else."

Julian is patient with my monologue. He nods thoughtfully, sipping at the Disaronno unhurriedly. When I get to the metaphor, he stands and begins ambling casually around the room. I stop speaking. He nods to himself in the silence before pointing to a framed collage of magazine clippings with his drink hand.

"Let me see if I can guess the next part," he says. "In a flash of recognition, you grasp the metaphor. Then, you begin to experiment with 'rearrangements,' as you call them. You apply your insight into the nature of relationships to other arenas of experience."

I can't hold back another smile. "Correct," I say, "more or less. I begin with images. I cut photos, as you can see, from magazines and arrange them to form something new. The only problem with images is the final result. Once you glue the clippings down, you are participating in the violence of language. You sever the breath from the composition. Sounds were next. But, I must say, my prime preoccupation has largely remained firmly in the realm of taste."

Julian continues to circle the room. Soon, he is almost behind me. I can smell his cologne. Calvin Klein, if I'm not mistaken. Something stirs, an electrical sensation, along the base of my spine.

"So," he continues, "where does tonight's escapade fit in?"

I sigh deeply. I still find the fact of tonight's failure impossible to digest. So much planning. So much work.

"It was to be my masterpiece, I'm afraid. I thought of it months ago. First, I began to leave the house again, to test my strength of articulation and seduction in the world of people. I was afraid I had lost my touch after so long. My fears, of course, were unwarranted. I still had it in me. I could tempt even the most suspicious of individuals into my own sphere of relations. I frequented bars, the more upscale establishments in the city, in order to, to use a disgusting idiom, 'learn the ropes,' you understand. My successes exceeded my expectations. I had no trouble approaching either man or woman. I suffered no anxiety. I simply allowed the false ontology of language to dribble from my mouth like an intoxicated foam. When you grasp the emptiness of language, when you are conscious of your tools, you wield them much more effectively. This part of the process nauseated me, of course, but I persisted. I dissociated into dreams of my masterpiece, even as I prattled on with dreadful locutions...

"Many men and women expressed a desire to further our relationship. I promised them, as I promised you, Julian, a cliché, 'a night they would never forget.' I arranged, rearranged, initiated negotiations and cancellations, until you all agreed to meet me on this night. I never would've imagined they would all be so ungrateful to find themselves in eager company. If only they would have allowed me to demonstrate."

Julian, directly behind me, places a thin, delicate hand on my shoulder. I reach up and clasp it between my own.

"I can still show you, Julian. It won't be as beautiful without them. But we can still..."

I allow my proposition to fade with the increasing throb of my heart.

"We can still what?" Julian asks.

"*Hors d'oeuvres* are in the dining room. Ham sandwiches. I thought we could all... make love... all of us together... that's why I needed men... intermingling the flavors of our biology, rearranging our cells, and then—"

I almost weep as Julian laughs.

"I thought you said this wasn't a sexual thing."

"It isn't," I hiss in fury. "It's the sweat. I just wanted to taste the sweat."

Julian's laugh is harsh this time, edged like a blade. I try to withdraw my hands, but he holds them firm.

"How sad," he says, strength rolling through his voice like a black surf. "I know a thing or two about 'rearrangements,' as you call them. I am something of an artist myself. First, I tagged you for one of them. A self-assured parasite, like the rest. Then, as you told your story, I thought you were like me. I thought your realization had delivered you to the brink of power. 'How grand,' I thought to myself, 'two monsters, together, a tandem nightmare darkening the nights of the world's weak.' I suppose I was wrong. Oh well."

Julian forces something into my neck. I quickly shiver with cold. A new taste fills my mouth. Strong and unforgiving, like heated metal. It could use, I realize, a dash of dill.

Gemini Lunch (a Sandwich Cries America)

Justin Short

stars come out as I try my thumb
but no one stops
for a sandwich in moccasins
I don't think about them
the stars, I mean
they're only dots, after all
and I have bigger things on my mind
like the hatred and bombs on tv
it's not that I'm a draft dodger
no, not exactly
I just don't open certain pieces of mail

my thumb retreats and I catch a bus
constellations fogging windows
as I bounce to the beach
gonna see my baby
gonna fix the world
with peace and love
and a hundred million tokes

beached policemen pause mid-bite
their silent words butter-knife knifing
commie coward crustless
try something I haven't heard
but they let me pass
miraculously unmolested
and I doorbell her deli door

my corned-beef mama waits below the glass
we go for a kiss
but a hairy-knuckled stranger screams between
register singing, he bags my baby
shoe soles squeaking
she's gone

sunburnt
as fires roar and Gemini burns
a trail to the stars
occupancy, three
Young, Grissom
and my corned-beef, star-crossed love
a small bite for man
but what about the famine in my soggy heart
she was my soul
my mustard my life

now nothing's left
but zero-g crumbs

stars over water
this time they hurt
sirens reflecting
my trashcanned freedom
free lecture on the ride downtown
I'm unfit un-tomatoed un-American
but the words don't connect
what more can you say
to a ham sandwich
in love with space dust

Re-Ham

Riham Adly

Every Sunday, on the park bench swathed in pink blossoms from the nearby dogwood tree, Pedro would bring me those salacious BLT wraps with crisp bacon, grape tomatoes, shredded lettuce and that really good smelling pink sauce. I would shake my head desperately after bringing the sinful temptation to my nose, smack my forehead.

"Pedro, no. Why can't you get it?"

He was cute, his nativity exciting, his perplexing accent a challenge—and boy, I loved a challenge, but I didn't like having to repeat myself over and over and over. That was it, I decided. No more Pedro.

"I like you." That's how it started. "I want you to teach me English".

You're the typical black sheep of the family who refuses to learn how to cook molokheya soup and vermicelli rice, the insidious rebel who, yet still, faithfully abides to the teaching of her 1,400 year old "Book", the hopeless wallflower who would not agree to a preliminary groom viewing and would refuse trying any of her parent's "cheerful colors", only allowing herself the pleasure of being decked from head to toe in aubergine black, cherry black and even mulberry black—this one is reserved for all my headscarves, I have over twenty in this shade—that does not contrast well with my pewter complexion and almond-colored eyes. You'll begin to understand why I took on Pedro.

I've always wanted to perform in poetry slams but was too embarrassed of who I was and how I looked. I was a poetry major with no clear intensions or aspirations in anything whatsoever. I gulped Keats, Sexton and Plath like that BLT I could not have and splurged on, writing Rumi-like nonsense whenever I felt that itch for mysticism creep in. My best friend, Aisha, had urged me once to read some of my non-sense, and that's when I realized green-eyed Pedro lurked right behind us. Later that day, he asked me to teach him English. I was no English teacher, only a so-called poet whenever I deemed it, so I decided to teach him through poetry. Nursery rhymes at first, then simple quatrains and cinquains, before evolving to some serious villanelles and triolets. I was proud when he was able to discern my eclectic free verse. I would always sign every poem with my name, and he would always bring me BLT wraps every Sunday, on that park bench swathed with pink blossoms next to the Dogwood tree.

"Pedro, how many times do I have to tell you that Muslims don't eat ham sandwiches? Not even BLT?"

"But you always end every lesson with Re-ham. From what I've learned, re, means to repeat, and ham is, well, pork or bacon of sorts?"

"Pedro, what's my name?"

"You're the pretty Señorita in black."

"I don't have a name?"

"You are the Señorita in black."

"That's not my name."

"Señorita in black that asks for a re-ham every lesson." Yup, no more Pedro, and no more poetry, and no more BLT wraps—unless they had beef bacon.

Pigs Is Pigs?

Keith P. Graham

Jimmy sat outside the freezer at the Orgo-Life meat processing plant. He let his friend Tommy do all the work. The smell of dead pigs made him sick.

He could hear the whine of the forklift as Tommy loaded hog carcasses onto a skid. When he loaded up one skid, he moved it out to the loading platform where it could be moved into the truck. Jimmy's job, for now, was to keep count.

About noon, Frankie drove up to the loading dock with the truck and backed it up to the dock.

"You boys ready?" Frankie asked.

"Just about," Jimmy answered.

Frankie was dressed in dirty jeans and a black t-shirt with an old metal band logo on the front. His left sleeve was rolled up to hold a pack of cigarettes, revealing a tattoo of a howling wolf.

"How many?" asked Frankie.

"Well, so far ten pallets at four carcasses per pallet. That's forty, and they said we could have fifty pigs, so we're almost ready."

Tommy rode out with another pallet and drove it right into the back of the truck. He jumped down.

"There ain't many left," he said. "The manager said we could have fifty, but I don't think we'll make that many."

"We're supposed to get eighty carcasses," Jimmy said. "Randy's going to be pissed."

When they had finished, there were forty-nine dead porkers loaded in the back of the truck. Jimmy found the warehouse manager and got a receipt for the corrected number. He got the manager to write on the slip that they'd loaded all that were available so he could cover his ass with Randy.

The hot Texas summer air made the dead pigs smell even worse. The crew had to get to the ranch as quickly as they could before the meat went south.

The Double Bar-X Ranch Bar-B-Q, on the outskirts of Austin, Texas, served about seventy-five pigs a night in the form of ribs, chops, and steaks. The Double Bar-X Ranch had stopped raising hogs twenty years before in order to concentrate on the complicated task of smoking, cooking, and serving barbecue.

Randy Meyers met Jimmy at the doors to the Ranch refrigerated storage.

Randy took the clipboard from Jimmy as Tommy and Frankie started unloading the truck. He frowned as he inspected the scribble on the purchase order.

"What the hell? Only fifty?"

"Forty-nine," Frankie said.

"Whatever. These are the special porkers for the Sunday Specials. We need eighty. Damn!" Randy spat.

"They only had forty-nine. We took all that they had," Jimmy said.

"I'll give 'em a call. I need those pigs," Randy said.

"What's so special about these pigs?"

"See here? These came from that biotech company Orgo-Life. These are special pigs, grown for organ transplants. They are raised on milk and honey. The flesh is so sweet that grown men cry and hungry women faint when they take a bite. They sell the organs for transplants and the leftovers are good eating."

"I'll call up the manager and give him hell," Randy said.

Randy helped Frankie and Tommy unload the truck. They hadn't finished by the time Randy came back.

"Look," said Randy, "they got a labor problem down at Orgo-Life. They can't get me the pigs unless I can loan 'em some men. They have a bunch of porkers ready but not enough people to finish processing them."

Jimmy nodded his head.

"You and Frankie go up to Austin and pick up twenty men," Randy said. "Take them down to Orgo-Life. With twenty men they say they can fill the order by eight tonight."

There was an illegal day labor market down in old Austin in front of an abandoned McDonald's. Men stood in a line sharing smokes and waiting for any job from anyone hiring. It took Jimmy five minutes to fill the truck. The men got in and squatted against the wall, ready for the bumpy ride. A few women followed their men. Jimmy let them ride along.

"Everybody out!" Frankie yelled, as he jumped out of the truck. He and Jimmy herded the men into the warehouse.

"I'll stay with them and get them started," Frankie yelled to Jimmy through the truck window. "You've got more pickups to make."

It was 7:30 p.m. when Randy sent Jimmy and Tommy and back to Orgo-Life to pick up their order. Jimmy had been working all day and was hungry, so he grabbed a ham sandwich to go from the Ranch kitchen.

They had to wait for the manager to get the keys and open up the freezer. The sign over the warehouse read "Orgo-Life" and under it "Human Compatible Organs from Special Pigs".

As Tommy went in to start loading up the pigs, Jimmy asked, "What do they mean by 'Special Pigs'?"

The manager answered. "These pigs are grown for organ transplants. Kidneys, hearts, and corneas and such. They've got human DNA in them to make them compatible with people. They're almost human. They even look like people—feet instead of hooves, longer legs and such." He chuckled. "That's why they taste so good." He winked. "They say 'long pig' is the greatest delicacy there is."

Jimmy's mouth went dry, and he couldn't think of anything to say. At that moment, an old woman came up to the two men. Jimmy recognized her from the truck ride.

"Have you seen my man?" she asked in broken English. She put her hands gently against Jimmy's chest, pleading. "He came here today to work and he never come out."

"Get lost," the manager yelled and moved to strike her. She moved out of his way. "I told you before that there ain't nobody here. They've all gone home."

"He told me to wait here. He would not have left without me!"

"Get out of here before I call ICE!"

The woman backed off to the street corner but didn't leave. "Please, please," she pleaded.

Jimmy turned away to watch Tommy load the truck. He was coming out with a pallet of pig carcasses on the fork lift.

Jimmy bit into his ham sandwich. It really did taste good. The manager was right, special pigs went into this meat. He ate it slowly, making it last.

"We got some heavy ones," Tommy said. As the lift went over a bump, one of the carcasses started to slide off of the pallet.

Jimmy moved to catch it with his free hand, grabbing hold of the front legs, but almost dropped it. There was a dark blue mark on the right shoulder, shaped almost like a wolf.

He stared at the mark and thought about Frankie, then looked down at the half-finished sandwich in his other hand. He took another bite, savoring the flavor, and whispered, "that's a shame."

Copy That

Holly Schofield

(a version of this story was originally published in Stupefying Stories *in 2014)*

"More salt, would ya," Colin instructed the restaurant 3D food fabber as he chucked his French fries in its tableside hopper. It whirred, then lit up with a thank you.

"There's a salt shaker right on the table." Miranda pursed her lips.

"Huh?"

"You could have added salt yourself." She waved her hand at the tiny plastic shaker before picking up her ham sandwich.

"I thought that was, you know, just decorative," Colin said, watching his fries reassemble themselves layer by layer through the greasy viewing window of the tableside fabber. "Besides, that wouldn't get salt all the way through each fry. Like, inside of them?" *Stupid fabber*. It should have got it right the first time.

Suddenly he wished he'd splurged on somewhere fancier than this Print & Go diner, like the Alto Heaven Eatery down the street. They had real human waiters who would scrape your plate off for you if you needed your dinner refabbed. If he'd taken Miranda there, she might be giving him one of those crooked smiles of hers right now instead of just watching the restaurant window gradually opaque as the setting sun struck it.

He wanted so badly to make her laugh again. This was their third date and so far she'd only smiled a little.

The fabber beeped, and he retrieved his plate of fries from the delivery tray before it had fully extended.

"Mmm, my most favorite kind of sandwich." Miranda bit through the bread's blurred P&G logo into the precise and even layers of ham, swiss cheese, and mustard. She swallowed and raised her cute little eyebrows. "How was work today?" She'd asked this question on their other two dates, and he was never sure why.

"Some guy wanted original wiper blades for his '14 Chevy-Dai." Colin chuckled at the memory, juggling a fry between his hands. "Ouch, now they're too hot." He contemplated running his plate through the fabber again at a cooler setting but settled for blowing on each one instead. "I said he should wait a month until the windshields with the new 4D responsive coating are available. Who needs wipers when the windshield turns water-repellent in the rain?" A wink seemed too much so he delivered the punch line deadpan: "I told him he should take his old wiper blades and stash them with his buggy whip."

"Huh? Oh, you mean they're outmoded now. I get it." Miranda's smile was brief. She put down her sandwich. "Colin, have you ever thought of trying for a different job, one that isn't just…" She laid a hand on his, and his heart thudded.

"Isn't just what?" He could have sat there for hours, enjoying the touch of her fingers.

"Never mind, sweetie. Change of topic—I went to see Grandma today." Miranda bit her lip. "I need to talk about it, I think."

Her grandfather's death two weeks ago seemed to have hit her hard, probably since the old guy had died of liver failure six days before Federal template approval for internal organs had come through. Miranda hadn't laughed since.

Colin swallowed and groped for the right words. "Has your grandma settled in at the retirement home?"

Miranda nodded and picked at the ham layer but didn't take a bite. "She finally unpacked her stuff, including a ton of photo albums. She showed me a picture of Grandpa in a suit and tie for one of their Saturday night dates. He used to give her wild daisies wrapped up in a sheet of newspaper and homemade chocolates. Isn't that the sweetest thing?"

"Yeah, copy that. Your gramps had style. And your grandma could keep the newspaper to remember the day's events by." That was one of the functions of newspapers back then, Colin was pretty sure.

Miranda beamed and ordered a coffee refill.

Nailed it! Colin kept going. "Too bad your gramps didn't have gene-modded flowers back then, all those crazy colors and shapes. And, hey, a home printer—he could have made customized wrapping paper. They had 2D printers back in the 1960's, didn't they?"

Miranda's face fell. *Crap*. He'd said something wrong again. He reached out a hand towards her, but she drew back.

"You just don't get it, do you? Not everything has to be fresh-printed." She poked a finger at his head. "Is there a real you inside there, or is *that* fabbed?" She grabbed her purse and stood up. The *beep* as the screen presented the bill to Colin was drowned out by the restaurant door closing behind her.

•

The hairdresser's door chimed as Colin entered. The mirrored room seemed larger than it was, ping-ponging the reflections of the five stations into infinity. The five customers, their hair wet and messy, looked up from their chairs. Two skinny male hairdressers glanced over, then resumed their work. Miranda, in a pale blue form-fitting tunic, stood by the farthest chair, brushing something purplish onto the hair of a large woman.

Colin, using the courage he'd found after three sleepless nights, walked the gauntlet towards her, keeping one hand behind his back.

He cleared his throat against the stink of chemicals. "Can you take a break?" The eyes of the watching women tickled the back of his neck, and he fiddled with today's earring, an exact miniature of his favorite reality star wearing last night's costume.

Miranda didn't even look up. "No, Colin, I can't. Whatever you have to say, say it here."

"Here? Uh, okay, if you don't mind your customers overhearing. Don't want to lower your, uh, prestige."

"Prestige? You think I'm a hairdresser because of *prestige*?" Miranda glared at him, still brushing vile-smelling goo on the woman's head.

"You've got a great job, one that requires a person to do it. Like me with my automotive supply advisor position." He brushed his knuckles across the Vehicle Hands logo on his uniform shirt.

"I'm not in it for the prestige, Colin. I'm in it for the people I meet. Copy *that*?"

Damn. But he'd come this far; he might as well finish it.

"Here. For you." He thrust the paper cone of flowers at her, shifting the square parcel to his other hand. The customer craned her neck up and clapped her hands with glee. Her long nails, fabbed like dragons' talons, clacked together. Behind him, several women chuckled and said things he didn't listen to. Miranda froze, and the paint from her brush dripped on the floor.

"I got the newspaper in an antique store," he said, the words spilling out of him. "Nineteen sixty-seven, that's when your grandparents were first dating, right? And it's got a summer date, June 23rd, that's about when daisies bloom, isn't it?" The yellowing scrap of newspaper had cost him a week's pay. He could have fabbed it for pennies, but that didn't matter. The light in Miranda's eyes—that mattered.

"Those aren't daisies," the customer said, violet rivulets running down her neck, staining the white towel.

Colin kept his eyes on Miranda. "Yeah, these ones are all yellow. I couldn't find daisies anywhere. No template or anything." He sounded stupid to his own ears, but all the women nodded and murmured among themselves. "No more weeds. Even crab grass is disappearing," one woman said, "now that sidewalk slabs and artificial lawns are fabbed so tightly."

It was hopeless. But he kept talking anyway. "Then I thought of the zoo. The animals have those open fields they roam on, so I climbed a stone wall into the Africa zone —"

"You went into a lion cage for me?" Miranda interrupted him. Her mouth was all screwed up. *What did that mean*?

"You picked dandelions!" exclaimed the gray-haired lady one chair over, her curlers bobbing in her enthusiasm. "I haven't seen any in years!"

"Yeah, sure, that's what they are." He laid the limp bundle on Miranda's hairdressing stand. The whole thing seemed silly now. No point in even giving her the other gift still behind his back.

"Colin! You gave me flowers! Like Grandpa used to do." Miranda's eyes filled with tears.

"I'm sorry. I didn't mean—" He broke off as Miranda stepped closer and took his hand.

Her mouth twisted into a smile. "Dandelions! From the lions!" She kissed him then, long and tenderly, and he could have sworn his heart melted like cheese.

He held out the second package, a bit soggy and limp now. "I know your Grandpa used to give chocolates. I tried but I couldn't get them to come out right. I'm sorry."

"What's in there, young man?"

"Come on, open it!"

He'd forgotten all the customers watching and listening.

Miranda gave him an encouraging nod. A piece of lettuce fell to the floor as he unwrapped the second piece of newspaper. The bread had crooked edges and mustard had soaked through in places. Ham dangled out in uneven shreds. "It was hard to make. I can do better next time, I know I can."

She took the sandwich and clutched it against her tunic, heedless of mustard. Her laughter, when it came, was rich and sweet and seemed to bounce endlessly back and forth between the mirrors that surrounded them.

The Not-So-Mysterious Mystery of the Disappearing Ham

H.A. Burns

My bright blue eyes well up with tears as I moan my regrets through the bars. I am caged. Locked away for my sins. The people walking by have no mercy, only malice in their cold eyes. Oh, how long will I be punished? Please let me go! I whine pitifully. I am shushed and ignored. My cries fall on deaf ears, and I cry anyway—in misery.

It all started with a smell, wafting through the air into the den. I had been sleeping peacefully, napping in the early morning on my favorite couch. I was sprawled out with the fireplace crackling near. I had the perfect life, and it was a perfect day.

That smell! It drove me crazy. It was coming from the kitchen, and it was getting stronger by the minute. I resisted it. I tried to sleep. But I found myself going into the kitchen to walk around the island in the center. The island with the oven. The island with the smell. The impenetrable island.

I went back to the den, tormented. Oh, how long I waited! The smell getting stronger. The rumbles in my tummy stronger still. Still, I waited. Finally, I saw it. A ham. It came out of the oven in the island in the kitchen. My eyes were wide. My mouth opened. I drooled uncontrollably. I licked my chops.

I knew they knew I wanted it. That ham. They teased me, made a sandwich in front of me. Ate the sandwich in front of me as I sat there, begging. They looked down on me as I was licking my lips. Looked down on me as the sandwich disappeared slowly into their gaping maw. Piece by piece, none for me. To tease me more, they let me lick the crumbs from their fingers. Pathetic crumbs.

The sandwich was gone, and its crumbs only whet my appetite for more. My stomach rumbled for more. I looked to the island. That beautiful ham! Oooooh, how I drooled. It was so close now. Somehow my feet took me straight to the smell. I was summoned by the nose.

Please, can I have some ham? I whined. People? Please? People? Where are the people? Did they leave? They're gone! Oh! I am alone... with the ham.

That's the last thing I remember clearly before I was cast behind these bars. There was a blur of movement, and a satisfying gulp. Bits and flashes of teeth and flesh. I heard screaming. I think I know what happened to the ham, but I can't be sure... it disappeared so quickly. Really, it's a mystery.

Forty-Nine Hours of Breado

Calder Hutchinson

The problem with pissing off really weird mob guys is that you end up getting killed in creatively awful ways. When they say you're going to sleep with the fishes, you assume it'll be a quick cement-shoe plunge, a gulp of salty water, and a mercifully brief finale. But no. Not *these* guys. Not the guys who caught Tommy the Rat in a huge spring trap. Not the guys who sent a whole rival gang through a death-maze they'd spent two months building. I sometimes think they treat the whole syndicate as a kind of extended art project.

Which is why I, a small-time fence with a mouth too big for my own good, am now sinking into the Marianas Trench in a triple-reinforced bathyscaphe with forty-nine hours' worth of oxygen, several high-powered flashlights, and a crate of water and ham sandwiches.

Actually sleeping with the fishes. Hah hah. Slowly going nuts in my little spherical prison, watching god-knows-what swimming by with the aid of hyper LED illumination, waiting for the oxygen to run out or—hopefully—to discover in a final heartbeat that the invincible sphere has developed an unnoticed crack someplace, a crack weak enough to allow crushing oblivion to enter in a rush of water and shattered plastic.

But that seems unlikely. These goons know their business, for some reason. Down, down, I sink, watching the water get darker. I wonder if someone will find me someday, some Jacques Cousteau character looking for squid and finding a bizarre coffin with my skeleton pressed against the window. I wonder how well I'll be preserved, what with the oxygen being limited and all. I guess I don't really know how decomposition works.

I nibble at a sandwich, the weird blue of the LED battling the pitch-dark, listening to the creak and groan of my metal vessel. No possible way out of this one. No hope of rescue. I wonder for a moment if perhaps they've attached a chain to the thing, if they're planning on yanking me back to the surface after three-point-five days. The most lengthy and bizarre mock execution of all time. I wouldn't put it past them, except that my eyes had darted over every inch of my metal prison just prior to me being sealed into it and had failed to clock not only a life-preserving umbilicus, but also any possible point of attachment for such a thing. I bet the dickheads all crowded around the rails to watch me sink into the depths like a giant marble, exchanging guffaws and high fives as I vanished into the black. They'd probably painted some whimsical slogan on the top of the thing, something to focus on as I disappeared.

I briefly consider seizing a sandwich and shoving it down my throat, deep as I can, asphyxiating on ham and saving myself a few days of deepening madness. I get as far as an experimental thumb-push, trying to gauge how unpleasant intentionally choking to death on ham might be without actually doing it. I cough mildly, spraying a few sodden globs, and decide that "very unpleasant" is the appropriate category.

My morbidity is interrupted by a soft and sludgy impact. The bathyscaphe rocks, shifts slightly, rolls down some kind of muddy incline and... starts falling again. Maybe I hit the peak of some underwater mountain or something. At least they weighted this thing well, or I'd probably be tossing all over the place.

CRUNCH. A sharp impact and a tumble to the right. I shine the flashlight again, illuminating a cliff face, dizzyingly close, its features a blur. Somehow the speed of it causes my heart to race even faster. For a moment, I feel a powerful urge to go truly mad, to begin ricocheting around the interior of the craft, bloodying my fingernails on the screws. I relax and it passes. I wonder if they've put a camera in here. Almost certainly they have, though I'm not sure how well it could transmit through seven miles of ocean.

"I know you're listening!" I shout, just in case. I make lewd gestures at random, hoping a camera will pick one up. And then, with a sudden, jarring collision that knocks me off my feet, the bathyscaphe settles at last onto something solid, and lies still.

A quick check out the window with the LED shows... nothing. A featureless plain of sand. I feel the panic setting in again. The journey is finished. This is where I'll live out the rest of my life. Eating ham, staring out the window at a barren landscape, until my tiny spherical world can no longer sustain me. I wish I'd brought a book. Actually, I wouldn't be surprised if they'd sent one down with me, *Moby Dick* or *Twenty Thousand Leagues Under the Sea* or something. That would be just their style. I look around the walls of my prison, searching for hidden drawers. I look in the cooler, rummaging among the sandwiches. All I find is a tiny slot in the wall with a picture of a steaming cartoon turd on it. A little torpedo tube for waste removal, I suppose. How oddly courteous of them. I wonder if I could somehow mess with the equipment, jam the thing open and let the water rush in. I wonder if I'd have the courage to do so even if I could.

I sit on the cooler, munching another sandwich (pretty good, actually—probably the work of "Breads" Malone, the mob baker), staring out at LED-illuminated nothing. I remain that way for a few hours, long enough to have two finger-bloodying panic attacks and to use the torpedo tube once. I also see one fish and one bug. The window is close enough to the tube that I can watch my own waste settling gently to the ocean floor. Eventually, I fall asleep.

When I wake up, there are more fish outside the window. They look blind; I doubt the light brought them. More likely, the smell (is that what it's called, underwater?) of excrement aroused their curiosity. They are hideous and alien, but I find myself unreasonably happy to see them. Eagerly I stare out as they nibble at my leavings. Eventually, disinterested, they begin to swim off, and in a sudden panic at being left alone I find myself cramming a ham sandwich into the torpedo tube, jettisoning it into the black water.

The effect is more or less immediate; the fish wheel about, closing needle teeth around the crushed mass. Somehow, the sight of the alien beings consuming what I'd always considered to be comfort food brings home the reality of my position. I start to think about the ham sandwiches my mom would pack in my lunches at school and then realize I am teetering over another psychological precipice and dismiss the memory, symbolically flushing it out into the abyss with another torpedo-tubed sandwich. I watch the fish have at this one, too, and imagine they're swallowing my memories along with the pressure-crushed sandwich. I picture my regrets vanishing down the gullets of these bony fiends and am delighted to find the image holding.

I'll never see the sun again, I realize with a chill. Never mind—out goes the sun, out the tube with a half a sandwich, to be devoured by the unrecognizable life forms, Rahu catching Surya at last. My friends and family go next, and I find myself removing slices of ham from sandwiches and sketching their likenesses in mustard on the flesh-coloured slices. I work in reverse order of pain, dismissing lovers and close relatives first, occasionally shedding tears over a smeared-yellow face on a floppy bit of slaughtered meat. I kiss one before tubing it and tell myself as I lick the mustard from my lips moments later that I've forgotten who it was. The fish eat that memory too.

By the second day, the helpful demons outside have eaten most of what I am. I sit, smiling vacantly, looking out the window, thinking of nothing. Whenever a thought or memory pops into my head, I put it in a sandwich and send it out the tube. All the details of my life, surrendered to the blind hunger outside my inverted metal womb. By hour forty, I've forgotten about hunger, and the sandwiches are now only thought-vessels, dutifully carrying facets of my life to the jaws waiting outside.

Now I find myself in the forty-ninth hour, knowing in a dreamy way what the numbers on the countdown mean without really recognizing them. The final sandwich waits in the tube, waiting to take whatever is left of me out into the dark. I've decided to flush it in the last minute before the oxygen runs out. Earth goes first, then air, then fire. Water will have to take care of itself.

Five minutes to go. I stand, empty as can be, and the sphere tips towards my hands. I try to remember and am pleased to find that I can't. I caress the bread, once, and then carelessly flush it away, watch the demons surround and consume it. I sit back, smiling, and feel a jarring shudder pass through my tiny home. Placid, I feel the sphere pulled upwards, watch the demons wave their fins in farewell. A chance encounter with a rocky outcropping tilts me enough to see the slender cord, nearly invisible, pulling us both upwards, towards a shimmering roof of gradually increasing light. Still smiling, I wonder vacantly who I will be when we break the surface.

Ham: The Lunchmeat of Our Lives

Gerri Leen

Ham on bread was nothing new
Not as ubiquitous as bologna for school lunches
But still ordinary
A ham sandwich was made one way in our house
With butter, on white bread
Rye if Mom felt really daring
No lettuce—what was a tomato?
If you wanted cheese, it was Colby or mild Cheddar
We always had cheese in the fridge
But nothing exotic—these were the seventies
Foodie Culture hadn't been invented yet
Mayo and Miracle Whip fought to
The death for preeminence
But in our house, butter reigned
Even if I longed for more

If we wanted daring
We went to lunch with my aunts
Who loved Monte Cristo sandwiches
It was hard to argue with how beautiful they were

But I didn't like French toast
Or grilled cheese
And that sandwich resembled both
So I steered clear
And denied myself the first taste of Swiss cheese
That thing that makes ham sing between
The slices of any bread, but especially rye
It wasn't till—irony here—Switzerland
That I had my first taste of ham and Swiss
Mom considered it rubber, not cheese
I was in love—how had I missed this all my life?
But it was never in the house
And that's how we learn when we're kids

Years passed, I ordered Swiss at delis
But it never found its way to Mom's fridge
She considered it tasteless
Even if it was the joyful secret to the fondue that
Everyone bought pots for in the seventies
(Except they only cooked meat, not cheese or dessert)
Until fondue went out of fashion, the pots packed away
Waiting for The Melting Pot to make them fashionable
again
But in the eighties, the new shiny thing
Arrived in Seattle, changing the ham landscape forever

Honey-Baked, Spiral-Cut ham
A crust like candy
Served as an entrée at all the best parties and holidays
Plenty left over for sandwiches, oh the taste of them
Thick hearty pieces—always my preference over the
Dainty dance of the shaved slices
That would come later and conquer the deli counter

Do you notice something missing from my sandwich?
I'll never like lettuce or tomato
Between bread, anyway, so it's not that
I'd replaced butter with mayo
But mustard was an unknown quantity
And the bright yellow goop Mom pulled out
Every summer to go with hot dogs
Was disgusting
She didn't like real mustard
Dijon was just a commercial with two rich guys
So again, I learned from her choices
Until decades later a colleague from work
Proud of his new bread machine
Brought in ham sandwiches for the team
On rolls he'd proudly made
Obscenely thick-cut ham with honey mustard
Oh, oh, oh—the dance of complementing tastes

How had I missed this?
How lucky was I to now have it?
The ham journey I was on, always a new discovery

Finally, I discovered Southern Europe's answer to our
Pale pink, mild-tempered ham
Prosciutto, Serrano, Capicola
Marbled with fat, ranging from greasy to dry
Explosions of goodness in the mouth
But impossible to eat in a sandwich
The first bite pulls out far too much meat
It resists playing along
And you can't stuff it back in
Better to just roll your cheese in the ham
A low-carb wrap
And yet, I miss the bread
So I keep trying
Especially with Serrano, this queen of ham
I've yet to warm up to it on tomato-rubbed bread
But my father's family was from the Netherlands
And we'll pair mayo with anything
To any Spaniard's dismay

So many memories, for such humble fare
I can't think of similar for turkey or roast beef

Corned beef hasn't thrilled me, pastrami was a phase
Tuna fish—well, just ugh
Egg salad? So many more things you can do with an egg
Like fry it, and put it on a sandwich with cheese
And ham—lovely, lovely ham
Over easy, the egg provides a curtain of orange
Over hard, it behaves less messily
I'll make one now
Bite in
Close my eyes for a moment
Such harmony: the warmth of the egg, the coolness of the ham and Swiss
The mayo—did you think I'd forget that?
Excuse me while I meander down Memory Lane
With my ever faithful sandwich

Hamming It Well

Julia Wang

The entire premise of *The Ring* was bullshit, and I knew I could prove it. Sure, you could hold on for more than seven days at the bottom of a 20-ft. well if you had survived the initial fall, which must mean there was water at the bottom to cushion the fall, which means there was water. No matter how contaminated it was with dead horse carcasses as shown in the movie, you could survive just fine for over seven days if you had over seven cups of water to live on.

That was the reason I jumped into the well. I would stay here for seven days so I could write about it in my blog. It was going to be great.

I told my assistant where I was and what I was doing, of course. I'm not an idiot.

Day 1:

Popped my kneecap in the fall, but that was the extent of any injuries. Didn't bring any painkillers, of course. That wouldn't be authentic. It's very cold and damp in here. Been trying to scale the walls, not to climb out, which I can't, but to exercise, prevent hypothermia, and just to pass the time.

The water here is stale, as expected in an unused well in the middle of rural Maine, but water is water, and life with diarrhea is still life.

Day 2:

Explosive diarrhea from both ends. Losing fluid rapidly. Better drink more water.

Day 3:

Both knees are swollen, but the icy water helps keep the swelling down. Although I think I remember reading somewhere that dirty water is bad for an open wound. Can't be sure.

Day 4:

Something smells rotten. I think it's my knees. The right one is starting to ooze green and sticky pus. Stings like hell, too. Better wash it with some cold water.

Assistant came by today for a checkup. Swore to fire him if he calls in any cops or EMTs or psychiatrists. This is important.

Day 5:

Knees no longer hurt. Must have lost nearly 20 pounds already. I've always wanted to lose weight. This is a win-win.

Still Day 5:

Starting to feel chillier. Or hotter. Can't tell. Can't stop shaking either. But shaking is good. It's only when your body stops shaking that you...

Day 6:

My assistant—I think it's my assistant, can't see his face well—is looking down on me from the top of the well. He just stares and doesn't answer when I call out to him. What a weirdo.

Still Day 6:

He's back, and he just tossed something down the well. No warning or anything. It plopped and sank, and I had to fish around for it. Looked like a kidney. Turns out, it's a sandwich. The ghost girl from The Ring never had a sandwich, so I mustn't eat it. Besides, it's *ham*. Eww.

Still Day 6:

Ate it, but will not mention it in my blog.

It's not bad. For ham.

He's still staring.

Day 7:

Day 8:

Day 9:

...

The Cost of Perfection

Irina Slav

Let me start with the bread. It is where everything begins when you seek perfection. I always have, so it shouldn't come as a surprise to you, as a professional, that it took me three months of trial and error to produce the perfect loaf of rye bread. Don't even try to tell me about whites or wholegrains. If you want the perfect ham sandwich, you need rye bread, take it from me.

Getting the dough right was a challenge, I have to admit. It was one of the many I encountered on my way. But I live for challenges, including those that present themselves in the shape of unhelpful, even outright rude salespeople. I know this is what you want me to write about, but you will have to bear with me and let me tell the story as best I can. There is really no other way, is there?

It should go without saying that perfection requires the best ingredients. In search of these, I had to face people assuring me their flour was as fresh as if it was milled on site and as pure from any artificial additives as the morning dew. All this when I could *smell* the flour they were trying to peddle. I could smell it was dying a slow and painful death from all the chemicals they had stuffed it with to make it last longer. I could feel its pain. I shared it. I suppose this is part of the quest for perfection, though, so I didn't give them undue attention. I dealt with them quickly —verbally, I mean—and never went back to their stores.

The perfect loaf took me six attempts. Bread is a living creature, and it needs gentle care. I supplied that as best I could, letting the sourdough breathe, being very careful just how much honey and salt I added to the first-day mixture, making sure there were no pockets of dry flour on day two, when I made the final dough. Here is something you might find interesting: I slept with the sourdough.

Yes, I put it on my nightstand, the bowl covered with a wet cloth so it wouldn't dry, and I shared my warmth with it every night for a week, until it acquired that fresh, subtly sour scent that whispers the promise of a hearty loaf, a piece of life so delicious you would be grateful for just being alive when you tasted it.

When I put the dough in the oven, I felt a certain degree of reverence and I am not ashamed to say it. Bread deserves respect and, yes, reverence. It is a cornerstone of civilization that we have come to ignore or even hate and despise because we abuse it. You will have to forgive me for the lyricism, but you did ask me to be as honest as I can. I have no problem with honesty, unlike those people you want me to write about. Again, you will have to bear with me. It is my mind you want to take a glimpse into, isn't it? So this is it. I am open wide because I can see; I can feel you strive for perfection, like me. This is a disposition I have rarely encountered, and this has made me appreciate it even more.

I have all the respect in the world for bread. I also love a job well done, so when I opened the oven and smelled that sweet and sour scent, I felt dizzy for a moment. You think I'm going over the top? Try it and then tell me how it is. Only you can't, of course, because I'm not sharing my recipe.

Let's be clear about this before I go on. I am not one of those attention-seeking home bakers who are only too eager to share their mass-use recipes with as many people as possible, fishing for compliments, always hungry for praise. No. My quest for perfection in food was my own endeavor to honor my father's legacy. My father died six months ago of stomach cancer. He was the one who raised me to always seek perfection, no matter what it cost me. "All right" would not do for him. "Okay" would not do. I was consistently reminded that I could do better, in everything. So I strove to do better, in everything.

My father's favorite snack was ham sandwich, as you would have surmised by now. He taught me what it takes to make it perfect. It's not a lot as far as ingredients go but, like I said, it takes dedication, care, and respect to combine these ingredients in the perfect way. I'm sure you have noticed by now how important it is for me to do everything properly. You might even conclude that I am something of a pedant, and you would be right. I'm not embarrassed or bothered by it. There is no room for improvisation when you seek perfection.

Finding the perfect cut for the honey glazed ham is as difficult as finding the best flours for the bread. Sometimes I suspect salespeople are put in stores to make life harder for other people, not easier. Or I'm simply too different from other shoppers, and they are incapable of adjusting to this difference.

Here is something that might surprise you. I don't really expect much from people. I have met enough of them to know that high expectations invariably lead to disappointment, and disappointment hurts. I do have some minimal expectations, though, and these include the ability to accommodate more than one single worldview for at least a short period of time, such as the few minutes it takes to talk to a client if you work in a food store.

Here is what I mean. When I ask "Is this ham fresh?" I expect an honest, truthful answer. I don't expect a boilerplate "Yes, ma'am." I can *smell* it. The same goes for the eggs, for the mayonnaise. Do you know farmers' markets can be even worse than supermarkets if you are sensitive to outright lies?

You might wonder why I bother asking about the freshness of the produce at all. This is because I'm curious about people. I want to know if they are being honest with me. I can't shake off the hope that once, at least once, someone might surprise me pleasantly. I regret to say that so far I have been invariably disappointed, but I try to not overburden myself with such sad thoughts. I deal with the problem and move on. That's how my father raised me.

Now I have a confession to make. I like you, really. You are one of the very few exceptions to what has become a rule of disappointment in my life. Besides, putting all this on paper feels good. It feels like a release from months of unbearable tension, which in a way I suppose it is. So I will make you a concession. Since I'm sure you are not interested in the perfect thickness of the ham relative to the other ingredients, I'll be quick with the rest of the story.

The only ingredients that I came by in a stress-free, problem-free way were the tomatoes. The reason is simple: I grow them in my garden. Bull's heart—this is the best tomato breed for a ham sandwich. Why breed? Because they are living creatures, tomatoes, just like bread is a living creature. Mine were lovely—they had the perfect shape and rich, bloody-sunset color; they smelled like heaven probably smells; and they tasted of ambrosia. I do believe if there was such a thing as ambrosia in reality, it would have the taste of freshly picked bull's heart tomatoes.

The mayonnaise took only three attempts until I achieved the perfect balance between fluffiness and substance without compromising the flavor. I consider this one of my better achievements. After this, all that was left was to assemble the sandwich and taste the result of my efforts. It sounds so simple.

It is difficult for me to talk about this part. It hurts. Still, since you asked me to tell you the whole story—and you asked politely, I might add—I suppose I will have to swallow the pain and continue to the end. I'm afraid I will have to disappoint you, but at least this will give you a chance to put yourself in my shoes for a moment. Disappointment hurts, and it leaves scars.

I never got to taste my perfect sandwich. The world caught up with me just as I was sitting down with it, almost trembling with anticipation. I felt proud of myself, I felt happy. This is another rare occurrence in my life. But I had achieved perfection, and the tasting would prove it in the most final way. This was what I was thinking about when the police burst in, shouting at me. I dropped the sandwich. On the floor.

The tomatoes scattered. The rest of the sandwich plopped ham-first on the carpet. Someone pushed me to the ground, too, but it felt like a dream. All I could see—my only link to reality—was my ruined sandwich, the destruction of perfection I had worked so hard to achieve. I heard my father's voice as clearly as if he was standing over me. *You can do better*, he said.

You know the charges against me, so I will not go into that. You see, Doctor Smorrebrod, ultimately, it all comes down to one question. Why can't everybody else strive to do better? Why are so many people content to be mediocre? This is what I could never grasp, never accept. This is what has gnawed at my brain ever since I began using it properly, around the age of four.

I suppose this is what drove me to kill those three people although I don't have clear recollection of the events. This is what I meant when I said I will disappoint you. You want me to tell you about the murders, and I would like to, but I really do not remember them. I do remember feeling a certain weakness in my right hand from exertion on three separate occasions, but I never attributed it to anything other than straining myself in the garden. I spend a lot of time in my garden, especially when someone disappoints me.

You will probably attribute my lack of recollection to memory repression. I don't mind, really. You may be right. Then again, you might—just might—have gotten the wrong end of the stick here. Don't you think that, well, maybe you can do better? I told you I liked you, so I will help you. Here it is. I have often felt that striving for perfection can justify a lot of actions that are generally frowned upon or punishable by law. At least, it can justify them to the extent that the one who performed these actions is not punished as harshly as they would be had the authorities known that it was not really perfection that drove them to these actions but other, less admirable urges. Perhaps some people simply like to kill. With this I leave you to your analyses and profilings. I look forward to our next meeting. I might even share my ham sandwich recipe with you.

How to Make the Perfect Ham and Cheese Sandwich

James Dyer

The troubling spiritual experience that you're about to have with this sandwich requires a deftly crafted physical frame. Most H&C connoisseurs suggest some kind of whole-wheat hamburger-style bun or French bread. Balderdash. Bleached white bread is cheap, common, and will make a sturdy base for just about any combination of comestibles you care to put between the slices.

Consistency is key here.

You could lay down two worldly slices of 12 grain, or slice into a loaf of exotic pumpernickel, but you and I both know that you'd be lying to yourself. You were raised on white bread. Changing up the formula now would be ridiculous.

Play it safe.

Place two slices of Wonder Bread to one side on the countertop, underneath that awkwardly visceral crucifix hanging on the wall that you keep trying to convince your grandmother to get rid of. Keep it out of sight, but always in reach.

In your family, Grandma cooks the ham.

As the oven warms, she'll explain to you that it's important to strip off all the fat so that the meat comes out tender and easy to digest. She'll talk for a very long time, and you probably won't get to ask many questions, so be sure to listen closely. This lesson on baked ham will be the most important thing that she'll ever teach you.

Your family cooks ham with Vernors because it's the right way to cook ham. Anything else would be absurd. Faithless. Sure, you could use a different kind of soda. Substituting Sangria and pineapple juice will give your ham a fruity kick. Trendy fusion recipes may reincarnate forgotten taste buds near the back of your tongue. Yet, no matter what you do, the ham will always just be ham. No need trying to get existential with the rear end of a hog. Don't worry about it now, Grammy will say, as she closes the oven door. In time, you'll believe in her ham too.

And there the ham will sit, slow roasting between the hours of 9:00 a.m. and 3:00 p.m. on a baking pan atop the crossed slats of the oven shelf. After pacing the kitchen impatiently for six hours, Grammy will decide that it has cooked enough. She'll stab the ham in the flank with a meat thermometer. The juices will flow and collect in the pan beneath.

"It is finished," your grandmother will say.

It will be sliced. It will be served.

But to make a ham and cheese sandwich out of a freshly cooked ham dinner is ridiculous. What you're looking for here are the leftovers, and you've now got a three-day window before those leftovers go out with the trash.

The cheese is the thing you use to glue everything together.

Use American for its gooey, childish familiarity. Cheddar works too. Place two slightly overlapping pieces atop the ham. Heat it in the microwave for forty-five seconds, or until the cheese is good and melted.

The right cheese is essential in any sandwich. You could find the perfect pig, the too-perfect pig, and slaughter it. You could rend the hide from the flesh and slice off a prime cut of tender meat from its hindquarters. You could preheat an oven to three-hundred degrees and use whatever kind of funky, hocus pocus, satanic, Church of the Gospel Shrieking Baptist Angels of the Latter Day Saints recipe that you want to.

You could crucify it.

You could put the whole thing on a bagel. But if the cheese isn't there to stick the whole thing together, it'll all fall apart the second you lift the sandwich to take a bite.

If your sandwich does fall apart, pick up the pieces quickly and quietly. Throw them away. Do not attract attention. In your famished, frustrated state of mind, you're susceptible to outside influences. Swiss may seem like an innocent substitution. Ciabatta bread may sound exotic and intellectual. But they are, both of them, chock full of holes. Who knows where they'll lead?

Be safe. Start over from scratch and stick to the recipe. Follow it closely, combing for steps you might have missed. Don't change a thing, no matter how many times everything falls apart. Albert Einstein once said that the definition of insanity is doing the same thing over again and expecting different results. Or something. It doesn't matter. Einstein was a vegetarian.

Repeat.

Repeat until you get it right.

Repeat.

Repeat.

Let Me Finish

Chantal Boudreau

A sandwich is one of those things that has to be constructed with the utmost of care or it's just plain wrong. Building one the proper way is one of the three most important things in my life. And my favourite sandwich is a ham sandwich.

I had made sure to get only the best ingredients. The local baker makes a marble rye loaf that's sublime, and I had popped over just after breakfast. I had visited my favourite deli the day before and found the perfect black forest ham and the creamiest Swiss in the city. For greenery, I had picked up crisp romaine hearts and sliced dill pickles—the refrigerated kind.

Of course, I couldn't forget my condiments. I use only high-end Dijon, just a taste because it's costly, along with mayo I make at home—none of this "salad dressing" masquerading as the real thing.

Cleanliness and order are the second-most valued things in my life. With that in mind, when making the perfect ham sandwich, you need to start with a pristine kitchen, porcelain plates rather than plastic, and a sturdy knife. I prefer the multi-use kind, good for both slicing and spreading. A knife isn't the kind of tool that allows for compromise. It has to have a keen blade and a razor's edge. I never skimp on that either. My knife should be an extension of me, and I deserve the best.

I had everything ready. I was in my zone, my kitchen clean and serenely quiet, with all my ingredients laid out before me. The Master was ready to begin—the time was right.

As I was about to slice into the rye, a terrible noise jarred me out of my pleasure. One of my neighbours, Scott Wilson, had decided now was the time to mow his lawn.

Now I already had a bone to pick with Scott. He never followed the homeowners' association rules. The day to mow his lawn should have been sometime in the prior week, but he had let it grow well beyond the maximum height. I had approached him about it then but he had been getting into his car, talking on his cell phone I might add, and he had waved me away with a motion of his hand, like I didn't matter. He had driven away without offering me any further acknowledgement. I have a low tolerance for rudeness.

And mowing on my sandwich-making day was also a bad idea. It was a bit of a scorcher, with no rain forecast for the next three days. The city's water conservation bylaw was in force, which meant no water sprinkler use. So by cutting the grass then, he'd either have to disobey the bylaw and risk a fine, or his yard would end up turning a yellowish-brown, marring the neighbourhood.

That was unacceptable.

The absolute most important thing to me is finishing what I start, and I couldn't finish making my sandwich under the current conditions. That, and I clearly needed to finish resolving the situation with Scott Wilson.

My sandwich knife still in hand, I marched over to Scott's yard. I waved at him as soon as he had turned the ride-on to face me. He waved back but otherwise ignored me. I called out his name, and I suspect he heard me, but he gestured at his ear, like he couldn't hear. I don't know if he intended me to catch sight of his smug, mocking grin as he once again turned the ride-on, this time away from me, but I did.

That was the final straw. I was tired of watching him break the rules, frustrated by his lack of consideration for his neighbours, and pushed to my limits by the fact that he continued to dismiss me like I didn't matter, with his back turned. All those things, and he had disturbed my sandwich making.

Scott would play the scofflaw no more.

When I finished my business with him, I turned off the ride-on.

I still had a ham sandwich to make. First, I put the knife under a stream of tap water. You can't finish a proper ham sandwich with a dirty knife.

Things I Do Well That Nobody Will Ever Pay Me To Do

Christine Sloan Stoddard

Staring up at the sky and renaming stars because even stars need to hide behind an alter ego sometimes.

Just remember—David Bowie had Ziggy Stardust. That fact alone proves that vulnerability and magic are not mutually exclusive.

Clipping my toenails so my little crescents don't shoot all over the room.
Stumbling over someone else's personal detritus is never pleasant.

Walking by houses and silently deciding how to redesign them. *Add another window there, move the chimney to that side...*

This has nothing to do with property values or even livability. It's all about the neighborhood's maximum beauty enhancement.

Refreshing my inbox so frequently that I see emails as soon as they arrive.

Then I give myself permission to not respond to them until I've drafted the perfect response.

Researching every detail of living in cities where I am certain I will never live.
But if I had to live in those places, I would know the average rent, how to simplify my commute, and where to find the most devastatingly delicious kebab.

Writing scripts for conversations I should've had but never did. I'm mostly referring to conversations I should've had with people I could've loved and people who have already died. A couple very special people fall into both categories. Only my notebook knows their names.

Collecting and redistributing mica because it's only right to share the shimmer.
I need to find someone to assist me in this endeavor, for it is a noble one. Could that person be you?

Making tea that is just right. Not too hot, not too cold. Not too rich, not too weak.
I will warm you up, but I will not burn you.

Planning elaborate funerals for woodland creatures for gnomes to one day enact.

Things I Do Well That Nobody Will Ever Pay Me To Do

Should they ever hire me as a woodland creature funeral consultant, I'm ready.

Stapling items exactly as they should be stapled.
No botched jobs. No staple removers necessary.

Traveling from Bed-Stuy to Harlem without squashing my ham sandwich.
I keep it tasting fresh no matter how packed the subway is.

Spotting stray hairs and discreetly collecting them.
I will never let you march into a conference looking disheveled, and I will always have what I need to mount my Victorian hair art.

Knowing where all of the alley cats live between my apartment building and the subway.
I also notice when I haven't seen one in a while and imagine it somewhere cozy and safe. The places in my fantasies always have the nicest scratching posts.

Putting on a blindfold and completely re-imagining my surroundings.
Somehow, butterflies are almost always involved.

Determining exactly what kind of merperson any human would be.
Because so many of us secretly wish we could escape to the sea.

Reconfiguring stained glass windows in my mind into abstract sculptures.
Something so glimmering doesn't have to remain so flat.

Identifying exactly which clumps of moss to coax from logs.
I never rip them. I pull them up as gently as I can.

Doodling on edges of paper that looked neglected.
Sometimes we need empty space. Other times, we need to fill that space.

Arranging the toiletries in my bathroom in the most welcoming way.
So friends, lovers, and other guests can primp and care for themselves with ease.

Fitting my vision of the future together like a puzzle and then dismantling it.
Sometimes I need to fret less, plan less. Life is a continuum.
Pleasure is a continuum.

Things I Do Well That Nobody Will Ever Pay Me To Do

Sitting on the toilet, putting my weight on the balls of my feet,
thinking deeply.
And not feeling self-conscious about it.

Swaddling myself in blankets until I am perfectly cozy.
Adjusting my optimal level of swaddling for my love when I
tuck him in on those nights I stay up later than him.

Painting my nails for relaxation more than beauty standards.
Those tiny brushstrokes tickle me into tranquility.

Disguising just how messy and cluttered my bedroom really
is.
I'm all for artful shelves, trunks, and boxes.

Twirling my hair out of nervousness until I've given myself a
salon-worthy hairdo.
At least I'm not biting my nails.
Tricking myself into thinking my subway car is actually a spa
or a garden or a temple and that there is no more peaceful
place.
Until someone jabs me with their elbow, at least.

Eating tortilla chips.

Christine Sloan Stoddard

I will go through bags until someone stops me. I am relentless, persistent, a real rat in a rat race, the very symbol of Capitalism.

Listening to hours of shit music that is shit for my ears and shit for my soul, but feeling no guilt or remorse.
Because my soul can't be saved, anyway.

Giving myself dozens of makeovers in my head with the skill of a Hollywood stylist.
Not that I plan on changing a thing about my wardrobe.

Turning my enemies (and frenemies) into small puppets in my mind and staging elaborate plays.
It's a shame I can't generate revenue from these shows when I have rent to pay.

Hugging unicorns in my dreams.
Frankly, if there were a champion of huggers, that champion would be me.

Picturing 10,000 versions of paradise.
And accepting that none of them compare to the sheer thrill of living in our strange world.

Pining for a world that is as wondrous as ours but kinder.

Softer. More luminous. As sparkling as the coats worn by wishes.

Doctor Jayne Herbert: Private notes on Patient 16

C. Cooch

14 May 1935

The new male, Dashiell, on my ward is a fascinating creature. He is not bright, but he is literate enough to tell some very tall stories. He is polite and most of the time obliging of conversation. He was sent to our mental asylum for committing murder but, as of yet, I cannot understand why he would do such a thing as it doesn't seem a fitting trait of his personality. However, he is clearly insane. The mention of his killing of a man seemed to frenzy him, and this is where the literateness ended. He tried to explain something along the lines of 'killing for living', but for the most part, it was unfathomable. I thought maybe it was in defence, and so I asked, but more of a gargled response followed.

His physique and features could be classed as attractive, but his face quickly contorts, and he twists himself into 'ugly' easily. His body shows signs of abuse, the best part may be from fighting, but there are whip marks on his back. Nevertheless, I will not rule out this as being just a pleasurable pastime as the patient has stated he likes pain. What brings me the most wonderment of all are the iron teeth he has. They are a full set, top and bottom. He said his 'Master' was a doctor and he had installed them.

24 May 1935

Patient 16 has my whole attention. I am growing more and more curious about these stories he tells. However, along with the days passing, he seems to be growing more restless with talks of his 'Master' and how the food stores would be running low. He proudly and with no reserve boasts of his butchery skills passed down from his grandfather to his father and then to him. Along with other talks of serving up food, it would seem he did have someone he provided for. He asked what my favourite food was; it took me off guard at the time, so the only thing that came to mind was a ham sandwich. He was probably thinking of something that took more culinary skills though he didn't let on and proceeded to explain how he would perform the cut from a lump of given meat to gain the ham. I have to add it is not an untruth; I do love ham sandwiches.

25 May 1935

Nurse Hattie gave me the keys to the main gardens today. I was able to explore the exquisite gardens on my own. I managed to sit for some time and enjoy the sweet scent of violas whilst observing a feral cat deliver a fatal bite to the neck of an unsuspecting mouse. I should have been ecstatic, but my mind kept drifting to Patient 16.

26 May 1935

Today Patient 16 has given way from his fretting to settle down and talk to me. He agreed to call me Doctor. However much I tried to divert, he retained an interest in me. He had noticed the weakness in my leg, a hip injury I sustained as a child. Then he tried to make a connection between the pair of us; this is not uncommon, and I have found similar with past patients. I am not like them. Anyway, at first, he figured us both liking pain, but I explained to him that I would like nothing more than to be free of this pain. He said he could help with that if I were to help him escape, that his Master, the doctor, would fix it.

29 May 1935

Today I helped in the kitchen. Quite a nice change from my patient rounds, but I missed him.

31 May 1935

I am going to try something rather unorthodox, to say the least. I will have to keep my notes stowed away safely in my undergarments from now on. There is another patient on the ward, no next of kin, a complete ass and savage. I am going to put him in with Patient 16, Dashiell. I feel more comfortable using his name now I know him better.

I will keep the savage in a straitjacket and... give Dashiell a knife. I acquired it from the kitchen yesterday. I don't believe Dashiell could be a murderer. Not that this can officially gain his release. I feel I am doing this more for myself, call it a morbid curiosity. I also have to add I don't really know if he won't kill the man, but I feel this savage's life has no worth; pardon me for saying so... I guess. Unfortunately, I do not have a way I can watch the room, so the plan is just to leave them until the morning. I will either have a mess to clean up or two men to segregate and trudge along as normal.

1 June 1935

There was a mess. However, I have mixed emotions! I honestly expected there to be two men when I opened the door this morning, which is what I am telling myself anyway. But the outcome has left me startled. Dashiell has shown compassion towards me that no one ever has. I think I am besotted, let me explain... My experiment was flawed from the start; what I forgot is that I had told Dashiell about the savage and his advances on me. So Dashiell was already biased against the man, how delightful! So with me handing him the knife, he may have thought I was asking him to kill the man. But the sweetest thing of all... there was a ham sandwich lovingly prepared! Though it was unlike my traditional ham sandwich, and not exactly edible. It was two halves of the dead man's moccasin and, at a guess, a sliver of his buttock, the area where Dashiell told me the ham is cut from. He had said the ham from a human tastes the best of all. But I understood... it was made for me, and my heart fluttered. As I took a step forwards, into that room, I foolishly slipped on some blood splatter but fell into Dashiell's arms. For a moment I melted there. So the stories he told me were all true, the slaughtering of humans for their flesh to feed his Master's exquisite palate.

I took Nurse Hattie's keys from her desk. Dashiell and I fled together, to The Master. Dashiell said the food stores would be low, or maybe all gone, so he wanted to hurry. My hip failed me, but he scooped me up and carried me when needed. And so, I am here... I have yet to meet this Master, and now Dashiell has left me to rest a while whilst 'they prepare'. Preparing, I assume, to fix my unbearable hip pain, but already? Well, he had killed for me and then cooked for me? My guess is that now he wants to rid me of this pain, and he did say he would do so if I freed him.

I will stow my notes, add more later... I think I hear them coming.

•

The County News, Wednesday 5th June 1935

MURDER AT AN ASYLUM AND TWO PATIENTS ESCAPE – A shocking murder occurred on Saturday at Berkley Mental Asylum. The body of Henry Potter, 25, has been found butchered into a variety of quality meat cuts! Dashiell Hall, 27, along with a second patient, Jayne Herbert, 25, have been missing since the grizzly event. Potter's body was found in room 16 of the new west wing, which happened to be Hall's residing area. It is understood that a female nurse allowed Miss Herbert certain privileges which may have led to the incident, and she has since been dismissed of her role.

The two patients who escaped from the Berkley Mental Asylum remain at large despite all attempts to find them. Caution should be taken in the surrounding areas.

The Chase Is On

Doreen Joy Graham

Sir Donald was making a sandwich
he layered with cheese, lettuce, ham.
Six dollops of mayo and mustard,
an elegant step up from jam.

He whistled a tune while he puttered
and pulled out a pop from the fridge.
A pickle or two was extracted
to spice his lunch up just a smidge.

Now enters the dog in our story,
a lovable black Labrador.
He hopped up to stand on the table,
delighted to eat up this score.

When Donald turned 'round for his sandwich,
he only saw Zeus lick his lips.
Confounded the dog with foul language,
then Zeus stole the pop from his grips.

The chase could have looked entertaining,

a dog with a can in his mouth.
Our Donald behind with fist pumping,
and that's when the game headed south.

Excited and feeling so happy,
Zeus wagging his tail on the run.
He chomped and the can started spraying
while Donald yelled, "Son of a Gun!"

But that can stuck on his incisor,
more spraying of pop just confused.
Poor Zeus was in need of assistance,
lost track of why he was accused.

At last the dog stopped his rebellion,
submitted, all covered in pop.
The can was pried loose and surrendered;
Exhausted, all chasers could drop.

Sir Donald sat huffing and puffing
while Zeus was a big sticky mess.
The neighbors all couldn't stop laughing—
they all learned a lesson, I guess.

Ham sandwiches need to be guarded,

so YOU eat it up, not the dog.
Those pets love the chase when they're followed,
and you'll be expected to jog.

Monterey

Kristine Sahagun

Saturday, December 16, 2012

It's 3:21 am and I have to be at work in five hours. Why am I still awake? I'm writing this letter that I've been putting off for a couple of weeks now. It's not that I didn't want to write it, and it's not that I was too lazy. It's not because writing it would make me feel sad. I mean, yeah, you going away makes me sad, but that's not the reason why I kept putting this off. I send you long and winded emails all the time. This letter-writing stuff should just flow out of me right?

So you're on a plane. Are you on a plane? Or are you waiting in one of those uncomfortable chairs that feel like they've been grafted with felt skin? I've always been scared of planes. Not terrified but just uncomfortable. Are you uncomfortable? Do you feel the tingly vibrations, those fluttering trills swirling around your insides? That sounded lame. Your life is going to change in a few hours. I think that's pretty amazing. You know what else I think is pretty neat? The fact that so much can happen in such a small amount of time. A year seems like forever, but it's really not, you know? Of course, you know. I guess I'm just throwing questions out here. Letting my fingers and thumbs do the thinking for me. Okay, this is what I'm going to do with this letter. I'm just going to write everything that pops into my head and not stop. I'll just keep talking and not stop. Even if things become grammatically incorrect. I always have this need to backspace but this time I'm just gonna keep going and we'll see if I find a point. It's not a goodbye or a hello, or a how are you, have a safe flight, don't eat plane food, but watch a good flick, get your shoes shined by a fellow with a yellow smile because he probably drinks several cups of coffee to get through the day not because he spends most hours on his knees shining shoes, though people would think that I guess. They'd look at the shoe shining guy—let's call him Jim. I always liked that name. It's short and sweet and friendly and strange. It's the kind of name that belongs to a guy everyone knows, but no one really knows what he's about, like if he really wanted to be a shoe shiner when he was a child or did he really want to be a pilot, but because he was colour blind he couldn't get into flight school. Is there any truth to that? Maybe. Maybe Jim had a dad who worked in the airport, or a dad who was a pilot and he'd take Jim to Pearson every—no! Jim's dad was a flight attendant who travelled the world. Who was tall, and doughy, and had soft, kind hands. I wonder what soft kind hands smell like. Maybe baby powder. Maybe Jim's dad used baby powder on the back of his neck every morning because it reminded him of the way his first wife smelled. I don't know what happened to his first wife. I don't know if Jim even remembers his mother, but every morning, when Jim was a boy, he'd watch his father shake some of that baby powder onto his soft, doughy hands, and pat the back of his neck. Jim would see the small puff of white and he'd think of fluffy clouds and planes that would take him and his father places. Maybe Jim hardly saw his father. Maybe Jim only saw his father in the morning, smelling of powder and rye, and Jim would go to school full of milk and a ham sandwich, watching the sky through the classroom window, wondering what sort of person his father was helping out on the plane. Wondering if this person was short, or fat or kind or cruel or smart or if this person had a dog that waited for him at home, anxious for the door to open and he'd step through again. When Jim grew up maybe his first job was at Pearson bussing tables at some tacky bar and grill with green neon lights and that endless stream of sports coming from the too small televisions. Jim wouldn't know it was green though because Jim's colour blind. If you're colour blind, how do you go through your world and make meaning? Maybe Jim liked the way things smelled. Maybe Jim saw things in smells and each brought a little memory of what he wanted things to be like, or how things were. When Jim didn't make it into flight school, maybe his dad tried to cheer him up by buying him dinner at a restaurant in between countries. Let's say it smelled like rubber gloves, grilled cheese and that faint musty smell of coffee breath after your first cup. But Jim doesn't feel sad. Jim stomps on that sadness. Jim pushes the sadness away when his father, now a little grey, orders Jim a soda because Jim doesn't drink alcohol. He can't stand the smell. So he's sitting at a table that has marks from children playing with butter knives and slightly bent forks. His dad orders a beer because all dads order beers, and when the funny waiter who smells like watermelons hands Jim his soda, there's this moment when Jim notices the bubbles kinda dancing inside his glass. The drink smells sweet and sharp, but it's the bubbles that Jim can't look away from. They're bright. They're… I don't know what they are, but that's what makes Jim push all the sadness and disappointment, and he imagines that when he takes a sip, when he swallows that drink, those bubbles will be inside him and they'll wash away all the grainy bits. They'll grind all the pasty, doughy stuff inside him and clear a path so when Jim takes a breath he'll feel taller, bigger. And even though he's not up in the sky, up above everything, even when years later he spends most of his days bent over, crouched by the tip a shoe, he won't feel small or insignificant. Even when days become heavy, Jim will sit back on his haunches, or sit up in that shoe shining chair and he'd let himself feel the heavy day run through him, but then he'd stop it from rising up, digging its nails into his neck. He'd inhale, suck in the smells of life and go on.

Okay. This is long. I have no idea where I was going with this. Jesus. I just read what I wrote and it's pretty damn sad. I didn't want this to be a sad letter. It's actually more of a ramble than a letter. Are you still reading this? Did you skim? It's okay if you skimmed. If you are skimming then I can write this: once upon a time there was a young man named Henry who packed his bags, picked up a plane, and sailed to the other side of the country where there were mountains and people and places and streets and cars and sights and sounds to see. He lived in a little pink house with pink carpets and rooms, one of them with a window barred so he couldn't leave its little pink palace. He lived with friends and a fireplace, and drank scotch in a hot tub, and wine on warm summer nights on the beach, climbed mountains, rode trains, went to school and made movies. Westerns! John Wayne westerns! Zounds! They wouldn't say zounds in westerns. They'd say, "That's awfully nice." or "This here's a stick up." or "Evening Ma'am."

This isn't much of a letter. I'm not handing you handy advice from my hand. I'm not telling you that I'll miss you terribly, that I already do miss you terribly as I'm writing the words: I miss you terribly. I'm not giving funny anecdotes of times passed or tossing little inside jokes. I'm not saying to meet a pretty girl who'll make you smile, laugh and be happy, who will listen when you speak, tell you when you're being an idiot, or be supportive when you need it. I'm not saying to meet pretty men who aren't too pretty but can be pretty to a friend who is typing out these words with her little fingers and thumbs. She will hopefully hop on a plane, trying not to be terrified of being lifted high up into the sky. She'll distract herself with music or shut eyes, and she'll press a book into her chest so she can feel something.

Can I say something else? Thank you for those three nights you stayed awake with me and we told each other stories. That moonlight tale, the memory naming colours, and that last night when you got drunk and your spelling went downhill. You helped me push my nightmares away, Henry. I won't forget that. I'm going to see Michael on Wednesday. I'm not sure what I feel about this.

Things are changing and everything is happening so fast. But it's nice, and when the year goes by I wonder what kind of people we'll be at the end of it. I want to send you 365 days' worth of good morning comrade messages. I hope your day is bright and beautiful. Warm and wonderful. Incandescent. Intoxicating. Your life is going to be amazing, Henry. Even on days when you don't feel that it is.

Do you have a window seat? Look out the window. Tell me what you see.

If you don't keep in touch, I'll cut you.
Celine

Henry folded the letter, leaned forward to stick it in his back pocket, then settled into his seat and shut his eyes. He heard a flight attendant pass with the refreshment cart and debated on calling her back for a drink. It was dawn and the plane tipped and circled above the sleeping city. Henry watched the cabin slowly drink up the light, which flooded waking faces with pink and gold. Celine would want to capture this moment somehow. The seatbelt sign glowed red and people shuffled back to their seats. A sea of clicks resounded through the space, and Henry inhaled deeply as if he could suck in all the sounds with his breath, holding himself suspended between places for a moment longer before his life unravelled and became new. He wondered where he should go after he landed and settled in at his new home. He wondered what Celine would think of it and of him. He wondered who they would be years from now, if their friendship would fade with distance and time.

If Celine was sitting in that empty seat beside him, she would say, "You think too much, Henry."

And he'd want to say to her, "Just stay and I'll stop."

But she was miles away, and all he had for now were her words in his pocket. He shifted in his seat again so he could hear the paper crinkle with his movement, whispering.

On the Side

R.D. Sullivan

Derick didn't find it hard to be "in the vicinity" when the call came in. His new partner, Mary, was still green enough to go along with whatever he said. So when he parked on a side street four blocks away, she didn't ask why.

"10-4," he said into the radio. "5-Adam-3, we're on Aloha and en route."

"Received," the dispatcher responded.

Mary's jaw was set tight and her knuckles white on the door. Every muscle in her tall, lithe body seemed tensed, her posture rigid.

"Don't be nervous," he told her. "Guy probably went on vacation. These welfare checks? It's almost never a dead body."

She stayed quiet but he was happy to see her relax a bit. Having his partner jump at every creak in the floor would put him on edge, too. Two skittish people makes it hard to do what needs done.

Of course, if she was scared of the body he knew they'd find, it would be easier to get her out of the room.

"Police. Anybody home?" They gave it a moment, looking around the neighborhood. It was on the nicer end of things, old homes lovingly maintained. They stood at the red door of a brick number, roses in the flowerbeds and grass trimmed short. No sound from inside. Derick knocked again, for Mary's benefit. "Police! Open up if you're home, we've been asked to check on you."

"Now we enter?" she asked.

In response, he tried the doorknob. It turned, just like they'd said it would, and he grinned. "That'll make it easy. Police!" he yelled again as they stepped in.

Silence from within the house. Derick pointed at the staircase. "You go poke around upstairs. Holler if you find anything."

"Got it," she said, and started climbing. He heard her yell her own "Police!" at the top.

Mary was proving to be a perfect partner. Sure, somebody also on the take would have been ideal, but the girl never blinked twice when he told her to do something. *Look that way. Go over there. Take a break and grab yourself a cup of coffee, sweetheart, I've got some business to attend to.*

They'd gone together on most of his side work, her never asking about any of it. Not on the errands he ran for Frank Evola. Not on the ones he ran for his new boss, Vic Salerno.

May the right hand never know what the left is doing, anyway.

And now, *why don't you go upstairs while I "discover" the dead body I already know is down this hall and two doors to the right?*

For the benefit of the lie, he opened every door in the hall before stepping into the dead judge's study. Still in his office chair, the honorable Judge Robert Hicks had died with his head thrown back and his hands on the armrests. The foam that had spilled out onto his cheeks had dried, leaving crusty white trails on his skin.

On the judge's desk was a plate, and on the plate, a ham sandwich. Hicks had only managed to get a few bites in before whatever they'd laced the meat with had taken him. It looked like it had been a painful way to go, too, but that's what you got for crossing the people Derick worked for.

No, he corrected himself, *that's what he gets*. Or better, that's what Hicks deserved for getting caught. Derick had nothing to worry about himself. Caution had dictated his every move with Salerno so far. Just a few more months and Evola would be gone for good, anyway.

Derick stood still for a moment, listening. Mary's footsteps thudded across the floor above him, and he heard a door open. Good. He had a few minutes to finish up then before she came back downstairs.

From the breast pocket of his jacket, Derick pulled out the bag he'd been given that morning. The sandwich inside was identical to the one on the desk—whole grain wheat, thick slices of ham, provolone, stone-ground mustard, lettuce and tomato. Minus, of course, whatever had been in Hick's sandwich that had laid him out.

Derick stood next to the body and lined up this second sandwich, matching it to how the one on the plate sat. He took a bite where Hicks had, lined it up again, and took a second bite. It wasn't until he was reaching to switch the sandwiches after the third bite that he noticed the sudden hammering of his heart. He stepped back, staring in confusion at the food in his hand.

"Cyanide," Mary said from the doorway. She leaned against the stained wooden trim, arms crossed, hawk eyes watching as he dropped the sandwich.

Cyanide? But how? Had he eaten the wrong one?

No. That wasn't right. Was it?

Derick couldn't tell. Everything in his head had become slippery as his heart sped up. He was breathing heavy and grasped at the desk for support as he raised his wrinkled brow to his partner. "But... what? I don't..." He shook his head but couldn't go on through the pain building in his chest.

"You thought my uncle wouldn't find out who else you've been working for?" She didn't move from the doorway as he fell to his knees. "Double-crossing sack of shit, anyway. I hope the money from Salerno was worth trying to sell my family out."

Frank was her uncle? Oh, God. He looked at the sandwich, understanding what they'd done. "Help," he said. "Please. Call for help."

She finally moved when he went for the radio at his shoulder. This quiet, compliant partner of his delivered one swift kick to his ribs and sent him sprawling on his back. When he reached for the radio again, she stepped on his wrist. Not that he could have used it. Derick couldn't breathe, let alone call for paramedics.

"Don't worry, big guy. Once you stop twitching, I'll be sure to call it in." Mary sighed as he coughed, foam spraying from his throat. She stepped back a few feet to avoid it, out of range of the hand that reached for her pant leg.

Derick wanted to crawl after her. Maybe if he could just grab her, connect with her, she'd have mercy on him. If only he could, but he couldn't. His body wouldn't even let him roll onto his side. He moaned low, but the sound refused to be shaped into words. It felt like there was an elephant sitting on his chest, stealing his breath. His left arm was numb.

"I'm almost impressed by how easy this was. 'We killed him with a sandwich. Here's a sandwich for you, just bite it like he did.' How did you make it this long, being as stupid as you are?"

Darkness pressed into the edges of his vision. Derick lay flat on his back, just trying to breathe now. He couldn't. He couldn't breathe.

Her footsteps seemed to come from all around him. There was the snap of a rubber glove. The sound of the ceramic plate sliding off the desk. A soft *thump* as she dropped his sandwich on top of Hicks'.

"Don't worry, Derick." Her voice was mockingly sweet. "I'll call for an ambulance in a few minutes, just as soon as I take care of the leftovers and dishes. You hang tight, buddy. And before you die, think about what got you here. It won't help, but I want you to know that you did this to yourself." Her voice was growing fainter, and he heard door hinges squeal. "Oh," she added, "Uncle Frank wanted me to tell you what a good thing you had. He was going to take care of you. Shame it came to this."

Derick heard the door click shut, though he couldn't see anything anymore. His whole mind was going dark like a flame deprived of oxygen, dimming by the second. He was dead, his body just hadn't accepted that yet. There would be no help. And yet, before his mind finally extinguished, he found a moment to admit she was right. He really had brought this on himself.

And to think. He didn't even like ham.

Havana

Selena Mercuri

Mom tells me to stay in bed and keep a cool cloth on my forehead to bring the fever down. Dad doesn't tell me anything at all. He is across the room, huddled in front of the hotel TV, moving the antennas to try and get anything but grey fuzz on the screen. He doesn't care about the grey fuzz in my head. I'm cold, but mom says I can't have the covers or I'll get worse.

"I'll move our dinner reservations to eight," Dad says. "I've had nothing but a damn ham sandwich all day."

"The lady at the front desk said there's a hospital just outside Havana. The taxi will be out front in an hour," Mom says. She pats my head with the cloth, and her long hair tickles my face. My eyes are heavy, and I'm worried they'll sink into the back of my head.

"I didn't pay all this money to spend the week in the hotel room. Can't even get the television to work."

"No one's stopping you from going to dinner, Tom, but I'm taking Sophia to the hospital with or without you."

"I'm fine," I say, getting out of bed. "Let's go to the beach."

My head starts to spin like a merry-go-round as soon as I get on my feet. Darkness. My eyes must be finally falling into the back of my head, like giant gumballs coming out of a quarter machine. I can't tell if I'm getting closer to the ground or if the ground is getting closer to me, but Mom catches me before I have a chance to find out. She lifts me back into bed.

"Get out," she says to Dad.

I've ruined everything.

"You'd still be living in this country without a dime if it weren't for me," he says. "But I'll leave if that's what you want."

Instead of going out the door, he walks around me to the night table and takes our passports out of the drawer. Mom tries to grab them from his hand, but he's too fast for her. He opens my mom's in half, rips it down the middle, and throws it at her feet.

"Find your own way home," he says.

Dad looks at me for a minute before storming out the door. He slams it behind him.

Mom and I are in the back of the taxi on our way to the hospital an hour later. She's packed us a pair of ham sandwiches we snuck out of the hotel buffet in her purse, but I'm too tired to eat mine. Dad and me used to make those all the time when I was little, before he got too busy at work to be around much. This one doesn't look half as good. I throw mine out the open window when no one is paying attention. Maybe dad will see it and know which way to come looking for us when he stops being mad at me.

The Crimson Pumpernickel

Andrew Giordano

"Yeah! S'whatchu git!" he exclaims, furiously mashing the left ctrl button on his keyboard. His character dances the crouching dance of mockery known as "teabagging".

'NO ONE BEATS PUMPERNICKEL PHIL!' he types in self-congratulation in the post-game chat window.

'Go fuck yourself' is the response from his esteemed opponent.

"Oh shit, it's getting pretty late," he tells his gaming group. 2:35 a.m. It seems like he's been staying up later each night. Hours in the arena pass as if they are mere minutes. He is transported each night by this game to another world, battling with anonymous virtual murderers in intense, adrenaline-filled fight & flight encounters.

"It's my morning to get up with the kiddo, so I gotta hit the sack. G'night guys!" He feels triumphant after this last victory. After cleaning his desk, he heads through the kitchen to bed, his eyes drifting unconsciously to the gorgeous new loaf of bread on the counter as he passes. With an alias like Pumpernickel Phil, he figured he ought to learn the art of baking a mean loaf of pumpernickel. His hands move on their own to cradle the loaf. Still warm, though it came out of the oven hours ago.

"Ooh baby… that's the good stuff," he mutters, his heart filling with pride. He lifts the loaf to his nose, inhaling the warm aroma of fresh bread.

"Huh, that's strange," he remarks. With the loaf so close to his face, he notices a hair poking through the surface. It must have gotten baked right into the bread. In mild revulsion, he tugs at the hair, but it breaks off at the surface.

•

He dreams vividly. He is performing some pleasant activity, working with ease and grace, enjoying the freedom and sense of flow. Slowly though, the task becomes harder. His hands fumble, and he loses his confidence. What is he doing here? How is this supposed to go, again? He is reprimanded for his clumsiness, told to work faster. He tries, but he just can't remember where he is or what he's doing. Time is running out. The world shrinks around him, closing in on what is slowly becoming a nightmare. He can't find the parts. Weren't they just right there beside him? And what happened to his progress meter? How is he supposed to know how much longer to work when there's no progress meter?

Something brushes across his face. He brings his hands up and disgustedly paws at himself, trying to brush away the sensation, but the subtle tickling stays, unaffected by his efforts. He is unable to see clearly, and his mind conjures thoughts of centipedes and horrible small hairy creatures, writhing and crawling. With a sickening sense of claustrophobia, he realizes that his hands have never left his sides, and that he is paralyzed. He tries and tries to bring his hands up, without success. What is this thing? And why can't he move?

With a massive effort of will, he breaks the paralysis and swings his arms up, making contact with a hard round object just inches from his face. In that moment, he wakes and realizes that it is his child's head, with its fine hair hanging down and tickling across his cheeks. In his panicked efforts to free himself from sleep, he has swung his arms a little too hard, and now they've collided with his son's small skull.

"WwwaaaaAAAAAAHH!" His son's cry pierces his heart. A vicious, throbbing headache punctuates the silence between sobs. He slowly sits up and cradles the boy, apologizing in mumbles while he puts the pieces of reality back together. His wife opens the door and pokes her head in to see if everything's alright. He tries unsuccessfully to put words together to explain.

"Sorry, Isaac... dream. I couldn't find the things... progress bar was gone... Paralyzed... It was an accident."

Her eyes narrow. "You've been up late again, playing that stupid game, haven't you?" The contempt is clear on her face.

"It wasn't THAT late..." he murmurs.

"What?" She can't hear him over the child's cries. "Never mind. I'm going to work. Please feed our son his dinner from last night. It's really important that we stick to what we say, or he'll learn that he can just eat whatever he wants, whenever."

She goes on, but he's unable to follow. He's inundated with pain in his head and what feels like a megaphone in his ear, amplifying his child's cries, the cost of his mistakes. Eventually she leaves, and the sobs die down while he offers small and insignificant apologies. He stumbles into the kitchen, carrying his child, slumping with the stiff back and poor posture that come from spending too many hours hunched in front of a screen.

"Hey, sorry kiddo. I thought you were something horrible. I was dreaming. I hope you're alright... Oh hey, here's the bread your Pops baked last night. Do you want to try some?"

He swigs some of yesterday's coffee along with some painkillers. He slices some of his new bread, its rich darkness the one bright thing in this trainwreck of a morning.

The deep flavour of the pumpernickel makes him feel a little better. At least I got one thing right, he thinks. It has notes of coffee, cocoa, molasses, caraway, rye. They dance together on his tongue, creating a perfect, tenebrous landscape. This is bread with a soul, he thinks. Before noticing what's happened, he's eaten two large slices of the bread, and so has his son. Ah, crap... I guess I'll have to eat that leftover dinner as well. It'll be easier than force-feeding it to Isaac after smacking him this morning. Also easier than explaining to the wife why it's still here...

The day, though difficult because of lack of sleep, passes uneventfully. When his wife returns, he decides to share his creation with her. She was once apprenticed to a baker and makes excellent bread herself. He has a vague thought that they might use this as an opportunity to connect in their ragged and fading relationship. Ever since having Isaac, there's never seemed to be any real time to connect, and the opportunities to fight just seem to be so much more plentiful.

"Here, hun, have a slice o' this!" He offers a plate of freshly sliced bread topped with cream cheese, ham, and capers, something that he saw a professional baker do while he was researching it online.

"I told you I'm not into pumpernickel," is her response.

"Yeah, I know, I just thought, you know, that you might like to taste my first real baking project. I think it turned out pretty well." She assents, taking the plate and having a bite. Her reaction is no reaction at all. He realizes that she's upset with him. Knowing that this is probably about something other than bread, he steels himself for a bit of digging. Keep it light, he thinks to himself. We don't need another heavy conversation about our relationship.

"What is it? Are you angry at me?" His mind races, trying to figure out what it could be that he's forgotten. Birthday? No. Anniversary? Fuck... he's forgotten their anniversary. The cogs of his brain skip a beat.

"You probably forgot to make our dinner reservation too." she scolds. "I even left a note on your desk—you know, the desk you spend your whole day at, playing your stupid game? And I reminded you this morning!"

"I'm sorry! I couldn't hear you over our son's screaming!"

"You mean after you punched him in the face?"

"I didn't punch him! I was dreaming! Jesus, I'm sorry, ok?!"

"Whatever. Your bread is dry." She thrusts the plate like an accusation into his chest, storming out and slamming the door.

He sees the half-loaf sitting on the counter and smacks it across the room in frustration. It bounces off the wall and falls to the floor. "Fucking pumpernickel," he mutters under his breath.

"Fucking pumpernickel!" Isaac repeats joyfully. "Fucking pumpernickel! Hahahaha! Fucking pumpernickel!"

He launches unsuccessfully into damage control.

•

With his son finally settled in front of dinner and his wife still not home after storming out, he sits at his computer to plan his new creation. In his research, he traces pumpernickel bread to its progenitor, a man known to his fellows as "Old Nick". He lived in France during the mid-1700's, and the name "Pumpernickel" was the bastardization of the phrase "pain pour Nichol", meaning "bread for Nichol". The man was a hermit and a minor figure in local lore. He commanded an enormous beard that was said to be able to engulf misbehaving children (or so the story was told). There were possible links drawn between this figure and the modern-day figure of "Saint Nick", or "Santa Claus". As he browses through paintings of this man, what is most striking (besides the gigantic beard) are the dark depths of his eyes. He stares into them, feeling himself drifting away...

He comes back to himself with a start when he realizes that his child has climbed on his lap. "Pops? What are you looking at?"

"What? Oh, nothing, darling. Just learning about where this bread comes from."

•

After putting his son to sleep, he realizes that his wife still has not returned. Well, so much for our anniversary, he thinks. Did I really fuck up that badly? Normally she doesn't care about that kind of thing... And so what if I missed it? I made that loaf for us! For the family. A Breadwinner, that's what I am. Literally! She should be thanking me for my hard work.

It was too early to start playing his game—his son had been waking up shortly after being put to sleep recently. So he continued in his research. He wanted to know more about the actual crafting of the loaf. He needed to master the art of the pumpernickel, to live up to his alias of "Pumpernickel Phil". One of the techniques he found was the "altes brot" method. In this method, a piece of the "old bread" is saved as a sacrifice, to be incorporated into the next loaf.

This is a kind of bread that gets sacrificed to its future self over and over, unendingly. How cool is that? To know that even if you escape being eaten, your fate is to be torn to bits and incorporated into the next loaf, only to have the cycle begin once again. God, that's morbid... I wonder if that's what drove Old Nick crazy? Well, I'd better go and slice off a chunk now as a sacrifice for the next loaf.

•

The games progress as they usually do, with Pumpernickel Phil sowing seeds of anger and hostility across the world with his "teabagging" and grossly bad manners in the post-game chats. This time, though, his friends also seem to be irritated with him for not playing as part of the team.

Still chuckling to himself afterwards, he packs his things up and gives a loving nod to his sacrificial slice of pumpernickel on his way to bed. His dreams that night are again vivid, though quite confusing. He feels flustered and panicked, not able to move forward in his mission. This time, he decides that he won't let a lack of tools stop him. He'll use whatever's at hand to get the job done. Building. Stitching. His vision is blurry, but his goal is clear. Some moments he appears to be in his house, some moments he appears to be in his workshop. He's holding a saw, now a ball of twine, now some old rusty wire, old scraps of wood. All these blend together in the folds of his dream to create something beautiful. Something perfect. A tribute. A temple. He mumbles in his sleep.

"Yeah… What you get… It's what… what you… what you… GET!" The last word comes out violently as his son wakes him suddenly by shaking him.

"Pops, get up! It's morning time!" A bright and impossibly cheery face greets him in his groggy state. He's trying unsuccessfully to dredge himself up from the dreamsludge of molasses and tar. Looking outside, he sees that the sun is not even close to rising. His son always does this to him. He checks his cell phone beside the bed—6:00.

"It's morning time! Time to get up! Time for… oakmeal!" His son has taken to calling oatmeal 'oakmeal', and it has stuck in the family because it is so adorable. His wife was the first to notice. His wife… where is she?

"Where's Mama?" Clearly, his son is also wondering what's going on. "Uh… well, uh… that's Pops' fault. Pops missed something really important yesterday, and now Mama is mad. She'll probably come back today."

Why is he so tired? He got at least four hours in bed. That should be plenty, right? It feels like he hasn't gotten any sleep at all. Like he's been hit by a bus. Achieving a standing position takes several tries. What happened to the days when his body was so spry?

The light comes on after a bit of fumbling, illuminating the kitchen like a crime scene. Tools and materials are scattered about on the floor and table. His first thought is that someone has come into his house in the night and made this mess. Scanning the room, he finds something built into the table. His heart lurches into his throat.

"Oh my god. How did this...?" He doesn't finish his sentence because he already knows the answer. The object that has been built into the middle of the table is a grotesque, patchwork hook. Hanging from the hook like a lifeless body is the sacrificial slice of his first pumpernickel loaf. His heart now sinks as he realizes that he must have done this in his sleep.

"Pops! What did you make?" comes the innocent and curious voice of his son. Oh god... he thinks. How could this have happened? Jesus christ... I was alone with my three-year-old all night. What if I had done something to him instead? Oh god. Oh god. Ohgodohgodohgod...

"Go back to bed, kiddo. Pops will clean up this mess."

•

All day his head is pounding, and this time it's not responding to painkillers. He must not have gotten any sleep at all—the hook, still embedded in the table, is fastened quite securely, and he can't figure out how to get it out without destroying the table. The external sloppiness belies its structural integrity and craftsmanship. The dark slice of bread still hangs from it. He figures he'll attend to it later, after he's had a good night's sleep.

They eat all the remaining food in the house that day, and he's too daunted by the prospect of making a shopping trip on his own with a small child. His wife normally does the shopping, but she still hasn't returned. The only thing that they still have ingredients for is more pumpernickel bread. Knowing that his son loves it, he decides to make another loaf, but he can't work up the energy to do so during the day.

That night, with his son asleep in bed again, his energy levels rise. He is determined not to be a terrible father on top of his failings as a husband. Besides, he thinks, nighttime is the best time to make pumpernickel. Confused, he tries to remember where he heard that. The question sticks in his mind as he grinds up the sacrificial piece of bread into his new loaf. He's so preoccupied with it, in fact, that he accidentally doubles the darkening ingredients—molasses, caramel powder, cocoa, and coffee. He notices grimly that this loaf is nearly pitch black. Unsure whether to be proud of or embarrassed by this, he begins to knead the dough.

Looking up at the clock, he realizes that he ought to hurry up if he wants to get any games in tonight. It requires more kneading now, due to his mistake.

"No time... no time. There's just no time to get this done." He curses under his breath. He works faster and faster, kneading with all his strength. The bread just won't seem to pull together and develop. The rhythmic motion of the kneading, combined with the lack of sleep, pull him into a trance-like state. He keeps working at it, ignoring the tension building in his shoulders. His muscles bunch and strain, and he grips the loaf like a strangler. His temperature rises. As he kneads and kneads, sweat begins to roll off his forehead and down his cheeks, falling off his chin and into the bread. An occasional drip turns into a steady leak. It runs down his arms and through the cracks of his fingers, into the dough. His head is pounding harder as he loses more and more of his fluids to the bread.

The dough finally starts to pull together and create a cohesive loaf. Coming out of his trance, he realizes that hours have passed. He is thirsty and drained. Now suffering from severe dehydration, he feels like he's got a hook through his skull. He can barely open his mouth, it's so dry. His throat stabs with pain. He drinks as much as his stomach can hold and is comforted as he looks at his beautiful dark loaf. Perfectly round and smooth, like a newborn baby. He feels immense pride at his work.

"Yeah! S'whatchu git!" He crows in delight. He dances a macabre dance around the kitchen, stretching his sore and abused body. He catches a glimpse in the mirror of the next room. The sight shocks him. The overhead lighting casts unflattering shadows down his face and body. He realizes with a sickening feeling that his hunch has worsened.

When the timer for the oven goes off, what he sees within snaps him out of his hot and seething thoughts like a sudden plunge into arctic waters.

The loaf, which began as a perfect sphere with smooth roundness, has been hideously deformed, twisted into a horrifying mockery of his intentions. It stretches malefically outward, almost seeking to escape itself. As if in protest of its unnatural existence, it has grown long, horrible tendrils that contort in agony, far away from its core. It fills him with fascination. Like watching a car crash, unable to turn away despite the horror. It is privacy exposed, guts wrenched out into the world for all to see.

•

With no other food in the house, father and son must eat the bread in the morning. His son gives almost no reaction upon seeing the mangled pumpernickel.

When his wife returns in the early afternoon, he knows he should be angry at her for leaving them for so long with no information. Somehow it doesn't feel like a surprise when she tells him that she's gone to stay with an old lover. He knows somewhere inside that he ought to fight, but he just doesn't feel like he has it in him. He is drained and filled with shame and embarrassment at his creation from the previous night. She notices, and rages.

She wants him to fight for her. She doesn't want this to be over—she digs the knife deeper and deeper, trying to provoke a reaction. When he fails to respond, a look of utter contempt fills her face.

"Jesus, look at you... You look like you haven't showered in days! Your beard is filthy. What the hell kind of example are you setting for our son? I bet you've been spending the whole time with your stupid game, haven't you?"

She makes her way to the kitchen. Feeling a sudden panic at the risk of being discovered, he bolts to head her off. Too late. Walking into the kitchen, she sees the hideous hook that now seems to be a permanent fixture on the table. She also sees her son hanging one of his little dolls on the hook and cheerfully calling it "Fucking Pumpernickel". She is speechless for a moment. Her eyes fall on the loaf.

"...What... IS... THAT?!"

"It's food. It's what we've been eating. I wouldn't let Isaac starve, you know. You may not have a very high opinion of me, but at least I can feed our son!"

"You... fed... THIS... to our son?!" She can barely choke out the words, they seem to disgust her so much. "Come on, Isaac, we're leaving."

Dragging her child around the house by the hand, she packs some bags with his things and leaves. His wailing is so shrill and piercing that his pops takes shelter in the office, listening to music on his headphones. He's trying to plan out how he's going to pull himself out of this one.

"Pumpernickel Phil always wins... fuck... how am I going to do it this time?" he mutters. He decides to console himself with a few rounds of killing random people in his game. He feels like a zombie—he ought to be sleeping, but he's not. He is in a half-awake trance, muttering his inane little victory statements. How long has it been since he had a restful sleep?

"Yeah. Fucked you up good. Shoulda known not to mess with Pumpernickel Phil..." The throb in his head grows impossibly. Why does it hurt so bad? He punctuates his games with trips to the kitchen to break off chunks of his grotesque loaf. On one trip, it finally hits him that his wife and son have left him.

His fists swing, smashing the plates and glasses on the counter, in the dish drainer. He flips chairs and knocks down shelves. The crimson shade of violence that fills his vision offers him no release. Holds nothing sacred or untouchable. The wedding gift from his parents, hanging on the wall, he rips off and smashes. His child's artwork he rips off the fridge and shreds. He tears the shirt from his chest, with the veins in his head pounding his skull. Pain, loss, anger, disappointment, shame, powerlessness, and abandonment all coalesce to turn him into another being. "Yeah! Eat it! That's what you get! What you FUCKING GET! NOBODY fucks with Pumpernickel Phil!"

The hook adorning the table becomes his next target. He swings his fist, makes full contact. The table legs flip momentarily off the ground, but the hook seems unaffected. He swings again. Nothing. He takes the table by the hook and attempts to toss it across the room. It is a solid hardwood table, not lightly moved. Despite his immense outpouring, the table doesn't seem to notice his efforts. His frustrated desire amplifies his rage. He swings blow after blow at the hook. The skin of his knuckles is becoming a horrible pulpy mess. Flecks of blood splatter the walls, staining his outrage on the paint. Pounding and pounding, blow after blow, savagely he tries to destroy the hook. One final blow embeds the hook in the flesh between his knuckles.

He screams in surprise and pain, tries to yank his hand away. The hook appears to be wrapped around one of his tendons. The red rage drains from his eyes. The hook is deep. It sickens him, and he retches on the floor. Carefully, painstakingly, he manages to extricate his wounded hand. He looks around and surveys the wreckage. Memories destroyed, treasures cast to pieces. A life of occasional but sincere joy, dashed on the rocks. He begins to tremble. He falls to the floor, tears streaming down his face. Lying in the mess of glass, wood splinters, and vomit, he rocks back and forth, muttering to himself.

"What you get. It's what you get. That's what… s'watchu git…"

•

That night, he stumbles from his bloodied keyboard to the kitchen. He's hungry. The entire loaf is gone. Sometime after he lost himself, he must have unknowingly torn a chunk and impaled it onto the now-bloodied hook in the wreck of a kitchen. Unthinkingly, he begins the ritualistic process of crumbling it into the new loaf. His head is pounding with an almost lethal pain. Hard to imagine that he still has enough blood for that, considering the size of the pools on the floor where he collapsed.

Mixing the ingredients, he begins to knead the bread. He is greeted with a sharp burst of pain in his knuckles. Bringing them slowly to his face, he realizes that he's opened the wounds again, and they're streaming fresh red pain down his forearms. Dumbly, he lowers them back to the loaf, grits his teeth, and resumes his kneading. Each turn, squeeze, and push oozes his life from his hands into the bread dough. Turn, squeeze, push. Turn squeeze push. The throbbing of his head and the bleeding of his hands join the chorus. Throb, turn, bleed, squeeze, throb, push, bleed, throb turn bleed squeeze throb push bleed.

The loaf, already dark, is beginning to take on the shade of coagulating blood. He notices and is unable to stop. Tears begin to stream down his face, and he prays that this is all just a dream. That he might wake up at any moment to his beautiful wife and son, and that they could all enjoy one of his treasured pancake mornings with bacon and coffee. Kneading, bleeding, throbbing, weeping, he continues his service. When it is time, he carefully places the loaf into the oven, muttering.

"What you get. It's… this is… it's what… get… s'what… you get." When it is time to remove the loaf, he doesn't bother with oven mitts. The loaf scalds his hands, but it's all the same to him now. "What you get... s'watchu... git." His vision blurring, he looks at his fresh pumpernickel loaf. It's beautiful. Round, gorgeous. It truly is a work of art. Every aspect of it is perfect. The deepest colour, the hardest crust, the fresh crackling sound like a symphony. Old Nick would be proud. He sways on his feet, head throbbing impossibly. The pain constantly threatening to overwhelm him, he holds on only to admire his bread. Is he imagining it, or is the loaf throbbing along with him?

"What you get. Whatyouget. This... swhatchugetwhatchugetwhatchugit." The loaf definitely IS throbbing. It seems liquid inside. With his knife, he pierces the loaf to check if it's done. A stream of red, crimson liquid comes rushing out. "What you get. It's what. This is... what... you... get." Blood, streaming from the loaf, runs down the counter to the floor to mix with the wreckage of his life. Faster now, it pumps from the bread, streaming to fill the room. It's up to his ankles. Now his knees, his waist, his chest.

"This is what... s'whatchu git." The blood from the loaf has reached the level of his face and pours into his mouth, suffocating his words into a slow gurgle, and then to nothing at all.

Across the city, his son sits bolt upright in bed, screaming. A slow ooze of crimson runs down from his nose, into his open mouth...

Hillary's Recipe

Sam Weir

"What *is* that?"

"What?"

"That *smell*. I keep catching a whiff of it. It smells sour."

"Oh, don't worry about it."

"It's distracting though. Do you have an open jar of pickles up here or something?"

"I'll put it outside then."

She got out of bed and let him watch her black-laced bum walk across the room. He winced as the bed creaked loudly—could the family who lived downstairs hear?—and then let his eyes drift over her skin.

She made her way over to the corner, bent over, reached under the desk and pulled out a bucket. Without addressing the cause of the smell, she carried the bucket out the door and left it a few steps down from the balcony. She left the door open a few minutes so that the cool air could freshen up the apartment and harden her nipples.

She watched him watching her. Thought about what might be happening downstairs. Then she closed the door and sauntered back to the bed.

"Better?"

"Much."

"Where were we, then?"

•

Earlier that evening

The bar was crowded, everyone was drunk, and the music was good for dancing. She started her rounds right away, cocktail in hand, looking for the right man for the night. She only ever had one drink on these nights; she wanted to stay sober to make sure she stayed in control. Inviting a man home could be a dangerous thing. You never knew what he might get into his mind, and she'd rather know that she would have her head about her if the need arose.

She usually knew when she saw the right guy. Most nights it didn't take too long. She would make her way around the room, assessing who was there with a girl, who was there with friends and who was alone. Usually the guys who had come alone were the best bet. Usually they didn't want to go home alone.

Tonight, she found him on her second lap around the room. He was not much bigger than she was, drunk enough that he wouldn't question her interest in him but not so drunk as to be sloppy. She made her way over and started moving her body to match his rhythm on the dance floor, moving closer when he noticed her. Without much delay, hands touched bodies and she knew that she had picked correctly.

Eventually, she motioned him over to a quieter spot in the bar and opened with her standard line: "You ever had a green tea in a dirty attic?" She'd learned the benefits of establishing right away that she was a little... quirky, we'll say.

"What are you talking about?"

"Sorry, I guess I should introduce myself first. My name is Hillary, how's it going?" Hillary smiled slyly, held out her hand jokingly for a handshake.

"I'm Jake." He took her hand, smiling back. He had been enjoying her dancing with him. He didn't often attract the attention of a woman.

"Hi, Jake. I'm thinking that I like the look of you, and I'd like to invite you home with me, but my apartment is dirty and all I've got to drink is green tea. I thought I should give you a heads up."

"Is green tea all you're offering?" He raised his eyebrows, hopeful.

"No, that's just all I have to *drink*." She guided his hands to her body, making it clear what else was on offer. She loved this part. She loved watching the eyes of her pick-of-the-night when she put his hands on her hips. Usually they lit up with hunger, or excitement or lonely hope. "Let's get a cab, if you're up for it?"

•

As they got out of the cab in front of Hillary's house, she whispered, "We have to be quiet. I live in the attic apartment, above a family with little kids. They should all be asleep by now, but I don't want to wake them up." She took his hand and led him through a gate to the backyard. "Sorry, the outside light burnt out and I haven't replaced it yet. I hope you can do the stairs in the dark." She showed him the way to the metal grate fire escape stairs that slinked up the house to the attic.

Jake approached the stairs cautiously. He didn't really like heights and didn't like the idea of climbing translucent stairs in the dark. However, he did like the idea of this woman and what she was offering him, if he could brave the stairs up to the attic apartment. Jake picked his way up the outside of the house slowly, holding tight to the handrail. He didn't notice that, instead of driving away, the cabbie parked in the driveway of the house, turned off the car and went into the house.

•

Once Dennis got inside, he called hello to the babysitter, paid her and made sure she got home safely, five houses down the street. He was hungry, and as he made his way to the kitchen, he decided on a ham sandwich. While he prepared his snack, he wondered what was happening upstairs. Hillary was good at picking guys by now, figuring out who would be a successful conquest.

He ate quickly and then climbed up to the second floor as he brushed the last crumbs off his shirt. With the bathroom light on, he cracked open the door to his son's bedroom. Man, he loved that kid. He watched him sleep for a few minutes and then went to get ready for bed.

Dennis had his eye on the time. He'd been home for close to half an hour, and usually it took Hillary about forty-five minutes to get to the good stuff.

•

"Better?"

"Much."

"Where were we, then?" Hillary asked softly as she crawled back onto the bed.

"Well, I think that you were right here." Jake smiled at her. He was stretched out on the bed and looking forward to feeling her weight on his thighs again.

"Ah, yes." Before straddling Jake's legs again, Hillary reached down the side of the bed and pulled a box up beside her. She opened it and pulled out some strips of satin and began to caress Jake's bare chest.

Jake closed his eyes. He hadn't had sex for almost two years, and he missed it. He took a moment now to drink in what was going on. The bed was creaky, yes, and the apartment was a mess, as promised, but he didn't care much about that. Hillary had lit half a dozen candles around the room, so everything felt warm and comfortable. And here was this rather attractive woman, sitting next to him in black lace underwear and a tank top. The satin felt good as she dragged it down his chest and back up. Then her hands were on him, sliding down his torso and undoing his pants. Oh, this was going to be a good night.

"I forgot to ask, are you into kinky?"

"Kinky like what?" Jake's experience in bed was limited to two long-term girlfriends who were definitely not into anything kinky. Of course, he'd watched some kinky porn, but it had just left him feeling disappointed, knowing that the girl he'd been with at the time was definitely not into anything kinky. But now, he remembered a particularly appealing scene he'd watched where...

"Can I tie you up?" Hillary interrupted his mental replay.

"Uh, well, I've never done that. But, uh, sure, I guess."

Hillary moved slowly still, despite her building excitement. They'd been here for close to forty-five minutes, and she wondered where Dennis was. Had he made it to their bedroom yet? Was he undressed yet? Hillary got Jake's pants off and caressed him up and down his body, alternating satin, hands, satin, hands, satin, hands. She made a slip knot in the end of the strip of satin and slipped it over his hand. She looked into his eyes to see how he was doing, hoping that the tranquilizer she had slipped into his green tea was working.

"Wait, a strong guy like you would rip this satin in a moment, wouldn't you? And part of the fun is letting me tease you, without you being able to do anything about it." She smiled seductively and trailed her hand from his shoulder down to the waistband of his pants. From her box she removed two restraint straps and, holding his eyes steady with hers, fastened his two wrists to the bed posts.

There was uncertainty growing in Jake's eyes. Hillary touched his skin softly, leaned in and kissed him tenderly to offer him some comfort. She caressed his skin, slowly making her way back down to the waistband of his pants, and then pulled them down his legs, enjoying every moment of anticipation. Once he was naked, she reached into her box for two more restraint straps and tied his feet to the bottom of the bed. Then she let her hands go back to touching him. Up his legs, over his balls and his cock, across his stomach, up to his chest and back down again, lingering where her touch made him close his eyes in enjoyment.

Jake wasn't sure what was coming next, but it felt so good to have soft hands on his body that he was willing to go along with pretty much anything so that he could have more. Two years felt like a long time to not be touched by anyone else, and he ached for the company.

Hillary got off the bed and slipped off her underwear, then swung her leg over Jake's and let him inside of her body.

Jake closed his eyes, savoring Hillary's warmth and the feel of her thighs against his body. He missed this feeling, being inside a woman. As Hillary began to move, stroking him with her body, he lost himself to the sensations she was offering him.

•

Downstairs, on the second floor, Dennis had heard the bed squeak a few times, and wished he could watch the unfolding of the scene. Hillary had described other nights like this to him, so he had an idea of what was going on, but he still wished he could see with his own eyes. However, he had a good imagination and found himself swelling without much effort. He got out of his clothes, thinking of his wife up in the attic apartment, capable and cunning, and began to stroke himself into full arousal.

•

Upstairs, Hillary felt ready to move on. She had been careful to keep the box close at hand, and now she quietly removed some string and her scalpel. Then she pushed the box off the bed, letting it bang against the floor. Jake startled. Dennis would know she was starting.

•

There was the thump—that was the signal Dennis had been waiting for. Now he knew exactly what was happening. Hillary had described this part to him many times and in such exquisite detail that he felt that he could picture it flawlessly. He kept his hand on himself, visualizing everything he could remember about it, pumping himself closer and closer, and then over the edge into ecstasy.

•

3 days later

Hillary picked up the platter and brought it to the table, where Dennis was waiting for her. Their son was at a friend's house, so she and Dennis had the evening to themselves.

Dennis smelled the air. "Mmmmm, I've been waiting for these. Your stuffed mushroom caps are always fabulous, but they're even better with like fresh pickled, ahem, *ham*."

•

Hillary's Ham-Stuffed Mushroom Caps

12 oz fresh mushrooms (about 24 medium)
½ cup butter, divided
¼ cup onion, finely diced
¼ cup red pepper, finely diced
¼ cup fresh ham, minced*
1 ½ Tbsp fresh parsley, minced
1 Tbsp fresh thyme
½ tsp Worcestershire sauce
¼ cup grated parmesan cheese
salt and pepper to taste

*For best results, let ham sit in pickle brine for 2-3 days before preparing recipe.

Remove stems from mushrooms. Melt ¼ cup butter in a pan and cook mushroom caps until just tender. Set aside.

Melt remaining ¼ cup butter in the pan and sauté onion and peppers for 5 minutes. Add ham, herbs, and

Worcestershire sauce. Heat through. Add parmesan cheese, salt and pepper.

Arrange mushroom caps on a baking sheet, hollow side up. Spoon filling into caps. Broil 5 to 10 minutes until filling is browned.

Enjoy immediately.

Grace

Sheilah Madonna

A pugilist face and the stance of a champion
despite what to her life has sanctioned:
Below minimum wage
Asbestos home
Polyester hand-me-downs that gave her hives
Worn out shoes with no arch support
Mac and cheese diet with no ketchup.
Even if she did not have a caved-in nose
that she won from a losing fight,
Because "No means No!"
she was not that pretty to begin with.
Slight underbite because dentists are expensive,
Premature wrinkles from squinting
because it's hard to see without glasses,
Permanent limp because she could not
run away fast enough from her mother.
"Loser, loser," the kids whispered behind her back.
Her breath smelled, her hair even worse.
But she's a champ
She would rather sleep in a house of cardboard

on a frozen field in the middle of Scarborough.
Because she's tired of saying no,
and losing fights mostly to her father, one time
to the principal, when she was only 12.
Exhausted from men clamouring over her when she slept,
but often too weak from starvation to resist.
She's a champ.
She worked the 4 to 10 a.m. shifts at the 7-Eleven
It was the only shift they would give her.
There's no street number on the vacant lot
beside the train tracks next to the presbyterian church.
They thought she needed the money to get high.
There was only enough to buy hotdogs
and butane for her gas stove to
heat up her cardboard home.
She's a champ.
Because despite, what to her, life has sanctioned,
she never forgot to say "please" and "thank you"
whenever she asked for the turkey because
she preferred it over the ham sandwich
that the presbyterian church next to her
gave out for lunch every first Tuesday of the month.
Her luck finally changed when two days ago,
she got approved for social housing!
She had to trade head and six months' worth

of Percocets with Norm the manager, for references.
She did not need to get numb to stay warm,
she can wean herself off the painkillers
that she legitimately needed for her limp,
If she finally got a house to go home to.
Yesterday she slept, dreaming of showers and a bed.
The wind kissed the stove and fire was born.
She went home sooner than later.
It was all over the news:
homeless
drug addicted
runaway
sex worker
young offender
She had a name.
Her name was Grace.
She had a pugilist face and the stance of a champion
despite, what to her, life had sanctioned:
She preferred turkey over ham,
She always said "please" and "thank you."
Her father, the principal, broke her nose.
Her mother broke her hips and damaged her spine
because she said she was still hungry,
The first time she got raped by a stranger,
he threw ten dollars at her after,

The last time was when she broke into a car
In an underground parking lot downtown.
It was the owner, who beat her after, stole her shoes
and then kicked her out, and it was -20 and
she walked for six hours to Scarborough
to the presbyterian church that was serving free lunch
because it was the first Tuesday of the month.
She had a name.
Her name was Grace.

Wish Granted

Gregg Chamberlain

The Literal Genius shook his head and slowly stroked a finger along a thin curling mustachio.

"Mad they are, these mortal humans," he said. "The things some of them ask for!"

One hand held up a thick Black Forest ham-on-rye sandwich. The Genius regarded the deli menu staple, sniffed at it, then took an experimental bite.

"Hmmm," he murmured, slowly chewing, then swallowed. He plucked up an "I Love NY" T-shirt, complete with a big red "heart" symbol, from a forlorn little pile of clothes sitting on the deserted stretch of beach along the Jersey Shore, and wiped his lips.

Half sunk in the sand near the discarded clothing was an ancient and ornate brass bottle. Its barnacle-encrusted stopper rested nearby, washed over by the incoming tide.

The Genius took another bite of ham and rye. His lips pursed in a slight frown.

"Perhaps," he mused, "a little more mustard next time."

ABOUT THE CONTRIBUTORS

Riham Adly
Author, "Re-Ham"
Riham Adly is an Egyptian writer. Her fiction has appeared in *Vestal Review*, *Connotation Press*, *Bending Genres*, *Spelk* and *The Cabinet of Heed* among others. In 2013 she won the Makan Award in Egypt and in 2018 she was shortlisted for the ArabLit Translation Prize. Riham Lives with her family in Gizah, Egypt.

Jayant Avva
Author, "Alimentary Mistake"
Jayant Avva is a Toronto-based author who writes fiction and nonfiction. He is a lifelong student of philosophy, science and learning. He can be found online at https://jayantavva.wixsite.com/website and on Twitter @JayantAvva

Lawrence Berry
Author, "Tavern Ham"
Lawrence Berry sold his first story to *Cavalier Magazine* and went on to have a 'best of' appearance in that publication. He is a specialist in horror fiction and the short narrative form, in print and podcast; you'll find a number of new stories and scripts in select anthologies and horror podcasts due for release in 2019. Lawrence writes two national columns: *Forbidden Words*, on the vocabulary of horror, and *Monstrous Friends*, monthly interviews with horror writers. For more on Lawrence, send him a friend request on Facebook at https://www.facebook.com/larry.berry.509 or check out his website: www.badweatherinventionfactory.com

Die Booth
Author, "Still Dawn"
Die Booth lives in Chester, England and enjoys painting pictures and exploring dark places. When not writing wild lies, he chairs a local writing group and DJs at the city's only goth night. You can read his stories in places like *The Fiction Desk*, *Shoreline of Infinity* and *The Cheshire Prize for*

Literature anthologies. His latest collection of short stories "My Glass is Runn", is out now, and he's currently working on a collection of spooky short stories featuring transgender protagonists. He can be found online at http://diebooth.wordpress.com/ and Twitter @diebooth

Harris Bor
Author, "Mist-taken Lunch"
Harris Bor is an English commercial barrister (trial advocate) and lecturer, with an interest in contemporary religion and the history of ideas.

Chantal Boudreau
Author, "Let Me Finish"
Chantal Boudreau is a Nova Scotian writer of speculative fiction. She likes to write about funny zombies, apocalyptic disasters, claustrophobic dystopias and gritty, realistic fantasy—oh, and ham sandwiches. She has more than fifty stories published with a variety of Canadian, U.S. and U.K. publishers.

Frances Boyle
Author, "Wrappers and Crusts"
Frances Boyle is the author of *Tower*, a novella (Fish Gotta Swim Editions), and *Light-carved Passages*, a poetry collection. Her work has appeared in many print and online journals in Canada and the U.S. as well as anthologies with topics ranging from love poetry to Hitchcock films (and now ham sandwiches!). A second book of poetry is due out in 2019, and her short story collection in 2020. Frances lives in Ottawa, where she helps edit *Arc Poetry Magazine* and writes reviews for *Canthius*. For more, visit www.francesboyle.com or follow her at @francesboyle19

Tim Brown
Author, "Words of the Lost"
Tim Brown has contributed photography and articles for *the Juniper Berry* and is currently at work on his first novel. When he isn't working, he can usually be found either playing video games or in a futile search for the perfect ham sandwich. Tim lives in Queens, NY and can be followed on Twitter @TimBrownWrites

H.A. Burns

Author, "The Not-So-Mysterious Mystery of the Disappearing Ham"

H.A. Burns is an engineer in the aerospace industry in the Seattle area by day and writes science fiction novels by night. It's like being a superhero with the power of a pen, which we all know is mightier than the sword. Her most recent work, the *Cyborg Dreams* trilogy, was published in 2018 and reads like a blockbuster movie—full of action, adventure, and fantasy in the form of dreams. As an engineer, she tries to incorporate as much realistic science as possible, while also speculating about the future of technology not yet realized. She can be found on Facebook and Instagram @writerhaburns, Twitter @authorhaburns, and her website at https://sites.google.com/view/cyborgdreams

Justin A. Burnett

Author, "Rearrangements"

Justin A. Burnett is a freelance editor and the Executive Director of Silent Motorist Media (www.silentmotorist.media). He's the author of *The Last Drug Trial on Earth* and *Esoteric Sausage and Other Malformations*. His work has been published on *Clash Media*, *Lost in the Fun House*, and in numerous anthologies.

Gregg Chamberlain

Author, "Wish Granted"

Gregg Chamberlain lives in rural Ontario, Canada, with his missus, Anne, and their trio of cats, who have everything that they could wish for from their human companions, although more belly rubs and kitty treats would be nice. He has about four dozen short fiction pieces in various magazines like *Apex*, *Ares*, *Mythic*, and *Weirdbook*, on the *Daily Science Fiction* webzine, and in original anthologies. He can be found online at www.facebook.com/gregg.chamberlain and on Twitter @greggchamberlai

C. Cooch

Author, "Doctor Jayne Herbert: Private notes on Patient 16"

Clara makes her home beside a wild and barren stretch of moorland in the mists of Devon, UK, with her husband and three hell-hounds. She has been published in various anthologies and magazines and is currently working on her first novel. She can be found online at www.ClaraCooch.com and on Twitter @C_Cooch

James Dyer
Author, "How to Make the Perfect Ham and Cheese Sandwich"
James Dyer is currently enrolled in a doctoral program at Texas State University, where he studies developmental education. He lives in San Marcos, TX with his wife, children, cats, dogs, hopes, dreams, and a trash-goblin named Casey who is just the worst.

Tom Fugalli
Author, "Café Zeno"
Tom Fugalli is the author of an online chapbook, *The Mind-Body Problem* (White Knuckle Press, 2018). His work has appeared in *Exquisite Corpse, Forklift Ohio, Right Hand Pointing, Voicemail Poems, The Western Humanities Review,* and elsewhere. He lives in New Rochelle, New York.

Andrew Giordano
Author, "The Crimson Pumpernickel"
Andrew Giordano is a doer of things. The list of things that he has done is very long. That list now includes being an author. It also includes creating a wooden espresso cup collection, renovating a bathroom, and raising a child.

Doreen Joy Graham
Author, "The Chase Is On"
Doreen Joy Graham lives in beautiful Calgary, Alberta, Canada. She is an award-winning poet who enjoys writing uplifting themes in traditional form poetry with metered lines and rhymes. She is a grandmother who often writes about her grandchildren. Graham is most proud of her first-place win in the Saturday Evening Post Limerick contest. Her winning entry, about bobbing for apples, was published in their January/February 2014 issue. Her first book of poetry, "The Gems In My Crown" is now available for purchase on amazon.com with more smaller poetry books to be self-published soon.

Keith P. Graham
Author, "Pigs Is Pigs?"
Keith P. Graham is a Computer Programmer, Beekeeper, Blues Harmonica Player and Speculative Fiction writer. His Websites include CthreePO.com, JT30.com and WestNyackHoney.com. He has published about 70 short stories in the last 20 years. He is retired and lives in the suburbs with Erica, four cranky cats, 24 chickens and about 200,000 bees.

Lionel Ray Green
Author, "Dill's Song"
Lionel Ray Green is a horror and fantasy writer, an award-winning newspaper journalist, and a U.S. Army gulf war veteran living in Alabama. His short stories have appeared in ten anthologies and two magazines, including Alabama's Emerging Writers, The Heart of a Devil, In Creeps the Night, and 22 More Quick Shivers. His short story "Scarecrow Road" won the WriterWriter 2018 International Halloween Themed Writing Competition All Hallows' Prose. Lionel ironically loves Bigfoot and hobbits, not necessarily in that order. He can be found online at his personal author page: https://lionelraygreen.com and his Amazon author page: https://www.amazon.com/Lionel-Ray-Green/e/B01KM4JLJE/

Shannon Green
Author, "Oh, Comely"
Shannon Green, originally from Carbonear, Newfoundland and Labrador, now calls wherever his wife and cats are home. When not at his day job, he enjoys ballroom dance, playing guitar, and drinking whiskey. He can most easily be found on Twitter as @HellTank34

Ethan Hedman
Author, "Famished Upheaval"
Ethan Hedman is a speculative fiction writer from South Florida, the land of heat, humidity, and hurricanes. He encourages a generous slather of mustard on the reader's next ham sandwich, especially if the condiment in question is both sweet and spicy. Ethan can be found online at EthanHedman.com

Calder Hutchinson
Author, "Forty-Nine Hours of Breado"
Calder is a capering conglomerate of chemicals which, if prepared properly, could likely be rendered indistinguishable from thinly sliced ham. He has mustard in his fridge, but you'd probably have to get the bread elsewhere.

Derek Kannemeyer

Author, "Argument Over the Lack of Ham in a Ham Sandwich"

Derek Kannemeyer's writing has appeared in scores of publications, from *Fiction International* to *Rolling Stone*. His 2018-2019 works include a book of light verse (*An Alphabestiary*), a poetry chapbook (as winner of the inaugural Blue Nib Chapbook contest), and more than twenty poems and short prose pieces in various online and print journals. He lives in Richmond, Virginia.

Jan Karlsson

Artist, "The Ham Sandwich of Doom"

Janne Karlsson is a Swedish illustrator/writer. When he's not busy creating weird stuff, he's either working at the psych ward or sipping cheap red wine. He can be found online at www.svenskapache.se

Regina Kenney

Author, "Little Bone-Brittle"

Regina Kenney is a former journalist for *Aviation Week & Space Technology* magazine. Originally from Minnesota, Kenney attended Loyola University Chicago, majoring in Communications and International Studies. She founded the literature website Literati Pulp with her brother Davy while in Chicago. Kenney then moved to London in 2016 and continued to write for several blog sites as well as technical aviation articles for MRO Network and ShowNews. Kenney now lives in Dublin, Ireland where she continues to write short horror stories.

E.E. King

Author, "The Cheddar-Ham Coast"

E.E. King is a painter, performer, writer, and biologist. Ray Bradbury called her stories, "marvelously inventive, wildly funny and deeply thought-provoking. I cannot recommend them highly enough." Her books include *Dirk Quigby's Guide to the Afterlife*, *Electric Detective*, *Pandora's Card Game*, *The Truth of Fiction* and *Blood Prism*. She's worked with children in Bosnia, crocodiles in Mexico, frogs in Puerto Rico, egrets in Bali, mushrooms in Montana, archaeologists in Spain and butterflies in South Central Los Angeles; lectured on island evolution and marine biology on cruise ships in the South Pacific and the Caribbean and painted murals in Los Angeles and Spain. You can check out E.E. King's paintings, writing, musings and books at www.elizabetheveking.com, and you can find her on Twitter at @ElizabethEvKing and Facebook at facebook.com/pages/EE-King

Gerri Leen
Author, "Ham: The Lunchmeat of Our Lives"
Gerri Leen lives in Northern Virginia and originally hails from Seattle. In addition to being an avid reader, she's passionate about horse racing, tea, and whisky, and her latest obsession is ASMR vids. She has work appearing in *Nature, Orson Scott Card's Intergalactic Medicine Show*, *Daily Science Fiction*, *Cast of Wonders,* and others. She's edited several anthologies for independent presses, is finishing some longer projects, and is a member of SFWA and HWA. See more at http://www.gerrileen.com or tweet @GerriLeen

Josh Lefkowitz
Author, "All of Us Atoms"
Josh Lefkowitz received an Avery Hopwood Award for Poetry at the University of Michigan. His work has been published in *Washington Square Review*, *Electric Literature*, *The Millions*, *The Canadian Jewish News*, *Shooter Literary Magazine* (UK), *Southword Journal* (Ireland), and elsewhere. His long humor poem "Saturday Salutation" was anthologized by Canada's Broadview Press. He can be found online at Facebook: https://www.facebook.com/josh.lefkowitz.357, Twitter: @jelefko, and Instagram: @jelefko

j. jewis
Author, "Pig Collector"
j.lewis is an internationally published poet, musician, and nurse practitioner. When he is not otherwise occupied, he is often on a kayak, exploring and photographing the waterways near his home in California. His first book of poetry and photography, "a clear day in october," was released in June 2016. You can find him on Facebook at www.facebook.com/poetryontap

Sheilah Madonna
Author, "Grace"
Sheilah Madonna is an avid street photographer and writer, and a bit of a crazy dog lady. She loves Fetty Wap and Air Supply. She prefers hamburger over a ham sandwich because it's more filling.

Selena Mercuri
Author, "Havana"
Selena Mercuri is a student of English Literature and creative writing at the University of Toronto. She has written articles for The Varsity, and has been a reader for both The Rights Factory and Transatlantic Literary Ageny in Toronto.

Edward Palumbo
Author, "The Zesty Garlic Pickles"
Edward Palumbo is a graduate of the University of Rhode Island (1982). His fiction, poems, shorts, and journalism have appeared in numerous periodicals, journals, e-journals and anthologies including *Rough Places Plain*, *Flush Fiction*, *Tertulia Magazine*, *Epiphany*, *The Poet's Page*, *Reader's Digest*, *Baseball Bard* and *Dark Matter*.

Virva Peikko
Artist, "He-Ham"
Virva Peikko is an artist based in Arizona. She loves making things that shouldn't exist. She can be found on Instagram @virvapeikko and her website at www.thekaterpillar.com

Robert Perret
Author, "Bedeviled Ham"
Robert Perret is a writer and librarian living on the Palouse in northern Idaho. He has written many stories across the pulpier genres, but this is his first ham sandwich–based piece. His work has been included in many Sherlock Holmes anthologies, as well as anthologies dedicated to C. Auguste Dupin, Solar Pons, and Nancy Drew. He has also written pieces of librarian fiction for *Two-Fisted Library Stories* and *Spicy Library Stories*. He can be found online at www.robertperret.com and Twitter @RobertP221B

Eric Potter
Author, "That Thin Fuzzy Line Between Ham Sandwiches and Bio-Terrorism"
Eric was born and raised in suburban Ontario and earned his master's in philosophy at Dalhousie University. In his youth, Eric tended to get into some trouble for his more inappropriate writings, and is now attempting to write full time. You can find more of Eric's writing on https://ericpotter.net/ and his recent comedy podcast, Eric Fabricates the News, can be found at EFTN Canada and on Spotify.

Kristin Procter

Author, "Disconnect"

Kristin Procter is a Canadian who currently lives in Massachusetts, where she collaborates on workshops and events for Motherwriters. She takes her lunches seriously and still hasn't forgiven the shop that contaminated her sandwich with tomato. Kristin can be found on Instagram: kmprocter

Kara Race-Moore

Author, "One Small Snack for Man"

Kara Race-Moore studied history at Simmons College as an excuse to read about the soap opera lives of British royals. She worked in educational publishing, casting the molds for future generations' minds, but has since moved into the more civilized world of litigation. Ms. Race-Moore first came to science fiction through Anne McCaffrey and is still grateful to her for showing an impressible teenager that women can be in and write science fiction too. Kara Race-Moore's short stories can be found on Amazon and Goodreads.

Rachel Robins

Author, "Eating the Earl"

An MFA graduate in Writing Popular Fiction, Rachel Robins is a self-professed medical mutant who lives a rich inner life with a steady diet of fiction, IFLS articles, theology, cat videos, drag queens and gluten-free concoctions. Her first novel features monsters and mindreading. And dear God, is she single. She can be found online at rachelrobins.com and Twitter @RSquaredWrites

Kelly Robinson

Author, "Read My Crust: a Brief Linguistic Analysis of Talking Ham Sandwiches"

Kelly Robinson is a freelance writer and researcher from Knoxville, TN with bylines in magazines like *Rue Morgue*, *Mental Floss*, and *Smithsonian*. She is a recipient of the Horror Writers Association's Rocky Wood Memorial Scholarship for non-fiction writing and was nominated for a Rondo Hatton Award for article of the year in classic horror research.

Kristine Sahagun
Author, "Monterey"
Kristine is a writer and editor from the grassy plains of Vaughan, where houses have the same face. When she is not struggling to perfect a downward dog, she can be found wandering the streets, dangerously caffeinated, or posting on social media for *The Puritan Magazine*. Her favourite writers include Dave Eggers, Richard Siken, Patrick Rothfuss, and Marlon James. Kristine prefers her ham smoked, and her bread toasted.

Holly Schofield
Author, "Copy That"
Holly Schofield travels through time at the rate of one second per second, oscillating between the alternate realities of city and country life. Her short stories have appeared in *Analog*, *Lightspeed*, *Escape Pod*, and many other publications throughout the world. She hopes to save the world through science fiction and homegrown heritage tomatoes. Find her at hollyschofield.wordpress.com

Justin Short
Author, "Gemini Lunch"
Justin lives in Kansas. His fiction has previously appeared in places like *The NoSleep Podcast*, *The Arcanist*, *Jerry Jazz Musician*, and *Dear Abby*. He can be found online at www.justin-short.com

David F. Shultz
Editor, Author "Hook and Grinder"
David writes speculative fiction and poetry from Toronto, where he also leads the Toronto Science Fiction and Fantasy Writers group, and is managing editor at tdotSpec, Inc. His more than fifty published works appear in venues such as *Abyss & Apex* and *Dreams and Nightmares.*

Irina Slav
Author, "The Cost of Perfection"
Irina is an energy journalist by trade and an urban fantasy author by calling. Her stories rarely have a happy ending but she can appreciate a good joke and so can her characters. Irina's first novel, *The Lamiastriga*, is out later this year. She blogs at Dezombify and is always happy to chat on Twitter as @IrinaSlav1

Christine Sloan Stoddard

Author, "Things I Do Well That Nobody Will Ever Pay Me To Do"

Christine Sloan Stoddard is a Salvadoran-American writer and artist living in Brooklyn. She founded *Quail Bell Magazine*, a feminist publication for real and unreal stories from around the world. Her books include *Belladonna Magic: Spells in the Form of Poetry and Photography*, *Water for the Cactus Woman*, *Hispanic and Latino Heritage in Virginia*, and other titles.

R.D. Sullivan

Author, "On the Side" and "Cold Slices, Hot Bodies"

R.D. Sullivan lives with her family and two solidly mediocre dogs in Northern California, where she runs a subcontracting business. Her non-ham sandwich work has been featured at *Fireside Fiction Magazine*, *Shotgun Honey*, *Killing Malmon* and the upcoming *Murder-A-Go-Go*'s anthology. You can track her down on twitter @RDSullyWrites or over at govneh.com

Chris Sumberg

Author, "Feral Lunchbreak" and "Ham Amongst Friends"

Chris Sumberg has had work published in *Bitter Empire*, *Southern Fried Karma/New Southern Fugitives*, *Broad Street Review*, *Chronogram*, *Urbanite*, *The Partially Examined Life*, *RealPoetik*, and other magazines. He has work forthcoming in *Pseudopod* and ChiZine's *War on Christmas* anthology.

Karen Thrower

Author, "Beware Brown Bags"

Karen Thrower was born and raised in Oklahoma. She is a member of Oklahoma Science Fiction Writers and serves as the President and Facebook 'Wizard', which she suspects has something to do with her young age. You can find the rest of her works on her Amazon Author page: amazon.com/author/karenthrower

Julia Wang

Author, "Hamming It Well"

Julia doesn't like ham sandwiches. She prefers turkey, but she'd eat a ham sandwich if it's there and it's cheap. She writes horror, historical fiction, mysteries, and sometimes all three at once. Her short stories have appeared in *Disturbed Digest* (2014) by Alban Lake Publishing and *Uncanny Adventures* (2013) by 8th Wonder Press. She lives in Toronto with a roommate who plays loud music, keeping her from writing. In no way has she ever plotted to poison his ham sandwich.

Sam Weir

Author, "Hillary's Recipe"

Sam Weir collects university degrees and new skills. Skateboarding and sewing are particular interests. Sam is new to the short story genre, working mostly in poetry, and enjoyed writing something out of the ordinary for this collection.

C.H. Williams

Author, "Ham Sandwich Recipe"

C.H. Williams is a full-time mum who writes adult fiction, contemporary romance, short stories, flash pieces and poetry. She can often be found with a jar of peanut butter in one hand and a bar of dark chocolate in the other, which coincidentally makes it rather difficult to type. Find her on Instagram @c.h.writes

HAMTHOLOGY
HAM SANDWICH LITERATURE

TDOTSPEC

43805458R00215

Made in the USA
Middletown, DE
29 April 2019